THE
CHRONICLES
OF NOE

The Chimera & The Grail Tree

THE CHRONICLES OF NOE

THE CHIMERA & THE GRAIL TREE

CORLIS C FRAGA

FRAGA
BOOKS

THE CHRONICLES OF NOE: THE CHIMERA AND THE GRAIL TREE

Edited by Laura Ownbey & Richard Storrs
Published by Fraga Books LLC
www.fragabooks.com

Library of Congress Control Number: 2025912117

ISBN 979-8-9926692-0-6 (Paperback)
ISBN 979-8-9926692-1-3 (Hardcover)
ISBN 979-8-9926692-2-0 (eBook)

Cover Art and Interior Illustrations Copyright © 2025 by Corlis C Fraga
Cover Formatting by Open Heart Designs

First Edition: October 2025

EYBOR NORTHLAND
8128 STATES
CHELYS SEA
NORTH ACHELON OCEAN
NAPE BAY
GULF OF PENDRA-NORTH
PENDRA-NORTH
28 STATES
REPUBLIC OF WICK
EBON BAY
NORTH BELLERO OCEAN
OUROBOROS GULF
BASILIC GULF
LONGSPEE CHANNEL
STATES OF SOUTH FLORENT
16 STATES
SOUTH ACHELON OCEAN
SOUTH BELLERO OCEAN
EYTHOR COAST (SUBMARINE) ICESHELF
EYTHOR SOUT

uirin

RUMFOOT HOLLOW

Stone Troll Wall

Mag Mell
Retirement
Wetland

The
Grail
Tree

Charon River

Stone Troll Wall

The
Star Fields

To the lionhearts who came
before me,

I hear you.
I cherish you. To the
lionhearts yet to roar, the
world needs you more than
it knows.

PROLOGUE

Surrendered magic of a Chimera's roar
is locked away in enchanted ore
until what was given to the pine
is bestowed to a child of the donor's line.

With this debt, honor is paid
to a world destined to be remade.
And what was locked away in enchanted ore
shall finally seek justice from a heartless war.

— TRANSLATION BY ABL V & PRP

CHAPTER ONE

THE MOST LEGENDARY VIEW
IN RUMFOOT HOLLOW

E nelope Noe, the two-thousand-three-hundred-and-first Chimera of her family line, reached forty-*ish* feet off the ground when the branch she grabbed cracked.

"There goes another one," Pemprin muttered as Enelope lashed her arms around the ancient trunk of the Grail Tree.

"Why would you say that?" Arcamo gasped.

The red snake-locks that covered the Forest-Oblin's head slithered across his crown. They coiled around the twigs of mountain laurel he tucked behind his ears and wagged their pink, reptilian tongues at Pemprin.

"Why not? No wonder there are so few Chimeras left in the Mundus if they pull stunts like this," she shot back.

"It's not helpful," Arcamo said.

"I didn't stop my important business to be helpful," Pemprin replied.

"Why did you?"

"As a future High Mage, it's my job to know what is

happening with my peers. If you're breaking the law, I need to be able to plan accordingly," Pemprin claimed.

Enelope ground her teeth.

"Watch out, Arc," she called below, perfectly at peace if Ms. Future High Mage got hit with a falling stick.

Arc jumped back. The branch hit the ground with a dull thud, landing two feet from where her best friend stood.

"She's not wrong, Enee. Remember the plan? Timing is important. The longer you climb, the greater the chance that someone will see you. The Accords may be old, but you'll get in serious trouble if someone reports you. A visit from the Guard kind of trouble," Arc reminded her. Again.

She loved Arc more than peanut butter and Mixed Magic Arts fighters, but the Forest-Oblin's gift for planning, mostly planning how to avoid disaster, came at a price. Worry. The Foblin generated an endless supply of it.

"I know," she said.

Enee couldn't turn back now. No risk, no reward. Besides, as a Chimera, she had a certain honor to uphold. Sure, Enee didn't look exactly like the legends. Who could live up to the exaggerated textbook definition of a fire-breathing monster with what appeared as a Lion's and a Goat's head and a Snake for a tail? *Please*.

Who ever heard of a real Chimera breathing fire?

Enee sighed. Pemprin could stuff it. But Arc? He'd spent too many afternoons humoring her scheme and tallying up the consequences for her to completely ignore the risks. Was *moderately* ignoring them a good compromise?

"Did either of you stop to think about what would happen if this woke the Grail Tree? It'll start spewing poison. That's the whole reason why the Alchem brokered the Accords during the Crusades. Leaving the Trees alone keeps us safe," Pemprin said.

The laugh that forced its way out of Enee's throat was so sharp it almost threw her off-balance.

"Those rules were only made to save face over a stupid war and the stupider idea of trying to cut down the Grail Trees to justify it," she argued.

Yeah, yeah. Enee's comeback made her a hypocrite, especially since she climbed the Grail Tree specifically to try to claim the one thing every Alchem king *said* they wanted during the Crusades: a Grail Stone. And where does a king find a Grail Stone? Stubbornly fixed to the very top of a Grail Tree's crown. In her defense, she didn't intend to poison Rumfoot Hollow. She simply aimed to collect on the debt the Trees owed the Chimeras.

She believed in this debt as surely as she knew the names of the remaining one hundred Chimera families. Their help in defending the Grail Trees centuries ago against the Alchem kingdoms was why only a Chimera could touch them today without, well, *dying*. Before the Crusades, the Grail Trees allowed everyone to touch them.

Back when they believed people were kind.

Back when they never imagined they'd need to transform into something more lethal than a war capable of swallowing the world.

Given that Enee felt fine and wasn't flailing around like an overcooked egg, this Grail Tree still remembered the Chimeras as allies, even if it was just a memory locked away in a sleep so deep that not even generations of horrors could find it.

"What history book did you get that lie from? As the next generation, we have a duty to honor the rules that protect us," Pemprin said.

"Oh yeah? Then what are you doing with *that*?" Enee retorted, glancing at the enchanted object Pemprin carried.

The air around the Tree had thickened with static the moment Pemprin graced them with her presence. *Magic.* The tangible, electric fingerprints of a triggered spell prickled against Enee's skin. Although Pemprin couldn't wield magic herself, *yet*, the Prayer Nut in her hands could.

Enee looked around the Grail Tree to see if Pemprin had brought anyone else. To her surprise, Keeper and the other girls who circled Pemprin at school weren't hiding in the bushes. She had come to the woods to practice magic alone.

"I—I was only rehearsing my spells, as every Alchem student preparing for the EMD should be doing," Pemprin stammered.

"Then where's your supervisor? Or is that one of those rules *not* meant to protect us?" she snapped.

Enee dug her nails into the bark until they threatened to chip. She needed to focus, and this wasn't helping.

Pemprin ran her thumb blindly over the ring she wore on a chain around her neck.

"Being supervised at this stage is unnecessary. Nobody can wield magic until after their Examination of Magical Dormancy and they receive a Familiar," Pemprin added, neglecting the part where anyone could wield magic with an enchanted object—even a magicless Chimera.

That is, if you could get your hands on one. Enchanted objects took time, *decades* if not centuries, and money to make. As a member of the Pendra family, daughter of the

6

country's current High Mage, the girl probably pooped enchanted objects while the rest of the Mundus got along with trinkets charmed with spells that faded over time like cheap print on a T-shirt. But Pemprin knew this. Moreover, she knew Enee knew. That meant only one thing: the would-be-mage was rehearsing her excuses.

Enee took three slow breaths to carve out a calm space in her mind. Pemprin wouldn't tell on her. She had gone to school with Pemprin long enough to know she cared how others saw her. Breaking the rules, or even witnessing the rules being broken and not rushing straight to the nearest adult, didn't speak highly of a future High Mage. Nor would reporting her make the girl any friends. No matter what Enee did, Pemprin didn't want to get caught either.

That had to be enough. She didn't have the luxury of believing otherwise. Enee needed the Stone. *Mama* needed it.

This task was all Enee had to offer, and she wasn't going to screw it up. If she couldn't help Mama somehow, how could she call herself a Chimera worthy of the family name? Having only one head and a body with a sad layer of peach fuzz the color of a baked rind didn't exactly make her heritage proud. At least she had a few snakeskin patches, mismatched eyes, and velvety ears. Otherwise, Enee looked like any other chump in the Alchem community. No offense to Alchem chumps.

Arc whined as another branch broke. He'd deny it when she came down, but nobody could fool her ears—being as long and soft as a Goat's had to have some benefits, after all.

"I will not begin my political career by being a part of a

Chimera scandal. But if she's still climbing when I get back from my practice session, I will report you both," said Pemprin.

"There won't be a scandal," Arc rallied, but Enee could hear the strain it took for him to say it.

Her climbs fell into the muddy middle of their friendship, the part where all his plans and her actions butted heads. But that's how a first-grade Arcamo Landem became friends with the wild-haired Enelope Noe. He came to the first day of school with a posterboard-perfect presentation on Glamour Snails. Enee came in with a sharp set of teeth that bit the classmate who derailed the whole thing by stealing Arc's work and sneering, "What's a snake-curse like you going to do about it?"

The words *feral* and *friend* met in that space, fitting perfectly hand-in-hand on that day. And every day since.

"Besides, there are probably better ways to earn money than this," Pemprin said, still rubbing the ring she wore as she walked away.

Only after Pemprin left did Arc speak up.

"Can we stop for today?" Arc suggested. He cradled the heads of his snake-locks as if to protect a pair of fledglings from the rain.

"Not yet."

Enee wanted to go farther than before. How did she expect to improve if she didn't go farther each time? But the wind that stirred the forest floor made the Grail Tree sway, catching on the needles that stretched longer than her arm. One branch, one step. She tried to ensure her long braid didn't snag on the way up. She couldn't risk having any evidence hiding in the weave that'd make Mama suspect anything. But that was easier said than done. Even bound in an industrial-strength golden cord, her hair went down to her calves.

She eventually passed the point where the crowns of the surrounding trees bowed beneath her. All the evergreens and oaks fell short of the massive Grail Tree. Here, she braced herself against a perfect quad of thick branches that faced the old, sleepy hills of Rabot County. The tree-speckled mounds hadn't had a growth spurt since the old Crusades when Drakes were said to be as large as the cargo carriages that rumbled along the tracks stretching from the nose of Pendra-North to the continent's dragon-like tail. Back then, the Drakes snatched full-grown Oblins from the fields. Today, the only things they stole came from feeders meant for feathery, seed-loving Aves and dumpsters.

Nestled in the cradle of slopes, Enee could make out the nearest town. The old brick of Rowbuirin's central square blended with the changing autumn leaves, accented with the chalk-white steeple of the Meetinghouse of Elmos and surrounding shops. Using the steeple as a marker, Enee gazed outward to find the town hall. From there, she found The Mitey Bean Cafe, the fire station, the WyrmMart, and all the other odd-and-end places she visited while Mama worked.

The farther out Enee looked, the sparser the buildings became, either hidden by forest or kept clear for swaths of farmland that spat out more rocks than squash. She found the paddock for the Night Mares that haunted Rowbuirin Castle, populated by the oldest and deadest family that descended from the region's namesake. Over the summer, the tourist trap was featured in the "Discover Rabot

County" campaign. The castle was a dot on a pilgrimage that began and ended with two major metropolises, where the Crusades in this country began and ended.

Enee wanted to turn around and see her corner of the Mundus, but to turn would mean risking a slip. So, for the moment, she let herself imagine the thousand-plus acres of Rumfoot Hollow and the hidden mushroom village of Porto Bello. She traced the footpaths into the wetlands that bordered the town line of Redwick. She flew over the school grounds and the Dryad Grove, spinning circles around the Landem Estate and gliding over the calm waters of the Churchmere and its liquid cathedral filled with the echoes of those who once lived.

The wind picked up again, and Enee hugged the trunk for support. At this height, she could wrap her arms around the Tree and *almost* have her fingernails touch. She still had what? Two hundred and fifty feet to go? The royal amethyst color of the gem was barely a speck against the paling afternoon sky.

"The wind's getting stronger," Arc called.

"I'll come down as soon as I reach the benchmark," Enee said.

She had to do that, at least. She kept climbing, staying as close to the trunk as possible. Twelve feet. Ten. Five. Enee passed the little notch she'd carved last time, reaching a new set of branches. Large patches of crusted gray sap guarded the base of the needles above her head.

Had the sap been this dark last time? Enee brushed away the thought. "I did it! I'm past the marker," she called, keeping as clear from the sap as possible. Even dry, that stuff could melt Arc's face off.

"Okay. Good. Climb down."

"Hold on. I need to make a new notch."

Enee pulled out a pocketknife. Steadying herself against the branches, she unfolded the smooth blade. Just one notch.

Please don't wake up, she prayed to the sleeping Grail Tree.

If seven and a half centuries hadn't woken them, a pocketknife wouldn't. Still, Enee didn't take the cut lightly. She only did it because a small cut was the easiest and least noticeable way to track her progress. If she used ribbon, there was a chance it'd be seen or taken by a roosting Drake. This way, the cuts were invisible to all but her.

As she cut, a drop of sap came out. That, she expected. She did not expect the sticky goop to be black. The change in the weather that came with the autumn had to have been the culprit. Right? Enee put away the knife and began to climb down.

"See, nothing to worry about," she called. Her muscles quaked, and the exhaustion made her laugh.

"Celebrate when you're on the ground," Arc said.

Enee sighed. Getting down meant dealing with everything, like the EMD or school. Only when Enee climbed, ran, or rode her Steed did the noise of the Mundus clear ever so slightly. She didn't worry about Mama as much, or her classmates' special blend of thirteen-year-old cruelty. All that stood before her were branches. An unmarked trail. A distance to beat. A Stone to claim.

The static filled the air again, and a shift in the light filtered through the canopy.

She looked down to see if Pemprin had come back, but

when she went to grab the branch she thought came next, her fingers wrapped around a fistful of air.

Amateur move. Both feet slipped out from under her.

"Enee!" Arc cried.

Everything was muted beneath a violent *hiss*. The hissing of the wind. The hissing of the branches as they slammed around her, offering only slick needles for her to tear apart. The hissing of—Snakes? Her stomach lurched, and the Grail Stone vanished from sight as Enelope Noe, the two-thousand-three-hundred-and-first Chimera of her family line, plummeted out of reach.

CHAPTER TWO
A TOUCH OF MAG-ICINE

E nee gave the deepest, dumbest sigh of her life. She couldn't believe it. Thirteen years without a single broken bone. *Over.*

"We're almost done," Dr. Sable promised.

He guided an elm wand across her arm. She could feel the break healing with each pass. The worst part of the process was the doctor's hand. Dr. Emery Sable had the bluest, coldest hand of any mage she'd ever met. Although every member of the Alchem had an Elemental ancestor, Enee had never met anyone who must have had a Land Elemental in their family tree from the iciest corners of the Mundus. A Yeti? A Snow-Oblin? Or maybe a Frost Giant?

Not even the doctor's Familiar kept his hands warm. The Drake coiled around his one blue arm as if to replace the sleeve of his lab coat. Hot vapor spiraled from their nostrils with each breath, making their scales glitter like a box of lit matches.

Dr. Sable caught her staring and smiled. "Her name is Ella. You can pet her if you want."

Ella cracked open a drowsy, purple eye.

"That's all right. Ella seems busy," Enee said.

The doctor chuckled. "So, what happened?"

Explain. Get the bone fixed. Get out. Before Enee started climbing the Grail Tree last summer, she and Arc had gotten their stories straight. Falling, broken bones, and even death were always possible outcomes. Arc drew out a table with every injury imaginable and matched it to an excuse. The table covered everything from sap stains to funeral arrangements. Scrapes? A slip on the Stone Troll Wall. Burns? An incident with a nest of Sun-Stinger Drakes. Bruises? A fall from her Steed, Knoble.

"I was climbing a tree with a friend. I slipped," she said.

True-*ish*.

Enee could have taken full advantage of the fact that she hadn't crossed paths with Dr. Sable before. He didn't know her well enough to smell the difference between her lies and the truth. After all, she'd only been to the doctor twice, and she didn't remember either time. Who wanted to remember being born or getting shots against the odd and end things that Mama deemed more threatening than seeing a physician? But they weren't alone.

Mama stepped around the observation table to face her. The Chimera stood a good two feet taller than Dr. Sable. Now, Mama looked like a true Chimera of legend. Well, almost. Disregard the two missing heads they lost in the years before Enee's birth. But even without Oma and Nama, and how they seemed ready to keel over from exhaustion most of the time, Mama was formidable and, for a brief moment, *skeptical*.

They refocused on Dr. Sable and watched him as if he

were covered in venomous fangs. They tracked every finger that ran over Enee's arm and noticed each shock of cold that made her flinch. Would cracking a joke help? She could bet Mama her favorite Mixed Magic Arts card that Dr. Sable had a great-great-great-great-great grandma Frost Giant named Nancy.

No Nonsense Nancy, the Brawler.

Mama wouldn't laugh. Not here. Doctors were dangerous. Dangerous enough that they refused to let Arc come with them to the clinic. They didn't even let their landlord, Mr. Loch, stay, and he *carried* her all the way to town after Arc's valiant search for help. The fewer people involved, the better.

Thick black rims surrounded Mama's weary sienna eyes. The rims carved a resting *I will eat you* expression onto their lion-face. Enee didn't have to be a genius to know what this face meant. Mama twisted the friendship bracelet Enee made nearly a decade ago in circles. She tried not to stare, but not staring meant her eyes fell on Mama's apron. One glance at The Mitey Bean's logo and Enee felt queasier than when she heard her bone snap like a riding crop.

The lies are necessary, Enee told herself.

The whole town would riot if she ever admitted to climbing a Grail Tree before she claimed the Stone. If something went wrong, Mama needed plausible deniability. Plus, they had enough on their plate.

"Take it easy with this arm for a few days. By next week, you'll be right as rain. As far as breaks go, this one was pretty fortunate," said Dr. Sable as he finished.

Enee dedicated her good fortune to rule number one: always have a spotter. The moment Enee began to fall, Arc must have whispered to the forest in his Foblin tongue, calling for anyone or anything to intervene. A wriggling horde of Snakes answered the call. They darted beneath the Grail Tree and cushioned Enee's landing. Thank goodness for Elemental friends.

"All right, give it a test drive," said the doctor.

Enee hopped off the table and stretched out her arm. A distant ache of pain shot along the bone, making her gasp.

"Easy. You still need time to heal. I only mended the bone. The rest will take time," he warned.

Enee grimaced. Every word out of his mouth needed to be taken with a grain of salt. No offense to Dr. Sable. A mage doctor could fix an arm on a good day without breaking a sweat. On a bad day, their decisions cost people their lives. Or their heads.

But he hadn't been horrible. Enee held out a hand.

"Thanks, Dr. Sable."

The doctor hesitated, glancing at Mama. When Mama didn't move, he smiled and accepted the handshake that made Enee temporarily experience the tundra of Eythor Southland.

"Are we free to go?" Mama asked.

"I'm ready," Enee said.

The sooner they left, the sooner she could lead Mama *far* away.

"I do have a few questions, if you don't mind. There are some gaps in your chart that I would like to fill. It'll make the process faster next time."

"There won't be a next time," Enee promised, more so to Mama than to the doctor.

Mama gave her a gentle nudge.

She sighed. If they were okay with staying for a few more questions, she would be okay with it, too. She hopped back onto the table and pulled the end of her braid into her lap. She twirled the hair at the tip and imagined it was the Snake she was supposed to be born with.

"Ask away."

"It says you're the latest Chimera of your family line. Correct?"

Enee nodded. Yes, a Chimera of legend. Part Lion, part Goat, part Snake—or, at least, what *looked* like these Elemental beings. Three heads. Three hearts. Strongest of warriors. Most loyal of compatriots.

"Fascinating."

Enee dug her nails into her braid. "Next question."

"Apologies, Enelope. You are my first Chimera patient. I want to be thorough. There's plenty of medical history on the Alchem and Elementals, but the field is lacking regarding Chimera health. I prefer to be prepared should you need to come in again," Dr. Sable explained.

"*En*elope. Or just Enee, like *any*," she corrected.

She bet all her MMA cards that curiosity had more to do with the questions. Only a hundred Chimera families remained. Before long, they would face the same fate as the Dragons. Was that what Dr. Sable noticed when he examined her ears and glanced at her snakeskin patches? Did he see what would one day become the footnote of a legend as he shone light into her mismatched eyes, which were so similar in tone that most couldn't tell one was green while the other was brown?

"Only one head?"

Mama twitched, and Enee made every effort to sit up straight.

"Yes."

If only she looked more like Mama, with a lion-face, eyes like a corn moon, and shoulders that could hold mountains. Scars from a "necessary" surgical decision that cleaved away two of Mama's heads made them seem like not even the Midst of the afterlife would dare keep them.

"Does she have a twin or triplet?" the doctor asked Mama.

"Only the one," Mama said.

Chimeras only had one cub in their lifetime. Sometimes, a twin or triplet. The rule of thumb was that if there was more than one, the cub usually had a single gender and a single head. Enee had no siblings. She had a substantial pair of ears that were long, silky, and prone to high-quality earwax.

"Yes, I suppose there's no golden rule regarding Chimeras," Dr. Sable said. "It doesn't seem like you've been in for any check-ups. Have you had any other illnesses or been prescribed any medications? I know most Chimeras are recommended to be put on stabilizers to help regulate any mood swings. Would you like me to—"

"No," Mama and Enee said it in perfect sync, making Dr. Sable jump.

"I am perfectly healthy," Enee added with a smile. She *was* perfectly healthy. As far as any doctor was concerned, that's how it had to stay.

"Right. And it says here that you're thirteen," said Dr. Sable, trying to clear the shake out of his voice. "Are you taking the EMD tomorrow?"

Enee sank a little. What a stupid question. Did she have a choice? "Yes."

She shouldn't have let the EMD bother her. If anything, the test was the least of their problems. Just look at Mama. They spent the last thirteen years straddling the line between being a Chimera *and* a probationary citizen of Pendra-North. And yet, Enee couldn't deny how the test made her feel. *Wrong.* She already knew what the EMD would tell her. Couldn't Enee skip the part where everyone else had to get confirmation that she didn't have a single connection to magic, unlike everyone else in the Mundus? Let the Alchem split themselves between those who can and can't wield. Let her Elemental neighbors stand in attendance, with magic already at their fingertips. Enee would gladly be anywhere else.

"Don't worry. It all works out how it's supposed to. You probably received a resonance test at birth to verify your missing connection. The EMD won't tell you anything new. Your part will take only a minute, two minutes, *tops*," the doctor promised.

Easy for him to say. He obviously passed his exam a million years ago. He literally just fixed her broken arm with a twig. Frankly, not having the potential to wield wasn't the problem for Enee. Like Dr. Sable, a member of the Alchem only had a *chance* of being able to wield magic. The rest of the Alchem lived on with their magic kept dormant, opening shops and running cafes with monthly poetry slams run by passionate, often messy, Muses.

Elementals had it simpler. They could wield from birth, and they could take up the professional title of *mage* with the right training. Arc had magic but zero interest in becoming a mage. Unfortunately, being able to wield meant he had to study as if he were to use magic professionally. The Mundus couldn't have haphazard wielders, after all.

The problem came when a creature popped up without a connection to magic. Do you know how many species in the Mundus didn't have a connection? One. The Chimeras. And the exam reinforced the idea that they existed as something *else*.

"Done?" Mama asked.

"Do you have a family emergency contact I can put down?"

Enee looked at Mama. Chimeras weren't like everyone else in the Mundus, with families all jumbled together with dads, moms, and generations that watched each other grow up. For them, family boiled down to one parent and their cub, or cubs if luck was on their side. And GrandMamas didn't usually make it long enough to be a part of the equation. Or didn't *want* to be a part of it.

"No. I may have another contact I can give, but I need to check with them first," Mama said cautiously.

Enee knew they were thinking of the Whittles. She wouldn't mind having them in an emergency, but why would they give out the names of the few allies they had to those who hadn't earned their trust?

"Done?" Mama repeated.

There were probably many more blanks they hadn't filled over the seven years since they'd moved to Rabot County from Camoya, but one glance at Mama and the doctor thought better than to keep them any longer.

"Yes, that's it. I'll send a report to the proctor conducting your EMD so they know about your arm. This shouldn't be a problem, but it's standard practice not to have any magical procedures done within fifteen hours of the exam to prevent a false positive."

Enee dug her fingers into her palms.

"It'd take a lot more than a broken arm to turn me into a mage, Doctor," she said.

The doctor led them back to the receptionist.

"Go on," Mama told her.

She didn't argue. Enee didn't want to see Mama speak to the receptionist. She didn't want to see how much this would cost them. Probationary citizens, like Mama, and their kids weren't covered for most medical stuff. Say, like, stupidly falling from a Grail Tree and breaking your arm.

Outside, Mama had propped their bike against the building. The empty bags Mama used for Mr. and Mrs. Whittle's weekly grocery run filled the bulky front carriage, leaving the rear-facing rack free for Enee to sit on. She waited until Mama came out before climbing on. Without a word, Mama wrapped their tail around Enee and pedaled away. The scarring left by Oma's absent head made the end of the tail pink and knotted.

"I'm sorry I made you come here. It won't happen again," Enee croaked.

She felt Mama's sigh—the sigh of a long day that not even caffeine and a month of sleeping in could cure.

"It will, and I doubt it will have anything to do with *climbing a tree.*"

Enee blanched.

"Just not too often, okay?" Mama said, too tired to truly uncover any of Enee's secrets.

"Okay."

Mama pedaled through town. Enee glimpsed the shops and the post-workday crowd. Rowbuirin wasn't big, but it had all the locals wanted. Lattes, second-hand clothing, books, pets for sale, a bank. The stores lined both sides of a four-way intersection stamped into the hill like a fallen cross.

"Do you think we could stop at the WyrmMart before heading home? I want to see if they have more tomatoes," Enee asked.

"For Arc?"

"Yeah."

She owed her life to Arc. What he'd done required more than a simple thank-you. A sack of rotting tomatoes would be perfect.

Mama veered towards the WyrmMart and parked on the sidewalk.

"We'll both go. I needed to go to the pharmacy for the Whittles today anyway," Mama said.

They left the bike on the curb, not bothering to lock it. Folks knew who it belonged to. If they didn't, they'd quickly find out.

The inside of the WyrmMart was, well, *wyrm-sized* and had nothing to do with the actual sale of such an Elemental. Several patrons inside caught sight of them and scooted out the door, nearly clogging the exit until they learned to take turns passing through. To them, a small space with a big Chimera smelled like trouble.

While Mama hunted down the pharmacist to check for Mr. and Mrs. Whittle's order, Enee found the manager's office. The door, as usual, was propped open. Nola Kannon sat behind her desk, scribbling her way through a stack of paper.

"Hi, Nola," she called, giving the doorframe a knock.

The store manager jumped in her seat, swiveling her beaked face toward the door. If Nola had intended to smile, she failed miserably.

"What a nice surprise. Hello, Enelope," she said.

"I'm sorry if I'm interrupting. I was in town and wondered if you had more of those tomatoes."

Nola looked over her notes before dashing to the back storage bins.

"Is Chalice, I mean, your, uh… Are you alone?" Nola asked, looking for Mama as she handed Enee a clear plastic bag filled with two dozen rotting tomatoes.

"*Mama* is at the pharmacy," Enee corrected, gently steering Nola away from the public name they never used. "Thank you for the tomatoes."

Enee added a smile, trying to keep her vibe as close to *don't worry, Mama won't eat you* as possible. Apparently, she needed to work on her vibes. Despite having known Enee since before her canines came in, Nola never seemed at ease with either of them. She still refused to call Mama by their personal name. Then again, so did most people.

"You have the EMD tomorrow, don't you?" she asked, keeping her breath shallow and quiet.

Nola's question killed her mood. Still, Enee nodded.

"Don't worry. It'll be over quickly," Nola said, who looked more than ready to sink back into her desk chair. "My daughter, Estel, and I will be in the audience. You know Estel, yes?"

Enee frowned. "Yes, I know Estel. We don't really hang out."

Nola relaxed back into her chair. "Ah, well, it's a big school."

Not big enough.

Enee desperately needed to run, climb, or ride until her lungs burst. Until her worries faded to just her and the dirt. Just her and Knoble. Just her and the next tree branch. The feeling must have been written all over Enee's face when she and Mama jumped back onto the bike. One look and Mama knew exactly what she needed.

"Fast?" Mama asked.

Enee clutched the bag of tomatoes. *"Fast."*

Mama pedaled with maddening speed towards the Hollow, leaving the town of Rowbuirin behind in a cloud of dust.

CHAPTER THREE

WELCOME TO PORTO BELLO, MIND THE CROCSWALLOWS

Stand on the tallest tree in Rumfoot Hollow, and *maybe* you'll find the entrance to Enee's apartment complex. The Hollow, however, knew how to hide things. To find Porto Bello and its towering mushroom buildings, you had to remember where you lived and how to get there. Luckily, Enee had a great memory. *If* the information proved important.

Mama stopped the bike where the road opened to the main entrance and its wide, hand-hewn sign.

"Go on ahead. I have some work that I want to finish for the Whittles before it gets dark," they said.

Enee knew they owed the Whittles a lot, and Mama showed their appreciation for all they did in the only way they knew how. Hard work. One of Enee's hearts wished Mama could work at the Whittles' apple orchard full-time, so they didn't have to juggle life around the whims of a job deemed *stable* enough for a probationary citizen. But that was impossible. The Whittles would have to go through a lot of paperwork to prove that an orchard could properly employ someone with a mountain of citizenship dues hanging over their head.

"Will you be gone long?" Enee asked.

She looked to Mama's calloused paws and followed the trail of scars that mapped their time as a cadet in the Guard and every odd job afterward. She counted each carefully made braid of their mane, girdled in shorter versions of her own golden hair cord. Mama used the crook of their finger to raise Enee's gaze to their own.

"Only for as long as I'm needed, lionheart."

Enee watched until Mama disappeared around the bend. When she claimed the Grail Stone, things would be different. A historian from the local university would pay big money to get their hands on a Grail Stone that revealed the past. Maybe not as much as a city-dwelling corporate hotshot, but the rumors she gathered from the Rowbuirin Castle tour guides who gossiped over their lunch break at The Mitey Bean said those kinds of buyers were only interested in Grail Trees that produced Stones that foretold the future. Even so, the Grail Stone she had her eye on would be enough to clear years of Mama's dues. Plus, those buyers would keep their mouths shut about how Enee got the Stone in the first place. Otherwise, they'd be in just as much trouble for buying the Stone as Enee would be for taking it.

Mama could work outside, set their hours, and never have to make a Smokin' Mochaccino again.

First things first, she owed a few people her thanks.

Enee hoisted the bag of rotten tomatoes over her shoulder and passed Porto Bello's threshold. The wards placed along the perimeter shifted, filling her nose with the musk of mushrooms, mixed with the smell of aging wood chips and Madame Huggle's nine-day stew pushing day eleven. Enee could see the mushroom apartments, some squat, and others lanky and crooked. White spots and the occasional borehole from the Wax Wyrms riddled the mushrooms' red caps.

As Enee made her way to Loop A, she caught sight of her landlord, Tobias Loch. He lumbered up the path with a handmade adhesive gun in his hands.

"Did they cut it off?" Mr. Loch asked.

"Yeah. Dr. Sable was able to regrow it, though. This time with super strength," Enee said. She balled her hand into a fist, ignoring the ache the break left behind. "All thanks to your quick rescue."

Mr. Loch snorted. It was a considerable sound, given that his nose took up most of his face.

"One-armed kids make for poor ratings," he said, his pore-pitted cheeks brightening with a bit of color.

Tobias Loch was one of the few people Enee knew who stood taller than Mama. As an Everlass, he was a Land Elemental, like a Foblin. Shaggy white fur covered his whole body except for his face, hands, and bare toes. A green moss cloak covered his shoulders, clasped at the nape of his neck. Salt-shocked hair hung over his back except for the little bun that kept the bangs off his wrinkled brow. Enee hadn't known Mr. Loch to move faster than a lumber, his tail always dragging behind him and creating trails in the wood chips. At least, not until he burst through the woods at a dead gallop to Enee's rescue with Arc a good two minutes behind him. Who knew her landlord could put a swift-footed Foblin to shame?

When Enee looked closer, she realized he was cradling something in his left hand. She didn't have to ask before he opened two fingers to show the little head of a Croc-swallow hatchling.

"This reprobate was eating through Mr. Soupmin's porch," Mr. Loch grumbled.

The hatchling thrashed its golden snout and tried to wriggle free, revealing the yellow down of its newborn wings.

"Where are you going to put them?" Enee asked.

She knew some folks ate Crocswallows, but Mr. Loch had been a strict vegetarian for three hundred and ten years.

"A crew is coming later next week to do a sweep and take him to a reserve. Until then, he's my prisoner, sentenced to watch me do paperwork."

Enee debated if paperwork stood as a better fate than being eaten. The sweeper crew did give Enee hope that they'd finally evict the Wax Wyrms from her ceiling. She knew Mr. Loch tried his best with the resources he had, but she didn't want to wake up with one of them in her ear again.

Although Mr. Loch had better things to do, he walked Enee to her building. They passed the registration desk with its connected shower room and turned down the entrance to Loop A. Apartment twenty was the tallest mushroom in the loop. The cream-colored stalk had small windows along one side and a red cap that had faded to a feverous blush. The whole structure leaned slightly to the left, and leaned even more when Mama stepped inside.

"Tell Mama I'm processing your latest request for a

ground-level shRoom this week. A few rumors are floating around about vacancies, so hopefully, I'll have an answer for you soon," Mr. Loch said.

After five years in Porto Bello, they still couldn't get a shRoom on the ground floor. Enee couldn't really complain, though. Five years here was comfier than the two she and Mama had spent living in a tent on the edge of Rabot County after they'd left Camoya. That didn't mean Enee couldn't hope for a space that didn't sway during a thunderstorm. Having an eight-foot-something Chimera as a roommate posed a slight problem. If Enee did any growing, their combined size would snap the apartment like a breadstick.

"I'll tell them," said Enee. "And, Mr. Loch?"

"Yeah, kid?"

"Thanks."

Mr. Loch blushed. "I did it for the ratings."

With that, he lumbered off, probably itching to put the Crocswallow hatchling down before it bit off a finger.

Left on her own, Enee stepped onto the porch and took the central door to the stairs. Up and up she went, until there were no more levels and no more rounded doors or shared toilet cubbies. Enee yanked a long string hanging from the ceiling of the very last floor. A trapdoor dropped down a row of stairs. She climbed up and pushed open a second door at the top to get into the apartment, leaving the stairs unfurled for Mama when they got home.

"Evening MuMu," Enee called.

She dropped the tomatoes next to the sandstove and knocked on the old breadbox she'd converted into a house for MuMu. The Kitchen Drake poked her head out and squeaked. She was cold. Enee looked up from the central pillar that pushed into the domed roof. A slight breeze poured over the platform that doubled as her bedroom. She had left the window open.

"Sorry, Mu," Enee said, giving the Drake a scratch on the nose.

MuMu curled back into her box and swiftly returned to her nap. Just as Enee took the first step that spiraled up to her platform, a tap came from the balcony. Enee looked to the door and smiled. She gave the sliding glass a good shove and stepped onto the spongy deck.

"Are you okay?" Arc asked the moment she reached the rail.

The Foblin crouched on the end of the tree branch across from the balcony. His snake-locks were all trained on her, their pupils the size of saucers.

Enee wriggled her fingers. "Good as new."

Twenty percent of the worry drained out of his face. "Are you sure?"

"Positive. Get over here before you fall," Enee teased, trying to lighten the mood.

Arc falling was even more unlikely than Mr. Loch electively running. His connection to the forest gave him certain protections. A tree branch would probably swoop down to catch him if he fell.

"I can't. The accident put my mom on edge. She only gave me ten minutes to see if you were okay," Arc admitted, pressing a finger to his lips before pointing to the forest.

The trees were listening.

"Ouch. I better be quick then," said Enee, knowing well enough to shut up about the Grail Tree.

Tree gossip always came in vague reports. The forest didn't really understand or care to understand the people who blundered above the soil. But if Mrs. Landem specifically asked the woods to listen in, why take the risk? She dashed back into the shRoom and grabbed the tomatoes, presenting the soupy mess like a polished set of family armor. Arc's smile brightened his eyes, which were as green as swamp moss in winter.

"For me?" he beamed.

"For your Snail army. I don't recommend giving yourself botulism."

Arc leaned forward and accepted the bag. He had two hundred and fifty pet Glamour Snails, give or take, all hungry for anything mushy.

"They'll love it. Thank you." Arc nibbled his lip for a minute. "I got something for you, too."

"What? Why?"

Arc pulled an envelope from his pocket and passed it over. "Before you say anything, I know you only accept the ones Mama gives you. But I didn't buy it. I saved it from a slow death by mildew and Wax Wyrm poop," Arc added quickly.

Enee opened the envelope and gulped.

"It's a 1983 edition MMA collectors' card for Dario 'The Hammer' Martel," Arc explained.

The Mixed Magic Arts fighter's profile had faded, but she could still make out his photo. Enee desperately wanted to build upon the thirteen tucked safely beside her bed. But the cards were Mama's gift to her. Enee passed the envelope back. She couldn't accept the card, especially when Arc had been the one to save her life.

"I can't," she said.

"Come on."

"No," Enee insisted. "Please don't be hurt."

Arc sighed and took the card. Whatever he wanted to say died beneath a half-mumbled, "I'm sorry I didn't do more."

Enee rolled her eyes. "You saved my life."

"All I did was get help. I should have had better contingencies in place. I didn't even wait in town afterward. I just went home," he said, practically whispering the last part.

Enee gave him a hard stare. Staying for hours on end wasn't an option, and not just because of Mama's worry. Foblins couldn't stray from their forest for long, and not having a forest wasn't an option. Well, not a *healthy* option.

She leaned over the rail and took his hand. "*My life.*"

Arc fell quiet. She'd tease him about it tomorrow when the whole thing wasn't as fresh. Maybe she'd tell him her arm had fallen off or something.

"See you on our walk to school?" Arc asked.

"It'll take more than a little fall to get rid of that tradition," she said. "Besides, I need someone to help keep me from running away before the EMD."

This time, Arc rolled his eyes. "You can stand still long enough to see the exam through."

"Easy for you to say. You're an Elemental. You only have to watch."

"Would you prefer your mom sticking you in a bathtub full of Pegasus milk on the roof?" Arc countered.

Enee snorted, pitying the person who tried to milk a Pegasus. In all seriousness, the tradition of the Foblins carried a downright depressing history. Their role during the Crusades had been a bloody one. And, odd or not, bathing in Pegasus milk on the evening of the EMD paid tribute to that past.

"I'd prefer a private ceremony. I know what the outcome will be anyway," Enee admitted.

"Think of it this way. After tomorrow night, you won't have to worry about it again."

That wasn't true. Enee would have to do this dance for the rest of her life in different ways. Plus, at school, Enee only had two courses with Arc as it was. Once she got the official *I can't wield magic* stamp of approval, they wouldn't have any subjects together. Although their friendship was stronger than a school day, the idea still stunk.

A branch full of leaves cascaded from the neighboring tree. Arc snapped his attention to the forest. Each of his snake-locks flicked its tongue as if it could taste what he heard.

"I've got to go, but I'll see you tomorrow," Arc said, sticking out his pinky.

She stuck out her own. When their pinkies touched, they let out a buzzing sound between their teeth. Arc jumped from his perch with the sack of rotten tomatoes. The mountain laurel at the foot of the tree had caught him and lowered him to the ground without a sound.

The moment he was out of sight, the trees stilled. Enee listened to the voices of her neighbors and the calls of the different Drakes and Aves nesting in the canopy.

MuMu began to whine. She still needed to close the window.

"All right. I'm coming," Enee called.

CHAPTER FOUR
COUNTING CARDS AND FALLEN STARS

Enee dreamt she stood with her back to the Grail Tree, holding a longsword in both hands. Not just any sword. *The Swan*. The same blade that hung above Mama's bed and posed as one of the few Noe family heirlooms she'd inherit now awaited her command. But the version of the Swan Enee carried wasn't Mama's sword. *Yet*. Nor did she stand before the Grail Tree as herself.

Enee gripped the hilt, twisting the blade. The metal showed the blur of her face. The Chimera who glanced back was older, darker, and muscled in a way that only fighting for your life could make you. Like Enee, their face was practically bald compared to Mama's. And like her, she had no doubt about what to call her host. *Family*. The helmet her host wore was the same one that hung next to the Swan, its silver sculpted into the likeness of a Gorgon. The Gorgon's body bent backward over the comb, and their snake-locks splayed across the helmet's brow. They were screaming.

This dream? Again?

The call of a trumpet widened Enee's senses. The Grail Tree looked—smaller? Younger. The forest felt thicker, swollen with mulch and mold and blood. She did not stand beneath the Grail Tree alone.

"A truce has been called," said her opponent.

If this had been any other time, Enee would have said an older version of her best friend waited before her. But if Enee was correct and her dream took place during the last Crusade, she stood in a time before the Foblins were cursed with the chance of having a child born with snake-locks. That meant one thing.

The person who surrendered their sword was a Gorgon.

This Gorgon's snake-locks were unbound but blindfolded, and he sported thick leather armor. Behind him, an army continued to bash metal against metal until their allies shook them from their stupor.

"The kings have called for a truce!" the soldiers echoed.

The battle slowed like a melting glacier. Most of the soldiers remained wary. Was this a true end to the war between the Alchem kings? The Crusades had lasted too long for them to hope for peace. Enee wouldn't have put faith in the kings who endorsed two hundred years of war, either. Only her history lessons had revealed this to be the last of the great wars. The Crusade of the Last Great Acre.

None of the other soldiers ventured as close to the Grail Tree as her, avoiding the seepage of poison sap that clung to her boots.

"I suggest we rest," Arc's doppelganger said, brushing chalky dust from his knees.

He waved to others with similar, slithering locks that were blindfolded to avoid accidentally turning their allies to stone. Despite the blindfolds, Enee still spotted rubble on the forest floor, the same color as the dust on this soldier's clothing.

"I will rest when your kings have signed and sealed the truce," Enee snarled, trapped in a script she had no power to change.

She could see the faded and broken crests of the royal families from the land that would one day be Pendra-North. The other crests she saw came from the Republic of Wick, Phlox, and Gattius. A few even looked to be of Eybor Northland. What distance they must have traveled, all for the sake of the promised land that the Alchem did not own.

The Gorgon took a step forward, snapping all into focus. Enee adjusted the aim of the Swan. Chimeras did not fight for a king. They fought for the Grail Trees. The trumpet's call for pause meant nothing to her should one of the soldiers decide to test her mettle.

"Do not think you can beat me, Gorgon. I know of your tricks. I know my reflection better than your snake-lock eyes. It is my ally in this fight," Enee's host said.

The Gorgon looked sadder than Enee thought her friend's face could. What had he seen during the Crusades? She could feel the same haunting weight on her ancestor's shoulders. How many bloodlines vanished in defense of the Trees?

Enee shifted her grip. She had to remain centered. Focused.

Perhaps she'd lose her life, but her conscience remained clear. The Chimeras were free, unlike many Elementals who'd chosen sides between the reigning kingdoms.

Did they really expect her to believe that, after everything, they'd call a truce? Just like that? Not a chance. The kings *wanted* something.

Let their want burn.

The Gorgon's gaze turned as sharp as shattered glass. "Are you sure?" he asked.

ENEE SHOT OUT OF BED SO FAST THAT IT TOOK HER A MOMENT to realize she stood on the platform's edge. From all the noise in her head, everything suddenly sounded too quiet. Too still. Only the sting in her palms blunted the silence. Enee moaned and rubbed her face. These dreams were becoming problematic.

She tried to curl back into sleep but failed to do more than tangle herself in blankets. Whether the blame rested with the old leftovers she found when Mama hadn't come home for dinner, her approaching EMD, or the freaky-vivid dream that'd plagued her for months, Enee couldn't get her brain to turn off. Sleep fell out of the question once her arm started to itch from Dr. Sable's healing spell.

Enee rolled to the floor.

One, two, three…

She tried doing her morning push-ups, but only hit twenty before the ache in her arm became too much. She ended up just lying on the floor, listening to the sounds of the shRoom and Mama's gentle snoring. Good. They needed the sleep. If Enee had to guess, they had been called back to The Mitey Bean from the orchard for another after-hours cleanup. She could smell their bagged dinner downstairs, long since gone cold.

Stupid poetry slams, Enee thought. Why couldn't Muses clean up after themselves?

Enee uncapped a charmed glowstone for some light and pulled out her treasure box. The box of peach wood and willow was the size of a loaf of bread and probably the best find Mama had dug up from the giveaway pile at the town dump in the last year. A stiff hinge kept the lid closed without the need for a clasp. Painted on the top were three pomegranates on a delicate blue sky.

She opened the box and dumped her MMA cards onto the bed. With them fell a braided lock of Knoble's mane, a river stone she'd plucked from the bank of the Church-mere, the worn remains of Mama's PT manual, a coin she'd found lodged in the Stone Troll Wall, and a round scrap of paper Arc used to sketch his snail-shaped business logo during one of his future planning sessions. All of her most precious treasures in one spot.

Enee set aside the lock of mane and Arc's sketch, trying not to think about the look on the Gorgon's face in her dream.

That wasn't Arc. Her mind had only stolen his face.

She pushed the dream away and focused on the cards. She had thirteen in total. They tracked every year she'd been alive, gifts from Mama for every birthday. That was their thing: the gift of a card and a fun experience. Sometimes, they hiked to a neighboring park. Other times, Enee held Mama's shoulders while scaling a cliff. Once, they swam to a small island on Lake Lore near the bottom tip of Rabot County and ate all the Goldfish they could catch. They got stuck on the island until the Charon River finished its weekly spirit drain, which made the experience even better.

She missed two glorious days of school.

Enee's first card was Maria "The Pure" Mettle, a Mixed Magic Artist from the States of South Florent. The card didn't have all the bells and whistles that the newer cards had, simply displaying the Artist's statistics under a kick-butt headshot. Mama read each card to her so she could commit them to memory. Arman "Of The Hour" Parisa from Gattius, Lady "Guerrilla" Rain from one of the Cemre Islands, Kitty "The Ox" Horn from Enee's home country, and five other Alchem mages from Phlox. Finally, Enee found the card she'd gotten on her thirteenth birthday. Olwan "A-Bomb" Yule, her uncontested favorite.

Yule was the first Elemental in the MMA and the first from Eythor Southland. The Yeti was a living legend with flawless blue skin, snow-white fangs, and matching fur combed into perfectly symmetrical braids. Yule wiped the floor with her opponents, holding six champion titles and smoothing the way for other Elementals to enter the MMA.

Enee scooped them together and put the cards back into the box with her other treasures. Part of Enee wished she'd taken Arc's card. But the cards were always Mama's gift to her. It didn't matter that the ones she had were dated compared to the newest cards printed on charmed stock and worth more than she'd make selling a kidney. Her cards were priceless, no matter what the other kids in her classes said, as they traded Artists as if they were candy scored on the eve of Saints Hallows.

She put the box next to her mattress. Sorting the cards did little to send Enee back to sleep, so she crawled over to the small window cut into the domed roof and pushed it open. The early autumn air felt nice. The shRoom stood tall enough and was placed in just the right spot for Enee to see out to the star fields on the far side of the Whittles' orchard. She relaxed against the window frame and scanned from fallen star to fallen star.

Some of the pieces that fell were as big as ships. A few even burned white or baby blue. In the halos they made, Enee could make out a Pegasus. The creature paused by a giant star, no doubt licking the minerals on the surface before moving on to wherever Pegasus liked to fly. She didn't know what kept them traveling, moving in circles around the globe. But she knew they'd always return to the fallen stars for their steady diet of dreams and wishes.

Aegis... Aja... Alma... Enee counted the stars with the names of the remaining Chimera families.

If only she had wings like a Pegasus. Chimeras did, once upon a time. She could reach the top of the Grail Tree without a problem if she had wings. Parts of Enee's dream flashed to mind. Stupid legends. The day the warring kingdoms and their allied Elementals swore never to claim another Grail Stone was when doctors used mercury to cure a common cold. Who were they to set the rules on the Chimeras' behalf?

Amell... Anapal... Atila...

Her ancestors died defending them. So, why couldn't she ask for something in return? The Grail Tree wouldn't die without it—at least, Enee didn't think so.

Aventure... Barlas... Bedelia...

Mama told her that pursuing the Grail Stones during the Crusades was an excuse. Could a nation argue with a king who held a Stone capable of seeing the future, proving the existence of a utopia that'd be obtainable if they had the right amount of land? Could an army argue with a leader who possessed a way to lay history at their feet so all could see their right to rule?

Cutting down the Grails Trees simply made the claims to certain regions final. Plus, if a Stone showed something an Alchem king didn't want the Mundus to see, getting rid of the Tree was a good way to keep another from growing in its place.

The Grail Trees' way of protecting themselves should have given the Alchem and Elementals what they truly deserved. *Nothing.* Well, nothing but a good poisoning and a bad reputation. Kings, however, knew how to turn disaster into opportunity. They became the heroes of their legends, swooping in to save the Mundus from the poisonous Grail Trees and their villainous Chimera. It's funny how easy it is to make everyone forget why their homes had turned to wasteland in the first place.

Absolutely hilarious.

Maybe Enee's plan did make her a villain, at least to the Grail Tree. But compared to the kings, her claim to this Grail Stone was practically philanthropic. How wrong could it be for her to sell the Stone to a private collector or someone who loved history enough to pay her price? She needed the money. She *needed* to free Mama from the mercy of others and their citizenship dues, preferably in a way that didn't require them to abandon the Hollow. Or, more specifically, Arc.

Belinda... Beroi... Cadel...

Mama deserved a better life. They deserved a proper

house, an escape from the schedules that had no end, and the hours that yielded more late nights than money for groceries. Everyone wanted a big hunk of muscle until they tried to squeeze them into spaces too small or asked them to handle objects so delicate they crumbled like sand. Then they called them feral. They called them unstable.

Carda... Cedar... Cheever...

But Mama played the game. They'd keep playing even when there was no longer a need for a Chimera in Rabot County. A day Enee swore to be ready for.

The Chimeras had helped the Grail Trees when they needed them the most. Once the EMD was behind her, it would be time they returned the favor.

CHAPTER FIVE

GLAMOUR SNAILS REQUIRE TOMATOES

Enee peeled herself off the windowsill like an overdone pancake. She had dozed off sometime after counting her one hundred and thirtieth star. The forest's Mourning Drakes cried to the dark sky as if to raise the sun. Enee rolled over with a groan and found a flat space for push-ups. Time to wake up.

One… two… OUCH. Stupid arm. Three… four…

Mama shuffled in the kitchen, wrapped in a puffy robe that could swallow Enee whole, except for the sleeves; Mama had cut those off at the shoulder. Finding a good robe wasn't easy for a Chimera, and having no sleeves was better than having small ones.

"Out," Mama cooed, coaxing MuMu from the breadbox with a lump of cheese.

The Kitchen Drake slipped from her lair and slithered over to the sandstove. She was long enough to wrap herself around the aluminum basin filled with two gallons of fine sand. With a steady supply of cheese in front of her little snout, MuMu ate her fill while her long, noodly body began to warm. After a few minutes, the heated sand made the air shimmer. While Mama took out a pan to fry a dozen eggs, Enee went straight for a jar of peanut butter and used the last of it to drown a bowl of fresh apple slices.

"Sleep okay?" Mama asked, taking a seat across from Enee.

She intended to mention her dream, but, like every morning, Mama's eyelids hung at half-mast. The rings of sienna behind them, once as bright as a polished shield, had tarnished with whatever little sleep they'd gotten that night. Mama didn't need the weight of Enee's dreams. They needed the comfort of their own.

"Not really," Enee admitted.

They finished cooking the eggs and grabbed a fresh apple from the bag they had brought home after visiting the Whittles. They may run out of peanut butter, but the apocalypse would have to burn the Hollow to a crisp before they ran out of apples, coffee, or eggs.

"We'll leave at eleven fifteen tonight," Mama reminded her as they sat down.

Right. The EMD.

"*We*? You'll be there?"

Mama nodded. "I will make sure of it."

Enee swallowed slowly. Was that a promise? They needed rest, not to be shoved into a grove with all the adults who had opinions about Enee and, by default, Mama.

"Why do you think Chimeras aren't connected to magic?" she asked.

45

They reached out a paw and tucked a few loose strands of Enee's hair behind her ear.

"Perhaps because Chimeras never needed magic to define themselves," they said after a long pause.

"But do I have to let everyone *watch* while I don't let magic define me?" Enee grumbled.

"According to the law," Mama said as they dug into a mountain of eggs.

"What about Chimera law?"

Mama grinned. "Finish your breakfast, lionheart."

One way or another, the whole thing would be over by dawn. Enee would step up to an altar and drop a precious item into a pool of water harvested from the Churchmere. A minute later, her object would come back *without* a Familiar. No fuss. No prolonged applause. She could slip back into the audience the same as ever.

With breakfast finished, they got ready for their day. Mama set aside the kitchen's water barrel as a reminder to fill it up later while Enee scrubbed her teeth. The only holdup was using the bathroom. They had to wait until the single stall downstairs was free. Plus, you never wanted to be the first to use the incinerator toilet. The Sewer Drake, who lingered in the dark corner of the pot, was not a pleasant creature first thing in the morning.

At six thirty on the dot, they left. Neither of them needed much. Mama only packed an apron since they got a free sandwich for lunch at the cafe, and Enee only brought what could fit in her pockets. A pencil (not that she used it), the token for the lunch line, and, when the mood struck, one of her MMA cards. She only took notes when the Treechers demanded she try, meaning they had to be the ones to literally push the paper into her hands. The only thing worse than her penmanship was her nonexistent reading skills. It took a few years, but the Treechers eventually found the right labels they needed to justify Enee's "limitations" on her report card. That didn't mean they didn't throw out the occasional test to make sure she wasn't faking it.

Mama told her not to worry. Her way of learning was *her way* and just as good as any other. So, she didn't. The catch? Enee had to remember everything the Treechers said and be able to spit it back out again when they asked it of her.

Today, Enee knew she'd need some extra *oomph* to get her to listen to the lessons. She pushed her Olwan "A-Bomb" Yule card into a hard plastic sleeve and hid it in her lower-right pocket before heading out the door.

"Ready?" Enee asked as Mama mounted their bike.

They smiled.

"Ready."

Mama kicked into gear, spitting woodchips into the air. Enee launched after them on foot, putting every ounce of speed into beating Mama to the complex's entrance. Mama didn't let her win, but Enee never made it easy for them to do so.

She huffed, puffed, and smiled a wildcat smile, eyes tearing up with the cold morning air. They tried not to run anyone over during their morning races, but accidents happened. The neighbors learned not to be in the way.

Mama kept straight once they passed the entrance wards, while Enee veered left. She traveled the road that bordered Porto Bello until she had no choice but to cross through the woods. The Landem Estate technically took Enee out of her way, but she liked running to school with Arc. The extra time it took to get to him didn't matter, since she always ran as if the forest were on fire. Plus, if she didn't physically exhaust herself before school, Enee would feel like she was the one on fire.

On the Landem Estate, the trees kept themselves organized. They turned into sentinels that watched over every creamy lattice and stained-glass window of the mushroom palace plopped in the center of the massive property. To be fair, the Landems needed the space. Arc's family consisted of five siblings, two parents, three grandparents, one aunt, three uncles, and four cousins.

Enee could hear their morning ruckus from the lawn.

"Finish your breakfast! Did Arc finish his? Arc!? Oh, he did. *Good.*" "Pants are for *every* day. Socks? Okay, no socks are fine." "Everyone, backpacks! Does Arc have his?"

Even if Mrs. Landem allowed her inside, Enee would rather get run over by Mama's bike than throw herself into the mess that spilled out of their blessed holy oak and mistletoe doors.

Besides, Arc wouldn't be there.

Enee cut through the rose garden and went around the pond towards the groundskeeper's cottage. Once she passed the old tool shed, Enee entered Arc's kingdom. A stone windmill half her size stood in the center of a hand-dug moat. Charmed stones surrounded the windmill. Nothing could stick to the stones, not even a wriggling horde of two hundred and fifty Glamour Snails.

Within the barrier knelt Arc. The Foblin watched the Snails swarm over a dish of rotten tomatoes. Enee wanted to meet the genius who discovered Glamour Snail slime to be the best spell neutralizer in the Mundus. All she could imagine was a mage trying to contain their wayward magic while practicing in the woods. When all hope seemed lost, they suddenly proclaimed, "Well, this is bad. Let's rub a Snail on it."

"Don't be pushy, Nome," Arc scolded, moving one of the bigger Snails to a second dish to keep them from crushing the others.

As Arc's friend and theoretical business partner, Enee had committed the Snails to memory.

Nome, Steeple, Bean, Tank, Gregory the Third (maybe the fourth), Pan, York, Dawdle, Ripper, Kettle, Spork, Bandit, Pocket...

Easy enough. Until one of them died, and Enee had to re-memorize the pecking order. The life of a Snail was brutal.

"All good in the kingdom of slime?" Enee asked.

Arc nodded. "Your tomato donation is greatly appreciated."

"I aim to please. Are you ready?"

"Yeah. I just need my bag."

Arc stepped around his Snail horde and jumped over the moat. The mountain laurel on the other side held out his backpack and an old rag doused in enough Slime-Be-Gone to strip the color out of the sky. A few jars of harvested slime waited at their roots for Arc to store them in the shed next to all the others.

"I think we almost have enough to put a notice in the Shopper's Guide," Arc said as he locked the shed for safe-keeping.

"Really?"

He nodded. "We just need to figure out how to convince Mr. Pool to print it."

Enee groaned. "Because that's totally going to happen."

The editor of the Rowbuirin Shopper's Guide treated the paper like the Rabot Gazette. They had tried requesting an advertisement last year, only to be told that Sir Illium Pool was not in the business of promoting kid lemonade stands.

"People can change their minds." He placed a hand on the trunk of an oak tree and whispered into the bark. "I'm off to school. We'll talk after I get back."

The message would pass from tree to tree, straight to his parents' ears. Benefits of being a Foblin. Super parental stalking powers. Enee just thanked her lucky fallen stars that certain *blind spots* existed in the forest, which allowed them to keep You-Know-What a secret.

"Talk about what?" Enee asked.

At first, Arc didn't answer, and she didn't push him. But when they reached the main bike trail, he sighed so long that Enee expected him to deflate. The Foblin slouched into his sweatshirt and pulled the hood over his snake-locks.

"My parents keep bringing up my bonding ritual," he finally admitted.

"Wait, why? You're thirteen. Aren't you supposed to wait until you're sixteen?" Enee sputtered.

Elementals didn't have to go through the EMD, but they had their own problems. All Elementals needed to be connected to the element of their lineage in some shape or form. And while every Elemental was born with a bond through their parents, eventually, that connection faded, and they needed to *resubmit*. To Enee, it sounded like signing up for a library card. If getting a library card required a blood oath. In her opinion, Foblins had it the worst of all. They had to stay within spitting distance of the specific plot of land they chose to bond with. Otherwise, spending too long away from their forest would be a death sentence.

"My mom doesn't want me to end up like my uncle. After all the excitement of yesterday, she got it in her head to try to reach out to him. I think your accident made her think she needed to check in on *everyone*. It turns out he was in the hospital," Arc said.

"Is he okay?"

"Yeah. He just stayed in a rental plot for too long and passed out on his way to work. His boyfriend got him help and found him a new rental before he got too sick," Arc said.

From what Enee remembered, she liked Uncle Tal. Rather than take the official blood oath at sixteen to bond with the Hollow, Uncle Tal hit the road with his friends and made temporary blood pacts wherever he landed. A temporary pact was the Foblin version of renting a forest.

But to make a temporary pact, the Foblin had to offer a bowl of blood to the land they decided to stay in. A couple of months later, when that bowl ran dry, their bond snapped. The Mundus didn't forgive those who made temporary promises. So, a blood pact only worked in a single spot once. If they tried again within a mile of the same place, the bond wouldn't stick.

"Do you think your mom will try to force him to move back to the Hollow?" Enee asked.

Arc shook his head. "Mom says he was born with more wander in his veins than water. The only way to make him stay would be to change him. If she did that, he wouldn't be the brother she loved."

"And yet, she wants you to think about your bond now?"

Arc shrugged.

"Do you want to do it early?" she asked.

Arc always had a plan. Flip the Foblin over and give him a shake, and Enee guaranteed a dozen different schemes would come out. Arcamo Landem's current plan involved building a Glamour Snail empire. He'd start it as a side hustle while working as a Green Squirrel Mail delivery person after graduation. Since Enee didn't have a plan, he incorporated her into his so she had a fallback in case nothing better came to mind. They would both make deliveries and sell high-quality Glamour Snail slime to licensed mages, maybe even earning degrees from the local university to help them look more official on paper.

Enee didn't have the heart to tell him that most universities probably wouldn't take a Chimera with *her way* of learning. So, she let herself sink into the ideas that helped Arc feel better about life. He liked to dream and scheme. He liked the Hollow.

"To be honest, I don't know. Part of me thinks, *sure.* Bonding early doesn't really change my plans. Another part of me worries about making a decision, like a real one, and not just something I can erase if I think of something better. And—"

Arc didn't finish, but Enee knew what he was thinking, because it was what she was thinking. What if she and

Mama left one day? Left and went too far for her to travel to the Hollow to see him. Enee turned the roar in her chest into a laugh and caught Arc in a headlock.

"I don't plan on leaving," she said.

"You don't have a plan at all," he countered as he tried to escape.

"Not true. My plan is You-Know-What," Enee pointed out.

"And what if that makes everyone in Rabot County mad enough to chase you out of town?"

Enee didn't want to think about it. She twisted her lips into a smug smile.

"I'd blame you."

"Nobody would believe that," he gasped, finally managing to wiggle free. "If I tried to climb You-Know-What, my snake-locks would melt off."

"Yeah, yeah, and the angry ghosts would take over your body until your mind turned into a puddle of mush and your toes fell off," Enee finished.

Foblin bedtime stories were undoubtedly graphic, which was probably why Arc carried around a small jar of Slime-Be-Gone and rubber gloves in his backpack so Enee could be sure to get *all* of the Grail Tree's sap off.

"Leaving only my ears untouched to be nibbled by Mourning Drakes," Arc recited.

"Come on, just a nibble?" Enee jumped onto a fallen log and balanced across its length.

"How'd you like it if they gnawed yours off?"

Enee rubbed the soft tufts of her long ears. "Maybe you have a point." She jumped off the log and gave her best friend a nudge. "Don't worry. No matter what happens, I won't leave you."

She stuck out her pinky. Eventually, Arc's face softened. They touched, making the same buzzing sound at the same time.

"Race you!" she said, taking off at a sprint.

Arc laughed and took off after her, showing no mercy.

CHAPTER SIX

THE SHOULDERS OF A TREECHER

E nee ran to the rolling drum of three hearts. She and Arc kept the same pace until she shot him a *don't you dare let me win* scowl. How could she get better if he didn't try? Arc picked up speed until she had a perfect view of his back. If only she could—

Arc stopped.

It was one of those spectacular moments where Enee had one second to think *this is going to suck* before they collided. She half-expected to run through him at the speed they were going. Instead, Arc flattened to the dirt like a toboggan.

"Ow," Arc moaned.

"What was that?" Enee gasped.

She rolled onto her back and looked at the ribbons of sky beyond the canopy. Did she break anything? Enee took a minute to flex her still-aching fingers. Nope. All good. Arc rolled to his side. Dirt smudged his shirt and face, but he looked unharmed.

"I saw something," he said once the daze wore off.

"So, you stopped?" she grumbled.

"Sorry," he added, looking away.

She sighed. "It's fine. Neither of us broke."

Enee got up first and helped Arc to his feet. As she suspected, they were fine. Besides, *dirt* was a synonym for *living* in her book.

"Well? Where's this dead-stop wonder?" she asked.

"Over there."

Arc guided Enee to the side of the road. A procession of six passed through the woods. She recognized five of them as seniors from school. Five *mage* seniors.

"I see Pemprin's sister," Arc said.

He pointed to a willowy mage with light, elegant hair. The girl could have been Pemprin's twin if not for the one yellow eye that contrasted with her chestnut one. Like Pemprin, Ellona was a Pendra prodigy. Come to think of it, all five of the students were at the top of their class.

"Maybe they're going to the ghost town?" Arc suggested.

"Without any supplies? I don't think so," Enee whispered.

Before a mage enrolled in university, they needed to complete a senior project. Most chose to create original spells, tame obscure Drakes, or write a massive report on the history of magic. Only the best students were offered the chance to spend one year in a ghost town. Goodness knew *why* the top students wanted to go there. Who wanted a career as a ghost psychologist? Not that it mattered. Enee would never be chosen to go. One needed to be able to wield, after all.

The sixth member of the procession only strengthened her suspicion. A proctor led the group.

"Proctor Pendra?" Arc voiced.

Yup. Proctor Ulyss Pendra, Pemprin's uncle. Ulyss carried a square box in his arms. There was only one reason a proctor would spend time with students. The EMD.

"Spying, now? You two are not building a good reputation."

They both flinched, making enough space for Pemprin to lean in. She gave them the once-over and huffed as if just looking at them proved her point.

"Where are they going?" Arc asked.

He stroked one of the snake-locks that slithered beneath the lip of his hood. Pemprin scrunched up her face and inched closer to Enee.

"They're going to the Dryad Grove to prepare for tonight," Pemprin said.

"Why do they need to prepare? They already took the EMD," Enee asked, holding back the bite in her words.

"It's not for them. They're preparing the Grove for us," she said.

The call of the would-be-mage's name came from up ahead. Keeper and the rest of Pemprin's gang waited for their leader. Nola's daughter, Estel, bounced among them, going from friend to friend like an Ave trying to find the right branch to roost on.

"Hey, Enee," Keeper called.

Enee frowned. "*Keeper*," she snarled back.

"You know, I met another Chimera," Keeper said.

Another Chimera? Here? Enee had never met another like her, unless you counted Mama. Did Mama know?

"Sselesu Retsnom. Do you know them?"

Enee racked her brain. *Retsnom*? There was no Retsnoms on Mama's rehearsed list of Chimera family names. Had she forgotten someone? Panic ate at her memory.

Over and over, she rolled the name in her mouth. Retsnom—

Arc tugged the edge of Enee's sleeve.

"Sselesu Retsnom. *Useless monster*," he whispered, sorting out the spelling of a name Enee hunted for by sound.

Pemprin shot Keeper and the girls who laughed around her a glance reserved for queens and servants. The look earned the would-be-mage a "What? It's funny."

"It sends the wrong impression, Keeper. Dignity is critical," Pemprin said, her hand clutched around her ring. "As for you two, don't be late for class."

"Just because we're not early doesn't mean we're late," Enee snapped.

Arc held out a hand, his praline palm slightly scuffed from the fall. "Come on. Let's beat them there."

They bolted down the road, blurring past the girls who squealed and jumped out of the way.

"Leash your pet, snake-curse!" Keeper shouted after them.

Enee twisted around just enough to stick her tongue out at them. Keeper had already turned to lock arms with Estel and the others, but Pemprin's posture remained perfectly unmoved. Not a single hair dared to stray out of place. And yet, her eyes watched, brimming with something Enee cringed over. *Want.*

What could a future High Mage possibly want?

Five minutes and a pair of burning lungs later, Arc and Enee made it to school. The school grounds were quite literally that. Grounds. Trees sheltered the main trail. Open circles meant for five or six kids at a time, each with butt-worn stone seats, branched off the main path.

The Treecher watched as the students found their seats. Camphor was like most Treechers. Tall. Wooded. Patient. He came from a line of trees that decided to take on a different mantle than their rooted kin. Enee didn't know why. If she had sprouted legs and learned the Mundian Common-Tongue, becoming a schoolteacher wouldn't have been her first choice.

"Ah, everyone's here," said Camphor.

Arc pulled his hood forward and tightened the draw-strings so all his snake-locks stayed inside. Enee gave him a nudge, but the smile she received was weak.

Here, Enee lost a bit of the Arc she knew. In school, he kept quiet, as if the silence turned him into a stone the others forgot was there. It worked. Kasim and Liesel bumped sneakers, seeing who could push the other furthest away, and Edom rattled off facts about the hour-glass she'd brought in to show everyone.

When the bell rang, the wards rose. A fog enclosed the circle, buffering the sound of the Hollow.

"Today, the subject of focus in all your classes will be slightly different than usual. I understand that none of you will experience the Examination for Magical Dormancy in the same way as your fellow Alchem students. However, it is still an exciting time," Camphor said.

"I guess. But everyone here is an Elemental except for

Enee. We already wield magic, and she'll never have magic in general, so it's really like any other day," said Kasim.

Enee sat on her hands until her temper turned to a simmer. She was the only one in this class who had to take the EMD. Arc, Kasim, and Liesel were all Foblins, with Liesel looking more like a beehive than a boy and Kasim sporting a heavy set of granite hands that made it seem like he always wore gauntlets. Edom was the only Sand-Oblin of the group, with warm sienna skin that rippled into gentle spirals over her cheeks.

"True, but today is still a time of transition for our community and an important remnant of the old Mundus. I'm sure the rest of you have your traditions at home. Plus, it means you can begin practicing supervised spells," said Camphor. "Except for you, of course, Enelope."

"Noted," she grumbled.

"Does that mean every class today will focus on the EMD?" Kasim complained.

Camphor laughed.

"Don't look so distraught. You might find what you learn to be interesting."

Given that Camphor taught history, Enee prepared for a thirty-minute lecture on the origins of the EMD. Instead, Camphor knelt.

"Who's up for a little trip?"

Everyone jumped out of their seats.

"Where are we going?" Enee asked.

"You'll see. However, before you can hop on, you must tell me the name of one of the Ages," Camphor said.

The group moaned. Their adventure turned into a pop quiz. But this was one Enee didn't mind. She knew the

Nine Ages. Mama had told her it was important to know how the Mundus saw time because so much of the Chimeras' past had been lost to it. What remained of their kin lived in the footnotes of the history written by those who could pay to be remembered the *right* way. So, Enee made a point to have her facts straight when she judged the stupidity of long-since-dead people.

Liesel stepped forward.

"The first Age was the Age of Foundation, followed by the Season of Empires," he said.

The Age of Foundation saw the birth of the Alchem and was a time when everyone began to spread out from the continent of Gattius and their Elemental homelands. The Season of Empires shortly followed, with dozens of new kingdoms starting to form as people settled into new lands, each striving to be the absolute best thing since the invention of cheese.

Camphor nodded and let Liesel climb to an enormous branch that stuck from his shoulders like a throne.

"Then there was the Age of Legends and the Crusades!" Kasim added quickly, eager to join his friend.

Both Ages saw the rise of the most legendary heroes in the Mundus. Murderers, thieves, and wielders of stupidly intense power who made their names through war, and all things big and angry and ugly.

For a moment, Enee could feel the Swan in her hands and the smell of sweaty armor. She dug her nails into her palms and refused to let go until it stopped.

"Next came the Age of Renaissance, followed by the Age of Unity," Edom added quickly, tucking her hourglass into her backpack to join the boys on Camphor's shoulders.

"Then the Seasons of Nations and the Era of Revolution," Arc whispered, surprising Enee over the fact that he didn't go last.

With Camphor's shoulders full, Arc sat in the Treecher's palm.

"And the last one, Enee? What Age do we find ourselves in today?" he asked.

Enee shook off the echo of her dream and stood at Camphor's side. She had no desire to be carried.

"The Age of Possibility."

The moment she answered, they took off. Camphor strode over the autumn brush and created a hole in the fog barrier big enough for Enee to jump through.

She should have known better than to think Camphor would leave his lecture behind. Throughout the walk, he spoke of the EMD. Since the EMD would technically be counted as the exam on the content Camphor talked about, Enee gave herself permission to zone in and out of the ceremony's history in favor of enjoying the walk to the Dryad Grove.

The Dryad Grove started just outside the school grounds. Here, the forest floor looked groomed between the trees. Well, not trees. Here, every tall, leafy creature was a Dryad.

Kasim snickered.

"They look like a bunch of wooden ladies minus the—"

"Kasim," Arc hissed, "Show some respect."

Kasim shot Liesel a look and wriggled his fingers like the rattling tail of a venomous Snake. "Don't get so worked up," he teased, turning Arc's expression back to stone.

Enee dug her nails into her palms.

Don't make a scene. Arc doesn't want a scene, she told herself.

The Dryads didn't give two hoots about control. One of the ladies animated long enough to swat Liesel and Kasim in the back of the head.

"Now, Lauris, they're just children," Camphor said.

"Children who need manners," Lauris scoffed before petrifying back into her tree-shape, her arms stretched upward as if ready to catch any falling stars.

The boys bit their lips and tried not to laugh. To pass the time on their way to the EMD site, they broke out their MMA cards.

"I'll trade you my Percival 'Jack-Pot' Jale for your Ima 'Making it' Od," said Kasim.

"Oh, nice. Sure," Liesel said, passing over a *three-time Mundus champion* from the unassuming island of Cane nestled in the nearly forgotten Welly Sea.

"I'd think on that trade a bit longer," Enee chimed.

She found the outline of her MMA card beneath the fabric of her pocket and traced a finger along the edge. Neither of their cards equaled hers, but still. She couldn't let such outright swindling take place under her nose.

"Nobody asked you," said Kasim.

"Hey, go ahead if you want to rip each other off. It's not my fault Liesel doesn't have the sense to recognize a bad trade."

"At least I have enough of a collection to trade. What do you have, five cards from your *mommy* or whatever you call them?" Liesel snapped.

Arc turned as if to speak up, but fell short of making the words come out of his mouth.

"Got some venom in those locks today, snake-curse?" Kasim teased.

She had no choice. Enee absolutely needed to hurl a stick at Kasim.

The aim was perfect. Spectacular, really. The stick impaled the middle of his spread deck, tearing through the card.

"Enelope, *no,*" Camphor snapped in a voice uniquely shattering from a Treecher. "Do we need to have another talk, or must I get Mx. Noe involved?"

Arc looked to Enee with *don't let them get to you* eyes.

"No, I'm sorry. It won't happen again."

Camphor grimaced. "Up front, no turning around."

She marched forward.

"Someone has to put a shorter leash on her," Kasim whispered.

"It's not her fault. My mom says without magic, Chimeras are born *unstable,*" Edom brought her voice so low her words crackled like settling sand. "It's why she can't sit still. She can't even read. Her body won't let her."

Enee clenched her fists until her healed arm felt like it would break again.

"That's not true," Arc croaked.

He said it so quietly, his chin tucked down into his chest, that only Enee could have possibly heard him. That was good enough for her. She didn't need him to defend her, and she refused to be ashamed of being a Chimera. She *was* a Chimera, cub of the greatest being that ever lived, descended from a family line that'd been around since the Age of Foundation. Why did that make her unstable? For the record, *her way* was just *her way.* Mama could read just fine, so Edom's mother could suck a basket of pickled Drake eggs.

"Here we are," said Camphor once they reached a small clearing within the grove.

A large stone occupied the center like a belly button. The site didn't look very impressive. Mr. Loch could have pushed the stone over. But looks didn't count for everything. Every hair on Enee's arms stood on end. Camphor must have felt it, too. When he reached the stone altar, he put the kids down and flexed his shoulders.

"This is where you'll be tonight. The person taking the test will approach the stone while the rest of you will take shelter outside the ring."

Enee gulped. She didn't want to be a curiosity for the parents to scrutinize within earshot of Mama. Nor did Enee enjoy the idea of everything that came afterward.

Arc squeezed her hand.

If she hurt him when she squeezed back, he didn't show it.

CHAPTER SEVEN

THE KNOBLE STEED

Arc left school before their last class. Apparently, a rooftop bath in Pegasus milk required a lot of preparation. He did promise to be at the EMD. If he didn't die from embarrassment first. So, with Mama at work and Enee's resolve not to climb the Grail Tree until after the exam, there was only one place she wanted to be once the school day finished. Sandwiched between the Landem Estate and the Whittles' orchard stood the barn of Phineas Rune.

The barn didn't look like much. The roof sprouted seedlings, and the windows lived in not-quite-white trim. Enee could see the edges of each faded red plank from the Stone Troll Wall that overlooked the pastures. But Phineas Rune was not a neglectful carriage master. Polished, live-edge beams kept the barn standing while second-cut hay filled a vermin-free loft, courtesy of Scoops, the barn's mostly blind Basilisk. Enee never found a sharp stone in the surrounding fields nor green slime in the Steeds' water troughs. The Satyr just wanted his farm to look old. He didn't believe in messing with the classics.

Enee pushed open the door. The heavy rollers rumbled against the concrete foundation, followed by a chorus of nickers and the rhythmic *shash, shash, shash* of an iron file.

"That you, 'elope?" Phineas called from across the aisle, his accent catching her name like a shell in the tide.

The carriage master stood by Sesame. The mare hung her head low, each side of her halter clipped to a cross tie. Phineas wore his farrier apron and ran a large file over Sesame's hoof, propped on an old stall jack.

"Nope. Just a thief looking to steal Mr. Knoble," she replied.

"You go for it. He was a beast to get his hooves trimmed," Phineas said, brushing hoof flakes from his apron.

Looking at the Satyr's cloven feet, they also needed a trim.

"Are you all by yourself? Where's Billy?" she asked.

Phineas rose long enough to give her a *do not ask about Billy* look before returning his attention to Sesame.

So, it's one of those days, Enee realized. The occasional spat came with the territory of a two-hundred-year relationship that spanned back to when a Satyr and a Charon couldn't sit next to each other. Let alone get married. Enee guaranteed they'd be over the whole thing by dinner.

"Make sure you don't go far. Just because I'm out here with the four-leggeds doesn't mean I don't know what day it is. If you miss your EMD, I can think of at least one person who'll string me up by my hooves," Phineas said.

Enee grinned. "Darn. There goes my escape plan."

With Phineas back to filing, Enee made her way to Knoble's stall. The other Steeds had already realized who she was and tucked their heads away. All but her leading man.

Knoble was the color of a freshly fallen acorn, with a mane as light as straw. He moved his head as if to talk, always looking to grab something with charcoal lips softer than powdered sugar. His six identical brothers, and sister, were carriage Steeds that worked the tourist routes in the summer when not carting waste bins from the various districts in Rowbuirin to the town dump or making local mail deliveries. That was the life he would have led if Enee hadn't fallen in love, working out a deal with the carriage master to muck stalls in exchange for Knoble. Enee could never afford an actual exchange, but Phineas was as honorable as a Chimera. He promised they wouldn't be separated in exchange for her work, remarking that finding a true partner in crime was a work of destiny.

"Who am I to poke fun at fate?" he'd told her.

She went for Knoble's halter, only to find it gone. In its stead hung a purple one with gold-colored hardware. She gasped, scooping the stiff halter into her hands. The material reeked like plastic, *new* plastic, and someone had stitched Knoble's name along the side in gold thread.

"Thank you," she beamed.

Phineas laughed to himself as he filed but said nothing.

With Knoble's fancy halter on, Enee brought him into the aisle to get polished for their ride. Sure, she always promised to wear a helmet, but she and Knoble were what she liked to think of as *free rein*. Plus, it sounded better than saying, "The cub who doesn't have tack" or "The rider too lazy to cinch a girth."

As soon as Knoble had been curried and brushed, his feet picked clean, Enee tied a lead rope to both sides of his halter and led him outside. She threw the lead rope over his head and half-leaped, half-wiggled onto his back. "All right, boy. Let's go."

Riding was simple. Not because of the balancing and leg cues, and ensuring you didn't get knocked off by a low-hanging branch. It was simple because riding made it harder for Enee's thoughts to wander. She felt *present*, with Knoble, on an afternoon in which she could spend an eternity. When there were hills, they scaled them. In the groomed fields, they'd go galloping as if into battle.

The sky burnished into a dark gold and striped the forest with shadows by the time they reached the midway point. Did she have to turn back? Couldn't they ride into the orchard and hide among the charmed apple trees? The Whittles would hide her. The exam wouldn't be until midnight when the full moon towered overhead, but riding in the dark had been nixed by Mama early on.

"Maybe just a little longer," she said.

Enee steered Knoble around the outer rim of the orchard until they reached the star fields. The stardust would be a pain to clean off his hooves, but it was worth it. Besides, the barn had a resident Basilisk. Enee could totally bribe her way to one of their eggs. One good egg bath, and she could eat off Knoble's hooves.

The Stone Troll Wall drove the road away from the late-season grass cropped by the Pegasus herds. Knoble let out a whinny to any Pegasus who cared to listen. Nothing.

"Don't take it personally. They're snoots and dreamers," Enee assured him.

A hole in the Wall gave them access to the field. They weren't trespassing. Nobody owned the star fields. Alchem law banned the owning of stars during the seventies. Back then, adding stars to clothing was all the rage. Which wasn't a problem until people started to eat them. Wild daydreams became a massive health crisis. Enee guessed lawmakers had a point, even if it made them incredibly dull.

Knoble slowed to a walk as they moved around a star the size of a sailboat. A group had gathered on the west side of the field facing the orchard. Enee needed only seconds to realize who they were.

The Landems.

The number of Foblins in Arc's family looked more impressive spread out on the field than crammed inside their mushroom palace. Half the Landems watched while the rest moved to rope one of the Pegasus mares. Among the wranglers stood Arc. He kept his hood up over his snake-locks and carried a bucket.

Enee snorted. *They're seriously going to make him milk a Pegasus?*

She pulled Knoble off to the side and watched. If Arc needed a rescue, she wanted to be ready. His family supported him like a bed of pillows. Easy to sink into. Easier to suffocate in.

The family of Foblins moved like the wind beneath the Pegasus' wings, even while wearing rubber booties. Her eyes could barely keep track as one end of a rope snared the closest mare. The Pegasus screamed and kicked and bit at anyone who neared.

Enee didn't know how the Foblins came up with this tradition. Did they think doing so made it okay that their ancestors slaughtered all the Gorgons, orphaning their Pegasus children? Did they think getting all cozy with the herds would lift the snake-curse some of them carried, a parting gift the Pegasus left behind out of anger? How about an apology?

"Hey, sorry we murdered your parents, but to be fair, if we didn't do it to save our necks, you wouldn't exist either," Enee grumbled.

Yeah. The apology sounded empty to her, too. No wonder some Foblins still carried the snake-curse.

Then again, Enee was a Chimera who participated in the EMD despite not having magic. The Mundus made no sense.

She kept watch as the Landems struggled with the mare. Others on the sidelines stepped in to help. Arc's older brothers took his bucket and had him stand at a safe distance.

"He could do it," Enee told Knoble.

Arc stuffed his hands into his hoodie while his family layered around the mare like a scab. Then, he left. Enee tracked him as he strolled around the nearest star, careful not to draw attention to herself. The boss mare with wind-made braids in her blue mane stood on the other side. Her colts watched from afar.

Arc lowered his hood so all his snake-locks faced the Pegasus, whose feathers were tipped in a red as deep as the locks themselves. The mare lowered her head for Arc. He said something that only the mare heard. They touched. Then she walked away, leaving only a feather behind. All the while, the other Landems had only started to get close enough to the other mare to try to milk her. Enee smiled. Suckers. Arc handled the important stuff.

Knoble became restless. He shifted from foot to foot and tried to bring his head to the grass.

"No grazing. You're not a Pegasus, bud," Enee said.

She pulled up his head, but the grass had started to move. The blades grabbed hungrily at Knoble's feet like Nightcrawlers. Enee searched for a breeze. Nothing.

She groaned.

Please don't be there. Please don't be there, Enee prayed.

She glanced back at the group. Across the field, one of the Landems stared back. Of course, it had to be her.

"No, don't—hang it all, she's coming over here," Enee grumbled.

Mrs. Landem moved across the field as gracefully as an Obolos Spider skittered over their web. And Enee wasn't being poetic. Delsie Landem had six arms and two legs, with flawless hair as dark as the ocean floor. If not for the fashion choice of wearing bright pink rain boots to keep off the stardust, she'd be terrifying.

"Hello, Mrs. Landem," Enee said with as much courtesy as she could muster.

"Enelope. This is a private affair. If you wouldn't mind leaving, it'd be greatly appreciated," she said.

She kept her expression light and *almost* friendly. "Right. I'm sorry to have crashed your Pegasus-milking. I suppose I'll just see Arc later."

"Yes, about that. I know that tonight marks a significant

transition. By next year, you and Arc will be taking different classes, seeing as you'll be grouped with the Alchem children who can't wield," Mrs. Landem said, with a voice as smooth as cornsilk.

Enee stiffened. "I don't see how—"

"I think it might serve you both well, given the upcoming changes, to try and branch out to other friend groups before the start of the new year. It's important to have good connections in this life."

"Nah, we're good. Nobody is a better friend than Arc. Not having classes together won't change that," Enee countered.

The smile on Mrs. Landem's face wavered. "He is priceless. Which is why he must be given every opportunity to succeed."

"And I plan to help him in any way I can," Enee countered.

"Yes, I know you care greatly for my Arc. However, I need you to consider that perhaps spending time with him is not in his best interest going forward."

Enee clenched the lead rope. Couldn't Mrs. Landem officially declare her dislike *after* the EMD?

"How is never seeing his best friend going to help?" Enee asked.

What started as a trap filled with honey had turned to vinegar.

"Arc needs to be as connected to his family and his proper place in Rumfoot Hollow as possible. And to do this, *all* of his connections must be carefully considered. Ones that will facilitate his future *here* in the Hollow. Not sabotage it."

Enee bit the inside of her cheek, positive that if she didn't, all the ugly words she wasn't supposed to say would come out.

"I'm simply looking out for my child's well-being, as any competent parent should," Mrs. Landem added.

The threads of the lead rope began to crack in Enee's hands, sending Knoble into a dance.

"Perhaps you should get moving. Please consider what I've said. For Arc," Mrs. Landem finished.

Luckily, Knoble kept his head and carried her away.

As if she didn't want to burn everything down today already.

CHAPTER EIGHT

IS TONIGHT THE END OF THE WORLD?

E nee ran as fast as she could for a glass of water. She took the stairs to the shRoom two at a time, grabbing the closest thing that looked like a cup and filling it with water from the barrel on the counter. Only after three glasses did Enee realize someone had left the shRoom's door open. Not only that, but the water barrel was full. Mama? Had they managed to come home on time?

Enee listened.

She put down the cup and crept towards Mama's bedroom door. Well, Mama's *curtain*. Through the partition, Enee could see all the usual bobbles. A bed, the polished armor above the backboard, an old chair they'd stripped to find a nice piece of furniture underneath the gaudy pink and silver paint.

Mama leaned against the chair while MuMu rested on the shoulder where Nama used to be. Enee knew the large scar that cut over their skin like a slit pupil would always ache. Bald and fleshy and raw. The Kitchen Drake glowed warmly while she gnawed on a wedge of cheese. Although

75

Enee couldn't see Mama's face, she saw them turn their threading bracelet around in circles.

Mama *was* strength. In Enee's eyes, they could take on the Mundus and win. But Mama had been in this battle since before moving to Pendra-North, and Enee came into the picture. Nobody could fight forever without breaking along the way. She needed the Stone before the Mundus truly broke her favorite person beyond what a runt like her could fix.

Hold on a little longer, Enee prayed.

She backed away from the curtain and returned to the front door. Mama must have been too deep in thought to hear her come in the first time. So, after giving them another few minutes of peace, Enee picked up the door and let it fall with a slam.

"Mama, are you home?" she called.

There was a pause. "Yes."

They left their room and carried MuMu back to her breadbox with one last piece of cheese. Mama stood tall and gave no hint that they hurt. So, Enee didn't treat them like they were. She barreled into Mama, squeezing them as tightly as possible with her iron grip. Mama squeezed back twice as hard.

"Ready?" they asked.

Enee picked at the floor with her toe.

"I'm not sure if that is the right word."

"Hmmm." Mama wiggled free from her grip and went back to their room. When they came out, they carried the Swan.

Enee's dream snaked its way into her thoughts, casting the echo of the war across the Swan's dulled edge.

Mama held out the sword.

"Take it."

She put one hand on the grip, another flat against the back of the blade. The sword weighed almost four pounds. How had her ancestors managed to swing it around for hours, often *through* people? Luckily, Enee's dreams didn't involve cutting people in half. Yet.

"This sword has seen what most believed to be the end of the world. Is tonight the end?" Mama asked.

Their message was clear. The EMD lasted one night. One test. Every Chimera since the Crusades had to do the same while the community watched. Enee did her best to make herself taller and gave Mama a fierce look.

"I'm ready to get it over with."

They laughed like a thunderclap and returned the Swan to its perch. "First, food."

Dinner turned into eggs with canned yams. Simple comfort food. Regardless, Enee found it hard to stay seated. Her heels bounced against the floor nearly as fast as her heartbeat. She felt warm and twisted and partially fantasized about a star falling out of the sky and demolishing the ceremony site.

"Do you want to talk or just wear through the floor?" Mama asked.

Enee swallowed. *Yes.* And no.

"The EMD feels like—a show. One that I know I need to participate in, but shouldn't be a part of. I want to run. I want to scream, and I don't know why this, of all the things I'll have to do in my life, makes me feel that way. I don't even *do* anything!"

Mama scooted closer, and Enee's lungs warmed to the smell of the balm they put on their scars.

"The Mundus is not always kind. It doesn't always make room for forgiveness. Sometimes, the spotlight reminds us of this."

Enee brushed her finger along Mama's paw.

You are cherished. You are whole. You are free. That's what they would whisper each night when they had slept in a tent. She'd been small, but she remembered. They didn't have much then, but Mama had always been there. They'd find the tallest rocks and hoist her up to the top. They'd watch the sunset. Now, Enee would be lucky to see them during the daylight.

All Enee wanted to do was tell Mama the truth. She wanted to tell them about the Grail Tree and her dreams. She wanted to tell them how angry she felt about, well, *everything*. But how do you tell the person that matters most to you something that'd only make them worry? It wasn't like Enee could change how people acted.

Instead, Enee would just fix it. All of it. And, at the pith of all she was, Enee knew she'd find the solution at the top of the Grail Tree.

"Does it bother you that we don't have magic?" Enee asked.

"Does it bother you?" Mama countered.

"Chimeras don't get bothered by such things. We get the job done and keep on," she said, returning to her food.

Mama smiled ever so gently. "So we do, lionheart."

Enee expected that to be the end of it. But as she set the plates on the sandstove for MuMu to clean, Mama fetched a worn pouch. They pulled at the drawstring and handed

Enee a stone and a rubber band. She ran a thumb over the stone. An enchanted object? Or was it simply charmed with a temporary spell?

"You need a precious item, too," Mama added.

Enee hesitated. She knew about this part. Enee had to give away something precious during the test to *tempt* a Familiar to approach the portal. Familiars weren't like the Elementals waltzing through the woods behind Porto Bello. During the EMD, the proctor would pour a pool of water from the Churchmere onto the altar in the Dryad Grove. The water would become a portal to the realm of the Familiars.

Reluctantly, Enee pulled out her MMA card.

"Are you sure I'll get it back?" she asked.

Mama nodded. "You tie the card to the stone," they clarified.

"So, it's like a weight? It'll sink my card, so it reaches the Familiars?" Enee guessed, hoping the process wouldn't damage her card.

Mama nodded again. "Don't worry. If the call is refused, the stone will come back."

"With my card?"

"With your card."

Enee dressed in her only set of white clothes, consisting of a button-down shirt and matching slacks, just after eleven. Mama topped the outfit off with an old gray capelet that Mrs. Whittle had planned to leave at the *up for grabs* table at the meetinghouse before she discovered Enee didn't have one for the EMD. They draped the capelet over her shoulders and straightened the cream-colored ribbon just below her chin.

By the time they hit the road, Enee felt ready–*ish*. Then her classmates started to appear.

They filed along the main trail with their parents, each carrying a glowstone to help light the way. Not everyone could have a Chimera's eyesight. Maybe that was for the best. Enee's entire grade pooled into the Dryad Grove. Mama had to hoist her onto one shoulder just to survey the scene. By sheer luck, she found Arc. He was bordered on all sides by his parents and grandparents, his siblings bouncing this way and that. His father put a jacket over his shoulders, while his grandmother picked dried milk out of his hair. Moon, the youngest of the Landems, handed him sticks and stones, while Ibree, the eldest, laughed and gave Arc a fisted nudge.

And Arc? He closed his eyes.

"Just breathe. We'll make it through this," Enee hoped.

Her classmates had already created a ring around the ceremonial altar. When they were close to the line, Mama knelt so Enee could slide off their shoulder.

"I'll be in the back but never out of reach," they promised.

Please let this go quickly, Enee prayed.

She tied her MMA card to the stone and filed alongside her classmates just as Proctor Pendra stepped into the ring. He had dressed in enough robes to shame a marshmallow, with a medallion bigger than Enee's fist over his chest, pressed with the insignia representing the Mundus. With the wave of a staff topped with a giant, smoky orb, the crowd settled into silence.

Enee twitched just looking at it.

"Please cap your glowstones. It's time to begin," called the proctor.

Shadow swallowed everything beyond the ring, making the faces of her classmates' families look like ghosts.

"Tonight, we are gathered for the most sacred of rites in honor of our finest youths of the Alchem kingdom," called the proctor, giving Pemprin a warm smile. He planted the staff into the ground so the orb's light could shine over the ring. "Tonight marks a new beginning for each of you. So may it be."

"*So may it be,*" echoed the crowd.

"Pemprin Pendra, please step forward," he announced.

Enee gulped. Weren't they going in order of their names? Pemprin strode into the circle dressed in a gown probably made by a hundred Obolos Spiders and a coverlet embroidered with twice as many pearls. Had she rehearsed this? Had she practiced lowering her hands to the altar where a hollow in the stone held a part of the Churchmere? Pemprin tied the ring she wore to her stone with a red satin ribbon. The stone slipped from her fingers and vanished into the pool.

Pemprin stepped back and waited for the proctor to proceed. From a leather pouch, he pulled out an old horn. When blown, the sound echoed as if summoned from another time. Enee could feel the music in her bones, and her hearts roared.

The sound vibrated under her skin as the light of the proctor's orb swelled. Something watched from behind the ore. Enee wanted to grab and break the sphere, beating the material into the ground like a drum to a song nobody else noticed. Sweat gathered beneath her hood, and she had to be careful not to break her stone accidentally.

When the sound of the horn faded into the night, a few solid seconds of silence made Enee wonder if Pemprin would get a Familiar. The same thought must have crossed the girl's mind because she glanced nervously at her uncle.

"It's okay. Just wait," he whispered.

Then, from the pool rose Pemprin's stone. Like Enee's, the stone was dark gray and smooth. As the stone made it over the water's surface, it became clear that a snout was attached.

A smile stretched across Pemprin's face.

A Familiar had answered the call, taking a form that literally could not have been more perfect for a brand-new mage. A Salamander. The creature's skin was as dark as fresh blackberries and covered in yellow spots. It had a thick neck, six legs, and spanned over a foot in length. Once the Salamander was free, it climbed down the altar, walked over to Pemprin, and presented the stone at her feet. Pemprin lowered herself into a graceful bow. She pushed both hands forward to collect the stone and allowed the Salamander to climb onto her arm.

"Ramil. You are Ramil," she said.

The crowd cheered.

"Now, now, folks. We've got quite a few to get through tonight, so please hold your applause until the end," said the proctor, even though it was clear he was happy with the result.

Pemprin stepped away with Ramil to make room for the next kid.

"Keeper Jinn," the proctor called, definitely not going by the all-mighty alphabet the Treechers favored.

Keeper strode forward with the same confidence and a coverlet as blue as polished sapphire. Their presentation was flawless, equal to Pemprin's in every way.

The horn sang.

The girl's face fell.

Keeper's stone jumped from the pool and landed on the altar's edge *without* a Familiar. No Familiar, no wielding. Keeper's magic was dormant and would remain so for the rest of her life. The crowd kept silent as she collected her stone and the Mage Maddie doll she'd tied to it. She slipped back into line with the others, wiping her eyes on the hem of her coverlet. When Pemprin offered Keeper her hand, she didn't take it.

Each time a kid stepped forward, Enee's hearts leaped. To make things worse, the orb's shimmer made her twitch. The more it swirled, the more Enee found herself staring at it. Could the orb be alive? If it was, nobody noticed. Classmates retrieved their stones, some followed by Familiars in the shape of feathery Aves of all sizes and colors, Drakes with luminescent scales, and even, beyond all Enee's comprehension, a Moon Bear.

"And finally, before we close for the evening's refreshments, Enelope Noe, please step forward," Proctor Pendra called.

Last. Figures.

Enee refused to choke on the whispers, "Is she in your son's class?" "There have been incidents." "I think I'll ask for my kids to be placed elsewhere next year."

She just hoped Mama didn't listen to them.

She squared her shoulders before stepping into the ring. She was a Chimera. Chimeras remained fierce in the face of all things. Warriors. *Survivors.* She would honor her family and stand tall.

She dropped her stone and the MMA card into the pool. "Have fun, A-Bomb," Enee whispered.

The sound of the horn turned into a haunting wail. Her body suddenly flooded with heat, as if she had been shot simultaneously with a dose of every emotion. The feeling hollowed her out, filling the space with everything three hearts could and could not contain.

Surrendered magic of a Chimera's roar is locked away in enchanted ore—

The proctor pulled his lips from the horn. Even as it quieted, Enee could still feel its song.

Child of the donor's line. With this debt, honor is paid.

The orb's light reached for her. She could feel the orb's hunger. It wanted something inside her and would gladly peel her apart to get it. Forest chaser. Tree climber. *Chimera.* Her stone flew from the pool. It hurtled through the air and hit her square in the face, breaking the orb's pull. Enee growled, one hand on her forehead, the other clenched in a fist.

"Ow!" she spat.

The crowd fell dead silent. When Enee searched her classmates' faces, none of them paid her attention. All eyes were locked on the altar and the two very fuzzy legs that peeked over the pool's surface.

CHAPTER NINE

THE PROCTOR OF IMPOSSIBLE

A Moth stared directly at Enee. Impossibly clear. Impossibly pink. *Impossible.*

A Familiar had answered the call of a Chimera.

Proctor Pendra fumbled back, knocking into his staff. The orb at the end clanged to the ground, disturbing the storm inside enough for Enee to feel the prickling static of magic scatter across her skin.

The crowd had broken into an avalanche of whispers. She caught some of the parents glancing back to where Mama stood, their eyes wide. But it was not the kind of look one gave in amazement. It was a look you gave to danger.

Fight, Enee's instincts told her. Then, her eyes found Arc. The Landems were in a fury of talking back and forth, with all his siblings tugging at his sleeves, as if he could somehow explain what had just happened. He didn't move. When he finally took in a breath, it was with both eyes wide open. Open and terrified.

Run.

So, she did.

"WAIT! You can't just—hang it all, housecat!"

The sound of the Familiar's voice nearly jolted Enee back. *Nearly.*

She could feel the pull of the Familiar behind her as if they were two ends of a string. As she ran, the Moth did their best to keep up, flapping frantically beneath the mother moon.

"WAIT!"

Enee didn't wait.

She bolted to the first place she could think of: Porto Bello. If there had been Nightcrawlers on the road, she probably mowed them over. If her neighbors were asleep, they wouldn't be for long as she tumbled through the front doors of her building and stomped up the stairs like a herd of Steeds.

"Calm down, will you!" the Moth barked as they entered the shRoom.

Enee grabbed the closest weapon at hand. A large block of cheese. "Get away from me. I'm not your mage," she shouted.

She swung the block, missing the Moth by a wingbeat.

"Thousands of years of waiting, and this is what I get? A psychotic furball?"

Enee swung again, this time close enough to cast a strong breeze that knocked the Familiar off-course.

"Wait. Wait! *Chimera*, wait!"

She paused just long enough to give Mama time to burst into the shRoom. Enee still had the block in her hands, half-cocked over her shoulder.

"It's a mistake, Mama," she croaked.

Mama knelt, their eyes carrying with them the same hollowing worry. "It's okay. We'll figure this out, lion-heart," they said gently, reaching for the block.

They took it easily, leaving Enee feeling hollow. No. Hollow wasn't the right word to explain how she felt.

"It's a mistake. Chimeras can't have Familiars," she repeated. And she *was* a Chimera.

Mama cradled Enee as if she were a star, holding her tight in the night sky and shielding her from the gravity of the Mundus. That is, until a violent wheeze came from the stairwell.

"Miss Noe, a moment," gasped the proctor. "A moment of your time."

They looked down to the floor below, where the proctor, swallowed in the haphazard twist of his robes, leaned against the railing.

"I—by virtue, so many steps. Yes, a moment, if you will. Perhaps some water. Yes, lovely, water," he gasped.

Mama got the water while the proctor climbed the remaining steps. He needed a moment to sit on the ground before getting into a chair.

"I can't stay—long. I have to see to—the closing remarks. However—goodness, *stairs*—"

Proctor Pendra guzzled down two glasses of water before he found the rest of his words.

"Dr. Sable sent me his report this morning. By all accounts, the charm used to fix your arm happened outside the time frame for the risk of a false positive. However, we must still do our due diligence," he said.

"Which means what?" Mama asked.

As if suddenly aware that he sat in a Chimera's home, uninvited, the proctor shrank into the seat.

"N—nothing unreasonable, I assure you, Mx. Noe. There are simply a few tests I can try that will be able to clarify if this is truly a false positive."

"It has to be," Enee said.

The proctor tried to smooth out his robes, nearly knocking his plant-like Familiar from their hiding spot within the folds. "By all accounts, yes. However, even a false positive isn't enough to bring a Familiar back to this extent. You've left the grove, and your Familiar followed you. In such a sense, you give every indication of being bonded," he said.

Enee grabbed a chair and set it in front of the proctor so she could sit directly across from him.

"Test me."

Proctor Pendra looked at Mama. They gave the briefest of nods without taking their eyes off Enee.

"Right, of course." Even then, he needed a minute to gather his wits and find the will to stand. He set the staff beside them, as if to allow the orb to watch. Enee's instincts screamed for her to grab the orb and shatter it. The smoky swirl of the material, which looked more like metal than any kind of glass she'd seen, raised every hair on her body.

From his pockets, the proctor handed Enee a two-pronged fork and a shiny stone. *Magisite.*

"Tap the tuner against the chair, then hold it at shoulder height while you hold the magisite in the other hand," he instructed.

Enee did as he said, finding it hard to believe she had done the same thing just days after being born.

The proctor watched in silence while the tuner rang. As the sound faded, the magisite crackled in her hand.

Enee clenched her jaw and kept still.

Mistake. This is only a mistake, she prayed.

And yet, the grey sheen of the magisite turned white. The proctor trembled and pulled out a little cluster of herbs from a silk bag. At the snap of his fingers, the herbs began to light. The trail of their burning scent wrapped around Enee, sending her into a fit of sneezes.

Although Mama made no moves to stop him, Enee could see the veins of their locked muscles.

If something happened, Mama stood at the ready.

If something happened, Enee doubted Proctor Pendra would survive it.

He stopped once the herbs burned down to his fingers. The look on his face filled Enee with enough smoke-tinged dread to choke a Dragon.

"How odd," he said, taking back both the magisite and the tuner.

"That's it?" Enee pressed.

"What does this mean?" Mama asked.

"It means Enelope continues to register as an individual with the ability to wield."

A Chimera that could wield? Impossible. Every theory, every model of the way the Mundus worked, rebuked the notion. After all, how could something wield a force they weren't connected to?

"That has to be a mistake," said Enee.

The proctor blew out from his lips and raked a hand through his sandy hair, clearly too stupefied to note that he was rubbing herb ash into his scalp.

"Yes, normally, given that you are a Chimera."

"Which I am."

That didn't stop him from glancing at Mama. Mama, on the other hand, only watched Enee.

"I have no evidence to disprove the results. However, although magic is not limited, a mage's use of it is. Magic, even in the hands of those who dedicate a lifetime to studying the craft, can be wielded imperfectly because working with a living being is more complex than working with objects," the proctor said, looking over Mama's scars.

Mama shifted and folded their arms, fully aware that, like their old surgeon's rash decision to save one head over the others, most mages didn't understand the complexity of a living being enough to know that cutting off a Chimera's head isn't as simple as cutting off an arm. No matter how infinite the magic, a mage couldn't heal cutting out a *person*.

"So, *you* could be wrong," Enee pressed.

The proctor pursed his lips.

"Yes," he conceded. "However, despite the possible margin for error regarding this unusual event, we should still follow the lay of the law until I can sort out where this error comes from. And in the eyes of the law, you are now a fledgling mage."

Enee dug her nails into the chair. At least he didn't lump her together with the Alchem.

"What do we do, then?" Mama asked.

"We continue as if Enee were a—" he paused, reading the room. "We follow the common procedure. I'll make the class arrangements with your school for next year."

Enee sank back. A student. A mage student. The

thought of it made her feel about as ecstatic as Proctor Pendra looked.

"Will that be all?" Mama asked.

He nodded.

"Yes, uhm, but perhaps I can sit just a moment longer. I, for the life of me, don't think I can get up right now."

Thirty minutes and two cups of tea later, the proctor finally found the strength to leave so he could give the EMD's closing remarks.

Neither she nor Mama spoke after. They shared a single glance as Enee went up to her platform.

"So, do I sleep here?"

Enee looked over to her nightstand.

The Moth sat atop an uncapped glowstone like an ominous ghost in the near-dawn light. Enee frowned. No more. Not tonight.

"Hello? Don't ignore me! I refuse to be—"

She didn't let the Moth finish. Enee scooped the creature up, trapping their torso in her palm like an overgrown Crocswallow hatchling.

"Unhand me!"

She pulled out her treasure box and dumped the contents onto her bed, scattering MMA cards and her other precious items across the blankets.

"Don't you dare!"

Too late.

Enee stuffed the Moth inside and sealed the box shut with the help of a hair tie. She could make out a muffled slew of curses and the beat of powdery wings through the wood.

Ignore them, Enee thought.

It was all a big mistake anyway, no matter what the proctor said. What did he know? Saying a "possible margin for error" was about as helpful as him saying, "I have no flaming clue and need to sit down before I pass out."

"I don't think your Familiar is supposed to be in a box," Mama called from below.

"They're not *my* Familiar. I broke my arm, remember? Dr. Sable made this happen," she said stiffly.

"Lionheart," Mama started.

"You heard Proctor Pendra. He could be wrong. This is all temporary," she interrupted.

"And if he's not?"

"I'm a Chimera," Enee snapped, her hearts rolling like thunder.

"You are. That doesn't mean that sometimes things, *unexpected* things, happen."

She didn't want to hear it, and she definitely didn't want Mama to worry about it.

All of this should have been over by dawn. She should have stepped up to the altar in the Dryad Grove and dropped her precious item into the pool. A minute later, her object should have come back *without* a Familiar.

This *shouldn't* have happened.

"It's a mistake," Enee declared.

CHAPTER TEN
A FAMILIAR OMEN

Every seat had a butt on Saturdays at The Mitey Bean. The wall-to-wall mirrors only multiplied the crowded feel of the cafe. The velvet booths along the outer edge were full to bursting, tended by a waiter who bustled back and forth to see who had finished. The sole table they didn't visit was Enee's, knowing well enough that she and Arc were only there to visit Mama. Usually, during her visits, she'd find something for her mind to latch onto—castle tour guides, for one, but none seemed to be around. Other times, she'd stir up a conversation with Arc to block out the creeping, spine-aching torture of sitting. Today, it was a Moth.

"Are you going to talk to me or are you waiting for me to turn into a Unicorn?" the Familiar grumbled from the rim of their porcelain teacup. They were too large to do more than sit inside, both wings spread out in full view.

Enee glared. "I'd believe you were real if you were a Unicorn."

Arc glanced up when she spoke. When he realized who

she talked to, he gave a quick scan of the room before returning to his journal. Only Enee could hear the Familiar since they were supposedly *hers*, as was the case for every other mage.

But I'm not a mage, Enee thought.

"Finally, she speaks. First, you abandoned me after the exam, making me follow you like a needy hatchling. Then, you stuffed me in a box overnight without saying so much as a word," the Familiar snapped. "A *smelly* box."

"I let you out," she argued.

Granted, when she showed up at the cafe with the Moth in what Arc cited as a *literal box,* her defense of the Familiar being a mistake didn't change his opinion that keeping them trapped constituted a horrible plan. So, out they came.

"Look, Mothy—"

"Omen. My name is Omen," the Familiar countered. "He/him pronouns, if you please."

"Since when?" Enee scoffed.

"Since you didn't give me a name when I came through the portal! So, I chose my own. It's a miracle I could come up with a good name that your ears would understand, considering how barbaric this Common-Tongue is. It literally took me two seconds to learn. Pitiful. Your era is cringeworthy, housecat," Omen claimed.

Enee dug into the seat, trying not to let his words work deeper into her already too-full brain. "Don't call me housecat, *Moth.*"

"Don't call me Moth, *housecat,*" Omen countered.

They continued their staring contest.

"So, that's it? Are you just going to ignore me for the rest of your life?" Omen barbed.

"What do you want me to say?" Enee snapped. "Chimeras do not have Familiars. They can't. That would mean they're connected to magic, which is impossible. And I *am* a Chimera."

Her voice broke a little at the end.

"What do you mean, Chimeras aren't connected to magic?" Omen asked.

Before she could grill him on how ridiculous his question was, another person walked up to the table. "Hi, Enelope. It's Enelope, right?"

"Yes. Hi, Lindy," Enee said. *Great, here we go again.*

"You know, if you ever need anything, you can always stop by the store. We'd be happy to help, no questions asked," Lindy said.

Arc stopped his scribbling. The pair of them knew exactly three things about Lindy. One, her name. Two, she was the granddaughter of the owner of the hardware store Mama had worked at before The Mitey Bean. And three, the moment Mama ever entered the same room as her, she left.

Enee smiled because she knew if she clenched her teeth hard enough, it'd keep her from screaming. Lindy was the fourth person to come over to ask if she was *okay*, all the while making sure Mama was well out of sight.

"Thank you, Lindy," Arc said, placing a clammy hand on Enee's balled fist.

"I'll be sure to tell Mama. They'll be happy to know we have the community's support," Enee managed to say.

Lindy flinched, "Ah, well, that's not what—"

Enee made her smile even wider. "I could go find them now if you'd like."

"No need. It's just something for you to keep in mind." Lindy put up both hands and dipped out of the cafe as fast as she'd appeared, just like all the others. Arc pulled back to his notebook and began erasing.

"What are you doing?" Enee asked.

"We clearly need a new plan. The old one doesn't fit now that you can wield," Arc said, flexing his fingers.

He had only been away from the Hollow for a couple of hours, and already the strain on his bond had started to take its toll. They'd have to leave soon, even if that meant leaving Mama behind to deal with the masses alone.

"Please don't. This whole thing is some twisted side effect from Dr. Sable fixing my arm," she said, glaring at the patrons who'd been watching her.

Or, more accurately, they had spent the morning watching her *and* Mama, stealing glances as if debating whether to call the Guard to investigate a possible kidnapping.

They could all burn.

"Didn't the proctor visit you? Did he test you to see if the results were wrong?" Arc asked carefully.

"*Powerful* mages can make mistakes," Enee said stubbornly.

She glanced across the room to where Pemprin's uncle now sat. Enee swore he was only there to keep an eye on her. She half-expected him to have come forward by now to verify he'd been wrong. He didn't. Proctor Pendra stayed in his corner of the room, reviewing piles of books and loose sketches. The current book in his hand looked old, with an orb pressed into the cover. The proctor mumbled over the text, occasionally glancing in Enee's direction.

"Is this because he's a Pendra? That doesn't mean he's automatically wrong. Maybe it's better not to be so quick to judge. We should consider all the options," Arc said softly.

All the options? Was he kidding? *Most* of the options sounded more bonkers than her wielding magic.

"I bet a lack of sleep caused whatever spell Dr. Sable used to stick to my arm than it was supposed to. Like when you don't get enough vitamins and cuts don't heal as fast," Enee said.

Arc put down his notebook. "You're not sleeping?"

Busted. "I'm just having dreams. Weird ones, but that's all. It's nothing to worry about."

"Weird how?"

Enee picked at her braid. "Just dreams about what I think are the Crusades. It's just exhausting, given it's been every night since—"

"Since when?" he pressed.

"Since I started You-Know-What," she confessed. When he went to press for more, Enee put up her hands. "That's the least of my problems right now."

Arc leaned back and stared at his notebook. "Maybe it'd help if you looked at magic as an opportunity."

"An opportunity for what? For people to spin wild stories about Mama?" she snarled.

Word had already gotten around town about what happened. Even Dr. Sable had sent a letter by Messenger Drake that morning asking if she'd come in for a follow-up exam. Mama let MuMu burn the letter to a crisp.

"An opportunity for us to be in the same classes," he offered.

The idea lightened the weight until Mrs. Landem came to mind. "Your mother would rather explode than let that happen."

"Who says she gets the final say?"

Who said she didn't? Gosh, Enee needed a run.

"I don't know what any of this means or what I'm supposed to do," she admitted.

She had no desire to spend a decade sitting in a library, puzzling over spells she couldn't read.

Arc reached across the table and stuck out his pinky. "You're still Enelope Noe. My best friend. We just need to really think about what we do next."

Enee ignored Omen's show of pretending to vomit into his teacup and allowed herself to smile, the first real one since last night.

A solid *thunk* broke their moment. A Crystal Mite fell onto the table. Once they recovered from the fall, the diamond-looking Mite stuck out six translucent legs and tried to make a run for it.

"What in all creation was that?" Omen exclaimed.

Enee pointed up to Loopla. The large Flower Drake was coiled right above their table. When Loopla slept, she kept her tail coiled around the brass ring bolted to the ceiling, so her back, covered in long, fleshy stalks capped with luminescent blooms, faced the ground. She made a terrific chandelier, with a few exceptions. First, the Crystal Mites. No matter how hard the manager, Dove Topher, scrubbed, Loopla always had Mites. They crawled along her back, nibbling on dead skin while her light reflected off their bodies like a million prisms. It was quite pretty. Too bad they also seemed prone to falling. Second, Loopla was a living creature. She needed to move, eat, and use the bathroom.

The Drake had started to wake up again, sensing that it was nearly time for her to take a lunch break. She shook her broad snout and long, floppy ears, sending the Mites across the room. The creatures skittered over tables, making their way into all the cracks and crevices the cafe offered.

Enee and Arc laughed. For a moment, life felt pretty good again.

Then Enee locked onto an old lady who glared from one of the neighboring booths. She had seen the woman before. The crone had twice as much nose as she did manners, with gold rings covering every finger. Usually, Enee saw her in the cafe on Sundays, when the tea leaves she used for predicting the week's weather forecast were freshly restocked. Whether by bad luck or bad sense, the crone had chosen today to be in the same room as Enee. She moved the cup between both hands in slow circles, her eyes locked on their table.

"Can you believe it? A Chimera who can wield," she whispered to the two silver-haired crones next to her.

"Do you think she's an Alchem child? She doesn't hold much of a family resemblance, if you know what I mean. Then again, she does act *unkempt*. Just the kind of thing you'd expect if the stories are to be believed."

"Nature versus nurture, I tell you. I wouldn't put anything past a Chimera, especially *that* one. I heard they were run out of Ledean by their own parent. Then again, from Camoya. I know a dangerous pattern when I see one, no matter what the Whittles say."

On any other day, Enee would have tried harder to swallow her anger. But their chatter spread to her hearts like venom.

"Take the spoon," Omen said.

"The what?"

Omen broke her concentration, but not with his usual grumpy tone. His voice almost seemed *happy*. Or evil. Evil happy.

"The spoon. Give that shriveled prune a taste of her own medicine," he said, pointing to the closest sugar spoon and one of the fallen Crystal Mites.

Enee took about two seconds to think, *If I am supposed to be the voice of reason, we are doomed*, before scooping up a Mite. She held it down in the belly of the spoon and launched the Mite at the crone. The crone jumped, sloshing her tea. Whatever weather report she had gleaned from the leaves was ruined. By the time the crone found the culprit, Enee had another Mite at the ready. *Bink!*

"Brilliant," Omen praised as the Mite bounced into the crone's lap.

The crone looked ready to get up and throw tea in Enee's face when Mama intervened. They lumbered forward with shoulders hung low and coffee grounds smeared across their apron. Mama placed a second cup of tea on the woman's table.

"Will that be all?" Mama asked. The way they said it didn't make the crone's answer negotiable.

"Yes," she said carefully. When Mama turned their back, the crone whispered into her cup, "Feral thief."

Nobody else saw, but Enee did. She saw the moment Mama flinched and redirected their might into something other than the assault of a four-foot-two grandma. Mama kept their stride and plucked a Mite from an empty table. They flicked the creature up and overhead with a single thumb motion. The surrounding mirrors guided their aim, sending the mite directly into the crone's second cup of tea.

Even exhausted, Mama was a legend. They tried their hardest to keep the smile to only their eyes as the crone sputtered, dripping tea down the front of her blouse. Then—

A customer jumped after finding a Crystal Mite in their sandwich, forcing Mama to step back. Just one step. That's all it took for Mama to ram into the table behind them, knocking over a brewing pot. Water went everywhere just as Loopla decided it was time for her lunch break, sending the Crystal Mites down in scores.

Mama didn't move. Enee couldn't even tell if they breathed. It was as if they became a statue while the world exploded around them.

"Noe," called the manager. "Help me get some towels."

Dove guided Mama gracefully toward the downstairs lounge, her white skirt, which somehow never got stained, and rich curls flowing behind them.

"I'll be right back," Enee said to Arc.

"Hold on. We can't be too far apart!" Omen complained.

Enee didn't feel like arguing. She reached into the teacup and scooped Omen onto her shoulder.

"I didn't say handle me," Omen grumbled.

Despite his complaint, Omen crawled onto her ear like a

big bow. They took the stairs around the corner to the lounge, but stopped before reaching the bottom.

"Gibbie just called out sick," Dove said, sounding just south of annoyed. "I need someone to cover her noon to five shift."

It was the kind of statement that doubled as a question without actually asking the question. There was a long enough pause for Enee to plead for Mama to say no. If Dove didn't ask, she didn't deserve to keep them.

"I have the five to nine," Mama pointed out, breaking the short standoff. "But if you need someone—"

"*Perfect*. You'll have fewer people to navigate in the afternoon, but there is a special coven gathering coming at four-thirty. Given the recent events, I'll have Boe handle that to avoid any mishaps. You can spend that time cleaning the altar until they leave," Dove practically sang, gesturing to the altar pressed against the wall that they'd made in honor of their failed EMD.

Events? No. Dove meant *rumors*. And nobody spreads rumors better than a coven crone. Enee wanted to run down the stairs and rip the ribbons out of Dove's hair. She didn't even ask. The worst part was knowing that, like every boss before her, Dove would use Mama until it became inconvenient, or because the paperwork required to hire a probationary citizen outweighed the benefits of having a Chimera willing to take on any job they threw at them.

Enee rehearsed the names of the Chimeras to calm down.

Cloud, Cordula, Cumalee, Cypress, Dell, Denzel, Donelle, Dust, Ebba...

"Want to light her on fire?" Omen asked.

Having such an idea come from someone else shocked Enee enough to settle her anger.

"I'm not setting anyone on fire. What good would that do?" Enee whispered, equally shocked that she was the voice of reason here. "Besides, I can't just snap my fingers and create fire."

"Sure you can. You can wield now."

Enee growled.

"Enee?" Mama called.

"I think Arc needs to go home," she said quickly, trying to cover up her snooping.

"Find me when you're finished," Dove said to Mama, passing Enee on her way upstairs, keeping herself as close to the wall as possible.

The amount of perfume the woman wore was enough to give Enee a headache. The scent lingered, even as Omen flapped his wings to dilute the wave of lavender and patchouli. Mama got down on one knee and gently raised Enee's gaze. They both knew Mama had to stay, so there was no reason to repeat it. Still, Enee picked at the ugly gray carpet with her sneakers.

"I'll bring back blueberry pancakes," Mama said.

All Enee could do was nod. Pancakes. Fine. Enee knew what she needed to do.

You bring the pancakes. I'll bring the Stone.

"Would your Familiar like anything?" Mama asked. Despite everything, they looked at Enee the same as ever. As their lionheart. Only this time, a lionheart with a Familiar.

"I swear, Mama's the only one with manners around

here. Butter, please. I want butter for those pancakes," Omen said.

Enee snorted. "Butter, apparently."

When Enee returned to collect Arc, his face and hands had a thick sheen to them.

"Come on, back to the Hollow we go. The last thing I need is for your parents to blame me for your spontaneous combustion," she said, scooping up Arc's pencils and putting them in his bag.

"Are you sure? What about Mama?" he asked.

But Enee just kept putting away his things until the table was clear, tucking her treasure box under an arm. He got the message. She was on a mission. As they left the cafe, Enee glanced at the proctor's table. He and his books had vanished.

"Can we talk about this *Chimeras don't have magic* nonsense?" Omen asked once they were outside.

"No." Enee broke into a run.

The jump caught Omen off-guard, but not Arc. The Foblin caught Omen and matched her speed, knowing better than to try to stop her.

CHAPTER ELEVEN
KEEPER OF MAGES

E nee needed to go faster.

The kind of fast that broke records. Or, at the very least, broke *bonds*. But no matter how hard she pushed herself, Enee knew she couldn't outpace a Foblin, not even one carrying a Familiar and a bigger-than-life backpack.

"I need to outpace you," she huffed.

"Then take your Familiar," Arc said, matching her pace to pass Omen to her.

She shook her head. When what she wanted finally dawned on him, all the color drained from his face.

"*Dumb ways to die,*" Omen began to sing, clinging to Arc's fingers.

"You can't test a bond like that! What if it breaks? Bonds are serious. Breaking them can break you," Arc gasped.

"I. Need. To. Try."

She looked ahead, pushing with everything she had to keep from losing steam. When she didn't slow down, Arc groaned.

"Fine," he said, dropping back.

The change in distance between Omen and her hit immediately. The pain started in her chest, tightening around her hearts with every step. The farther she went, the stronger the pull became until the pain radiated down to her toes. The forest muted, her vision blurred.

Think of Mama. Think of your goal to climb the Grail Tree.

A hundred breaths into her run, her knees threatened to buckle.

You can bear this, she scolded herself. *A Chimera can bear anything.*

Enee tripped, nearly sending her treasure box flying. When she hit the ground, the pain stopped.

Did it work?

She cracked a smile. A mistake, as she... Arc knelt beside her with Omen still in his hands.

No. She dug her nails into the dirt.

"Please, Enee," Arc begged, setting Omen between them. "We can figure out why this happened. Together. Just not this way."

Enee didn't want to figure it out. She kept her head down until the last of the ache subsided. Maybe the bond would fade on its own? Maybe she just needed more time? Time. Why did that seem like such a big ask? Patience wasn't exactly one of her virtues.

"Fine. Having *him* doesn't change the fact that I still have a job to do, anyway," Enee said, changing her focus.

Arc sighed. "I was afraid you'd say that."

He helped her to her feet, holding out an arm to keep her steady until her legs felt less like jelly.

"Ah, see. A nice stroll," Omen praised as they walked. "Not the worst thing in the Mundus, now, is it?"

Then, it was.

Keeper walked ahead with a good elbow-jab's worth of space between her and Pemprin. Two others from their group trailed behind. Myra, whom Enee only knew as the girl who only ever wore orange, and Estel.

"Maybe we can go a different way to get to You-Know-What?" Arc suggested, glancing into the woods, where the mountain laurel waited to welcome them into their haven.

"What's a You-Know-What?" Omen pressed.

Before she had a chance to answer either of them, the girls flagged them down.

"Hey, Enee. Are the rumors true?" Keeper called.

Enee clutched her treasure box so tightly that the wood moaned. Omen flew to her shoulder as the girls approached. They'd all lost the fancy capelets in favor of clean jeans and *new* vintage sweaters.

Pemprin shot Keeper a warning look, but did little to slow down whatever mission the girl was on.

Keeper smirked. "People are talking. After last night, there's no way your *mama* can keep their secret now."

"What secret?" Enee hissed.

Arc was right. They should have ditched the road for the forest the moment they saw the girls.

"That you're an Alchem kid who got stolen in the middle of the night by a Chimera," Estel said from behind, guarding Keeper's back with her long, ave-like talons.

"I even heard they were forced to flee an entire country," Keeper snickered.

Enee's blood boiled. She could practically smell the envy on her. That syrupy, dripping hunger for magic. If Keeper couldn't get it herself, then proximity seemed to be the next best thing, seeing as Estel was the only mage of the group, other than Pemprin, and simply because she was an Elemental.

"Don't worry. Now that the secret's out, we can totally ask our parents to help get you away from *them*," Myra chimed.

"My mom always said having a Chimera in town was dangerous," Estel added.

Pemprin stepped up and held out a hand.

"You don't have to be subject to your *parent*'s decisions anymore. Let us help. Let the *Pendras* help. We protect our people."

Enee slapped the hand away. "Don't touch me."

How *dare* they? She was a Chimera. A Chimera who wanted nothing to do with their *help*. Protect? What they were offering wasn't protection. They were only feeding a dangerous lie, built purely on the fact that she could wield.

Protect. Never had Enee hated a word more.

Keeper leaned closer, glancing at Arc before whispering, "Or maybe you like having the Mundus see you as a monster with a snake-cursed shadow. Monsters do get all the attention in the legends."

"Better a monster than a magic-hungry, Alchem brat," Enee said slowly, barely managing to weigh down her temper.

Keeper's expression changed. Ugly changed.

"Are you sure? Do you know what they do to rogue Chimeras? The Guard takes them away. Permanently. I'd say, given the rumors, it's only a matter of time before they're on your grubby doorstep. How much do you want to bet they'll take the biggest freak first?" Keeper said.

"Keeper! *Composure*," Pemprin snapped, trying to wedge herself between them.

Too late.

"Take her down," Omen said.

Enee dropped the treasure box and caught hold of Keeper's collar, pivoting the girl over her shoulder. Estel and Myra screamed as Keeper hit the ground *hard*. The wind rushed from her lungs, sending the not-mage into a fit of gagging coughs. Enee went in for a finishing punch when a Mundus-shattering, bow-breaking *"ENOUGH!"* sliced through the forest.

From behind ran Treecher Camphor. He'd dropped his shopping bags and, in one swoop, hoisted Enee off the ground as if she weighed nothing more than a toothless Drake hatchling and kept her lofted until he was certain Keeper could regain her footing.

"Are you okay?" he asked Keeper.

But Keeper was crying, letting Estel pull her into her arms.

"She just went crazy," Estel said sharply, echoed by Myra, who gave Enee a hard stare.

"That's not quite—"

Pemprin's words drowned under the sobs. Camphor was at a loss. He pulled out a rag and handed it over, letting the girls lead Keeper away from the scene. Only once they were far enough down the road did Camphor put Enee down.

"We've had this discussion before. Has nothing changed?" Camphor asked as he scooped up her treasure box and handed it back to her.

"They started it! They're spreading lies. Lies that could cost Mama and me *everything*," she cried.

"Rumors are just that. *Talk*. Nobody is threatening you, or Mx. Noe."

The fact that the Treecher genuinely seemed to believe that shook Enee more than anything Keeper and the others could have possibly said.

Treecher Camphor sighed.

"Do you think violence will ever result in a positive outcome? Do you think pummeling the other person will suddenly make their words disappear?"

She dug her toes into the dirt. "Maybe?"

"I know that the events of last night have left things unsettled, but that's no excuse for this behavior. As an—" The Treecher paused to find the right word, "*Mage*, you now have a greater responsibility to those around you."

"I'm not a mage! I am a Chimera, just like Mama, who's kind and strong and *good*," She fought to keep her tone in check. To be *good*. "This is a mistake. This Familiar doesn't belong here. Or, at least, he doesn't belong with me."

"*Gee*, thanks, housecat. And here I thought we had bonded back at the cafe," Omen said.

Treecher Camphor knelt and looked at Omen with a stare only a tree could give.

"There is no giving a Familiar back. The stone you used during the EMD, with your special object, opened the door for him to travel *here*. It does not work in reverse. They are linked to your spirit when they enter the Mundus. They can only go home when their mage dies, and both of their spirits are released into a Charon Well. So, for reasons beyond my understanding, this Familiar belongs to you. The question is, what will you do with him?"

"Put me in a box, apparently," Omen complained.

"If I catch you getting into another altercation with another student that results in bodily harm, more drastic action will be taken. Do you understand?"

She nodded. What else could she do? The one who left the bite marks was always the one to blame.

"I'll see you tomorrow, then," said Camphor.

Right. Their field trip. She'd completely forgotten about it. Part of her still wished that she still had. The last thing she wanted was to spend her Sunday with the likes of Keeper.

Once Camphor left, Arc came forward.

"If we keep our heads down, all of this will pass," he consoled.

Would it? What if someone, seeing Mama, called the Guard simply because of gossip? Or, what if Mama snapped and the incident got reported? Estel would undoubtedly tell her mom, and Nola would tell anyone and everyone who entered the WyrmMart. Enee needed to give Mama distance from the town. Not much, but long enough for another drama to steal everyone's attention.

She needed to set Mama free. *Now.*

Enee spared a glance over to the girls. Keeper looked livid, her face ruddy, while Pemprin seemed ready to vomit. Suddenly, she took a step back, offering Keeper a hand as if to lead her somewhere. Keeper pushed the hand away hard enough to make Enee flinch. She stormed into the arms of Estel and Myra, leaving Pemprin to trail after them.

Maybe she'd get lucky and they'd eat each other. That'd solve at least some of her problems.

She looked at Omen.

"Why do I have the feeling you're going to ask me for something?" Omen grumbled.

Enee pulled herself to her full height and let her drive devour the last of her anger. "How high can you fly?"

CHAPTER TWELVE

GOOD-ISH AND BAD IDEAS

"What is that?" Omen asked.

"A Grail Tree. Haven't you seen one before?"

"Not when I've been in the Mundus. And where I come from, everything is very different," Omen said.

"Don't Familiars live for," Enee almost said *forever*, but immortality didn't exist, not even for a Phoenix. "A long time? Didn't you see one during the Crusades?"

For centuries, the whole Mundus had talked about nothing but Grail Trees. If the kingdoms of the Alchem weren't bickering, they were chopping the Trees down and making a show of fighting over the spoils. How could Omen not have seen one?

"No," Omen said darkly.

What a grump, she thought. She wondered how his previous mages had lived with him. Since Familiars outlived their mages, they often went through several. As Treecher Camphor pointed out, when the Alchem mage died, the Familiar returned to their realm to start the whole process over again. No matter how much it hurt to admit it, she assumed the process would be the same for a Chimera. Elementals were the only other wielders she had to go by, and they didn't have Familiars.

"Enee?" Arc interrupted.

The Foblin stood far enough from the Grail Tree to stay out of the way without stepping beyond the blind spot the Tree created, shielding them from the spying trees. He looked less like he was about to explode than he did in the cafe, but he certainly didn't look happier. He scanned the soil and prodded the clumps of dry, brittle needles with a stick.

"Are you sure the Tree's okay?" he asked.

"Of course," Enee said.

The Grail Tree had been around for thousands of years. The fallen mat of needles was probably a sign of it growing again.

Arc didn't look convinced, but he didn't argue.

"Can you fly up there and get that Stone?" she asked Omen.

"Don't you mean, *will* you?" Omen prompted.

"*Will* you fly up and see if you can get the Stone?" Enee stressed.

She had heard that the Stone wasn't as toxic as the Grail Tree, but rumor had it that even the ones in museum collections needed to be handled with special gloves. That's why all the *sanctioned* collectors had first dibs. Historians in tourist towns, like Rowbuirin, didn't stand a chance at getting their hands, gloved or not, on one unless someone stole it for them.

And someone *did* need to steal it—especially if that person was a Chimera. The Stones had their own way of giving off some serious "don't you dare touch me" vibes, keeping away all the creatures of the Mundus. If it weren't for that, any Mourning Drake would see that shiny gem and think, *mine*. Not even the most obedient Messenger Drake would dare to snatch it.

So, what would happen if a Moth tried?

Well, they'd either succeed. Score. Or, Enee's point would be proven right, and Omen's bond to her wasn't what her Treecher claimed.

Enee flinched. *Am I really sending Omen to risk getting roasted?*

Everything felt on. Heightened. Every decision came with a hair-trigger and a bigger consequence. Omen flew onto her forearm. He looked at the Tree, feeling the change in the air with his yellow antenna.

"Fine. I'll try. Consider it an olive branch," Omen said.

Enee took a breath.

"Thank you," she said, "I'm sorry about putting you in a box, by the way."

"Oie, don't get sappy on me, now," he said and launched forward.

Omen flew in a tight spiral around the trunk of the Grail Tree. Enee stepped back to watch him ascend, flying higher and higher while darting between the branches. She could feel the pull on their bond, though the pain wasn't as sharp as it had been before. Each time he changed direction, weighing whether to land, rest, or keep flying, she felt a chill run down her spine and a deep pressure build behind her eyes.

Enee crossed her fingers.

Please work, she prayed, adding, *and don't wake up*, just in case. The last thing she needed was to be responsible for poisoning the town.

After a few minutes, Omen passed the point that over-looked the Hollow. The pull of their bond made her head feel like it was stuffed with cotton wrapped in thorns, making her ears pop as he inched his way to the tippy-top of the Grail Tree, where the Stone glinted in the Saturday sun.

Closer.

And closer.

And…

The wind picked up. The moment Omen reached the top, a strong gust threw him back.

"What's happening?" Arc asked.

"The wind's being a problem," Enee said.

Omen flew so close that his little feet nearly touched the Stone. He even tried diving headfirst from above to let gravity do most of the work.

"I can't reach it," Omen huffed.

Each time he tried, the wind drove him back.

"Maybe that's a sign not to climb today. We should go to the barn. You still have chores. Afterward, we can hang out with Knoble. I'll run, you ride? We can see who's faster," Arc suggested. She could hear the hope in his voice.

"I still need to try," Enee said.

"Wait," Arc said, grabbing her arm.

"You heard what Keeper said. I need to give Mama some breathing room. Not later, *now*. You can wait behind that tree if you don't want to watch."

Enee yanked her arm free and handed Arc her treasure box so he could put it in his bag.

"I hope you land on your feet, housecat," the Familiar called on his glide down, taking his place on her ear.

"If I don't, I guess you'll get a real mage next time," Enee teased.

"I doubt it," Omen said.

She was almost tempted to ask him what he meant, but she couldn't be stuck in her head while climbing. Every part of Enee needed to be present, especially given that her arm was still recovering from the last fall, and she couldn't rely on pure strength to make up for her mistakes.

Climb, her hearts sang.

Touch.

By the time Enee reached the lowest branches, her hands ached and were caked in black sap. Omen dug into her fur to hold on.

"Gross," he muttered.

Enee tried to ignore the oozing mess, but her hands kept sticking to themselves or the bark. Her head started to feel fuzzy again. She had just enough time to brace herself between a cluster of branches before a sharp sting shot through her palms, and a bright cloud swallowed her sight.

ENEE WAS HERSELF, BUT NOT. THIS CHIMERA WORE ARMOR. This Chimera carried a sword on her back. This Chimera stared out from the branches of the Grail Tree. The landscape before her was blank. No meetinghouse steeple. No Rowbuirin town square. Just forest, and a series of thin trails of campfire smoke dotting the hills.

Enee's ancestor looked up at the Grail Stone. The Stone

loomed above her, still glinting in the sunlight. Her fingertips ached, but she couldn't decide if that had been from the Tree or gripping the sword she'd wielded the last time she'd dreamt like this.

"Noe!"

Enee looked down. Mama? But the Chimera below wasn't Mama. Their fur was white, with a gray-streaked mane woven with beaded seeds.

"Come on, cub. The meeting is about to start," called the Chimera, this time from their goat-head, not their lion-muzzle.

Was Enee supposed to be somewhere? She kept expecting the Mundus to snap back to her own, with a worried Foblin standing where this new Chimera stood and Omen tugging at her ear.

Omen! Enee glanced around, but he was nowhere in sight. Instead, a serpentine creature no bigger than her hand sat before her face. A Blood Wyrm.

"It is wise to listen to Umber," the Blood Wyrm told her.

This Familiar had pink frills down both sides of their body. Thin rings of gold marked their spine, paired with two of the tiniest wings Enee had ever seen. Enee would have interrogated the Blood Wyrm and demanded to know what had happened to Omen, but her words were not her own.

"I don't remember anything about a meeting," she called below.

The snake-part of the Chimera laughed. "Kids," they mused. "This is what we get for recruiting them so young."

"War calls for it," said the lion-part. "Come along, Noe.

If you miss the council meeting, you'll scrub pots until the next Crusade."

"But who will watch the Tree?" Enee asked.

The kings had called a truce the last time she'd been in this dream. Had her mind decided to bring her into a moment of peace? Umber's snake-part laughed.

"I'd say the pine's been looking after you. It had stood for a thousand years, and if the proposed truce is true, it'll be here a thousand more."

The truce.

Another sharp pain ricocheted through Enee's body, ripping her back into the overwhelming fog.

CHAPTER THIRTEEN
LIAR, LIAR, TREE ON FIRE

"Enee?" Omen bellowed into her ear.

She shook herself from the—dream? A dream she couldn't control. This had to be the lack of sleep talking. Right? After several restless nights and the stress of the EMD, her dreams had become as impatient as the rest of her.

"I'm fine. Now hush, I need to concentrate," Enee scolded, more to herself than Omen.

She scraped her hands against the Tree's bark to try and get the sap off, but the pesky stuff clung. She needed some Slime-Be-Gone.

"Wait," Omen said, tugging at her hair.

"I'm not waiting, and if you keep talking, you'll end up with a new kid to bother before you know it."

Omen tugged hard enough to turn her head towards the ground. Arc had dashed to a neighboring tree, shooting Enee a single *move your butt or they'll see you* glance before digging out a piece of paper and a pencil.

Enee didn't hesitate. She ducked between two branches flush with needles and tuned in to the crunch of the underbrush, where the leaves and sticks below broke under the weight of a massive foot.

"Arcamo? What are you doing out here? This isn't a place for kids."

Mr. Loch?

"I'm just sketching the Grail Tree. It's for a history project," Arc said smoothly, showing Mr. Loch his paper. "I'm not an artist."

Mr. Loch laughed.

"Me neither, kid. Bonus points for trying. What's the history project on?"

"The Hollow during the Crusades," Arc said.

She grinned. Arc, the silver-tongued Foblin. Did he ever lie to her like that?

"If that's what you're after, you should meet my father," said Mr. Loch.

Enee bumped her head against a branch. Of course. How could she have forgotten? Mr. Loch's father lived east of the Grail Tree in a small wetland that had been converted into a retirement home. From what she remembered, Isaac Loch was an ancient Everlass born at the tail end of the last Crusade.

"Oh, I don't want to bother him," Arc said.

Mr. Loch waved off his reservations. "The old man needs something to do. He doesn't go anywhere these days. The conversation would be good for him. Fair warning, he tends to drone."

Mr. Loch guided Arc toward the retirement wetland. He

looked over his shoulder once to see if Enee was still there, but she had no idea if he had managed to see her.

Never climbing alone ranked pretty high among the rules Enee tried to follow, but she desperately wanted to keep going. Did Omen count as a spotter? Doubt it. The Familiar couldn't catch her if she fell, nor travel far enough from her side to get help.

"Do you know any spells? Ones for flying or that could act as a safety net?" Enee asked.

- Omen groomed his antennae. "So now you want to wield? Well, sorry to disappoint. I *could* offer guidance if you wanted to make it rain or blow something up."

Figures. If Enee wanted the help of magic, she needed to either learn the spell herself or find an enchanted object that could wield it for her, and she knew only one person with an endless supply of magical heirlooms.

Pemprin Pendra.

The idea of asking the mage for help made her cringe. The only reason she considered it was because Pemprin already knew about her climbs, and she'd have the chance to ask the mage about it tomorrow on their field trip. The Whittles had just opened their orchard to the public, making it the perfect chance for students to go apple-picking under the supervision of the Treechers.

But what were the chances that Pemprin would actually help?

She would if I said I was an Alchem mage in need of a rescue.

The thought was so vile, Enee nearly vomited. She leaned against the trunk. What would Olwan "A-Bomb" Yule have done? Practiced. And not just the physical stuff, but the mental too. Enee sighed and slowly made her way down.

Going down took her twice as long as going up. Once on the ground, she passed the tree Arc had stood by and found a small vial of Slime-Be-Gone. He had left it behind for her. Enee smiled and scrubbed off the sap.

"Alright. Let's go."

"How quaint, chivalry is still alive," Omen mused.

Enee closed her eyes and focused on finding the right smells to lead her to Arc. Cucumbers and wax. Warm skin and wool. Tomato pulp. Arc hadn't been gone long enough for the smell of him to fade. The moment Enee locked onto the scent, she followed the trail deeper into the woods. The wiser plan may have been to go to the barn, do chores, and hope Arc would meet her there. But Enee couldn't leave him behind. What kind of friend would that make her?

"I'm starting to feel considerably manhandled," Omen complained again as she moved him to her shoulder.

"If you don't like it, why did you choose to be a Familiar?"

"Choose? Nobody chooses to be a Familiar. We just are."

Enee paused. "Does that bother you?"

"Does being a Chimera bother you?"

"No. But, this couldn't have been what you wanted."

Omen kept quiet for a minute. "I wanted a chance to experience this place again, regardless of what that meant."

"So, you thought, *hey, let's pick the Chimera. She'll be a hoot,*" Enee snapped. She found a low-hanging branch and used it to swing onto a felled log. She balanced across the bark with her arms stretched out like wings.

"We don't choose who we get. You cast your stone, some of them calling for us to travel to the Mundus while others remain silent, then we decide whether or not to answer the call," Omen admitted.

"But you just said—"

"I said we don't choose to be a Familiar. Think of it like being an Elemental. They are who they are, but can choose whether they want to be a mage. Sometimes we can get stopped from bonding with a mage if our personalities are too *destructive*. But every Familiar eventually makes the journey to the Mundus," Omen said.

Enee rubbed her face. "Stinks for you because, even *if* I believed you're supposed to be my, you know, I'm not a mage."

"Uh, seeing as I'm here, I say you are."

"Am not."

Enee didn't feel magical. Confused? Pulled in a million directions? Sure. But did she feel like she could snap her fingers and conjure a hurricane? No.

"Oh really? Let's give it a test, shall we? Pick up that stick over there."

Enee looked to where a widow-maker had finally fallen from the canopy. The branch had splintered upon impact, leaving bits and pieces scattered across the ground. She would have protested in favor of focusing on following Arc, but an idea arose. Omen thought he was right about her being a mage. What better way could there be to prove him wrong and show everyone that she was Mama's full-blooded cub than for her to fail at wielding?

Enee chose the least soggy piece of the branch.

"Am I going to start waving it around and make things fly?" Enee snarked.

"This isn't some Alchem bedtime story. Besides, only doctors use wands," said Omen. He flew to a stump and directed Enee to face him. "The easiest thing a mage can do is create fire. A spell goes wrong; it makes fire. A spell goes right; it creates heat, sometimes enough to make fire. You can't go wrong."

Enee gawked at the stick. "You want me to light this on fire?"

The wood looked no more ready to burst into flames than Enee felt prepared to make it so.

"Well, I don't want you to eat it. Focus on the wood. Don't just look at it, but think about all its parts. Go layer by layer into the pulp."

She looked at the wood like a tree branch during a climb. Would it bear her weight? Never. But why? Enee let her thoughts burrow through the outer skin into the cambium, where wandering Elementals of the deep woods scraped for food when everything green had either died or was buried in snow. Her imagination dug into the pulp and ravaged its way to the pith.

"Now imagine you're inside. Trapped."

Enee felt herself collapse into the dark and damp wood. Her hearts raced, and a roar built in her chest. *Out. Get out.*

"To get out, you must shake the walls of your prison. Every bit of—what are you doing?"

Enee started shaking the stick, wagging it in the air to create a fan-shaped blur.

"You're not supposed to *shake* the stick," Omen criticized.

The prison of wood vanished, leaving Enee hot-faced and fuming.

"This is ridiculous," she said and threw the stick as far as she could.

"Don't be so stubborn, housecat. Try again."

"I'm not being stubborn. I can't wield. No Chimera can. This is just making me look ridiculous."

Omen stomped and ruffled his antennae. "Chimeras can wield! Or, at least, they could. I don't understand why you think otherwise," he said.

"No, they don't," Enee insisted.

The Familiar took a minute to compose himself. "I've gathered that they can't wield *now*, but all creatures are connected to magic. It's not something people own or create themselves. Alchem kids with dormant magic still have a connection to this power, even if they can't wield it. Wax Wyrms, Enelope. *Wax Wyrms* are connected to magic," he said.

"Not us. We are the exception to the rule," Enee said.

During her first year at the school grounds of Rumfoot Hollow, she was asked to draw a diagram that displayed the different creatures of the Mundus. Her Treecher instructed her to create an intersection among four circles, forming eight categories. The largest four categories on the outside of the diagram belonged to the Elementals, while the four inner spaces showed the main bloodlines of the Alchem. Of course, Enee knew genetic crossover in the Alchem was *way* more complicated in real life. But what remained true was that all these categories were bound at the center. A center that, according to the Treecher, was *magic*. Everyone in the diagram had a connection to magic.

Who wasn't in this picture? The Chimeras. Enee had drawn a little circle at the bottom of the paper so they wouldn't be forgotten. Mama had been proud. The Treecher had docked three points from her grade.

"There are no exceptions. I'm not sure what your generation of housecats did, but your connection must have been moved or disguised. *Something*," Omen said.

Enee snorted. Moved? You couldn't move a connection like that. Then again, what about enchanted or charmed objects? The object didn't just wield magic on its own. A mage had to make it happen. Could the opposite be true?

Enee shook her head. No way someone had removed all the connections belonging to the Chimeras of the Mundus. They would have put up a fight. At the very least, they would have remembered.

"Okay, for argument's sake, where did my connection go?" Enee asked.

"How am I supposed to know?"

Enee needed something other than his word to go by. They had known each other for less than twenty-four hours. He hadn't earned her trust yet.

"You're a Familiar. A literal anchor for helping mages wield. Can't you *feel* it or track it down?" Enee asked.

"Alright, missy, you got a good nose on you. Can you track down the exact Sol Ox that makes your cheese? Or the very plant that gave away its cotton for your shirt?" he asked.

Enee frowned. No way. Stuff like that had been processed, packaged, and shipped. Plus, there were like a billion Sol Oxen in Pendra-North alone.

"Not so easy, huh? Same problem with finding where

magic likes to pool. There are just as many sources as there are people, and even more ways magic has been packed up, pushed into objects, bought, sold, and grown. The more sources, the easier it is to lose manipulated connections in the shuffle," Omen argued.

Lose it? People lost their socks. They lost keys and left-overs. How could an entire species misplace magic? Sure, there weren't many Chimeras anymore, but it seemed a big thing to forget.

"But if Chimeras are connected to magic, why does everyone believe they aren't? Why are you the only one to tell me differently? Seems more likely that you're a liar," Enee said.

The Familiar hit a level of anger that bordered on comical.

He flapped and scrubbed his antennae, spewing vocab-ulary Mama had banned until Enee was old enough to drink coffee without it stunting her growth.

Maybe that was it. Perhaps the mistake of getting a Familiar wasn't on her end, but his.

"Do you want proof? All right, housecat. You asked for it," he bellowed.

Omen took to the air and attacked.

Every time his feet hit her skin, she received an electric shock. Enee yelped. He gave her another shock every time she tried to swat him away. Pressure built in her chest and burned its way into her throat.

"STOP!" Enee roared.

Fire came from her mouth. The force blew a soccer ball-sized hole in the neighboring tree. When her roar cut short, so did the flames.

The exhaustion hit Enee so completely that she fell over. All she could do was watch as the tree trunk moaned like a Leviathan, slow and aching until it snapped in two, landing with a thunderclap and a chorus of splintering branches.

Omen flew to her knee. "I'm no liar, *Mage.*"

CHAPTER FOURTEEN
DEATH OPENS LIFE LIKE A BOX

E nee stood over the smoldering tree with a Moth Familiar on her shoulder and the taste of thoroughly roasted dread in her throat. What had she done?

What am I?

Enee bowed to the forest and sprinkled an offering of soil over the offended tree. She'd seen Arc do the same when he accidentally crushed young saplings during their races. For good measure, Enee added a, "Please, for the love of MMA cards, don't tell on me."

When she finished, Enee walked away from the scene.

At least my only witnesses are a bunch of hardwoods, she thought.

Oak trees surrounded her. Hardwoods didn't gossip nearly as much as softwoods, especially if nobody asked them to. This didn't guarantee that someone wouldn't find out, but Enee did her best not to imagine the possibility. All she could do was walk away and lie like an Alchem king if people questioned her about the damages.

"Wait. That's it?" Omen asked.

It? Enee did not look at her hands. She did not open her mouth. She did not pay mind to the fire that burned in her chest. The questions she never wanted or imagined that she never wanted bubbled inside her. Why couldn't things simply be about her climbing? Climb the Tree, take the Stone, sell the Stone, and set Mama free. Pit-pat-*done*.

"I'm impressed. Just think about what you could do if you knew some better spells," Omen beamed.

A roar counted as a spell? Nobody had told her that before. Spells had only ever been words. And words were, well, not *her way*.

Enee took a deep breath and sought Arc's scent, desperate to escape the taste of charcoal that coated her tongue.

She wasn't the first wielder to lose control of a spell, nor the first student. But there was a reason why student mages could only wield under supervision. Accountability. Little spells could be hidden, and parents had the right to watch over their kids during such practices as long as they paid for any damages wayward spells caused. Mama would have defended her, but they didn't have the money to cover the fines for vandalizing the Hollow or the social capital to keep the town from thinking Enee would be better off under someone else's supervision.

She tried to be good, but her version of trying never seemed to come close to what others wanted. People only saw the violent parts. They never seemed to understand her intentions.

"Come now. There's no need to be scared. Chimeras are supposed to have magic. What you did was completely natural."

"Do you know how this will look if word gets around? And what do you mean by natural? It's not like I could do things like this before you showed up," she said.

Enee took a breath. She needed to calm down to a level south of *turn the forest to dust* and north of *I am one with the Mundus.*

"Of course not. You're not an Elemental, and while you're not one of the Alchem either, I'm assuming your ability to wield is similar to those who have that potential and need the EMD to provide them with the anchor to do so. That's where I come in."

Like Pemprin. Enee imagined the girl spending her evenings preparing for the day she could use magic openly. A legacy had to practice, after all.

Omen climbed onto Enee's ear and gave it a tap. "You did good. Don't worry about the details."

Enee clamped her eyes shut and took another deep whiff. She let Arc's scent lead her away from whatever details Omen had in mind. The trail eventually led her across the bridge that stretched over the Charon River to Mag Mell Retirement Wetland, where raised wooden walkways and mounded gravel paths webbed between a constellation of mossy islands. A nurse guarded the entrance. They watched for visitors with a basket of charmed entrance tokens.

Enee marched up to the nurse and tried to look official. The Golem was covered in hot pink moss that doubled as a pair of scrubs, and a Prayer Mantis clung to the center of their chest like a living broach. She could see the other Golems shuffling between islands, delivering medication, or guiding the retirees from one island to another.

"I'm here to see Isaac Loch. My friends are already here to meet with him," Enee said.

Between the mixed scent of near-dead Elementals and bog, Enee had lost Arc's trail. The Golem raised a smooth clay arm and dropped an entrance token into her hands. The metal was warm to the touch, charmed to track who came in and out of the area. Once Enee had safely tucked the token into her pocket, the Golem pointed her to one of the raised gravel paths, where another nurse waited to escort them.

"What is this place?" Omen asked.

"A home for folks who can't live independently anymore."

The Elementals who were wheeled along the paths or enjoyed a good soak in the heated pools varied from sixty years old to six hundred. Not every Elemental lived as long as an Everlass. Enee knew plenty who aged as quickly as the Alchem, looking at a good century of life until they used magic to keep them going.

The Golem stopped at a point where the path split into five. They gestured to the route farthest to the left and stuck out a sausage-shaped thumb to let her know that Isaac would be found on the left side.

"Thanks," Enee said, hurrying past.

The path widened and merged with solid ground. Like the Golem had suggested, to the left towered a stand of old grove trees, probably as ancient and moss-covered as the Everlass who lived there. Her landlord sat beside his father, looking like a mini version of Isaac. The size of the Everlass was even more striking when Enee looked at Arc. The Foblin stood as tall as the length of the Everlass' nose.

Enee looked on from a distance.

"Are you going to get any closer?" Omen asked.

"I'm thinking about what I'll say first. I can't let Mr. Loch know I was climbing the Grail Tree when he found Arc."

"Tell him you were looking for Arc and followed his scent. Lies are best when they're mostly true," Omen said.

"Enee?"

She flinched and shot her hand to a low-hanging branch like she'd been busy tending to the bushes.

"Smooth. If anyone asks, we can pretend you're the gardener," Omen teased.

Enee frowned. When she turned to greet the source of her discovery, she relaxed. "Hi, Billy."

Billy Glynn was the best Charon she knew. The fact that he was the only Charon she knew didn't change her opinion. The five-foot-eight solid gold skeleton wore his standard uniform: a gray T-shirt, a matching pair of plaid flannel pants, and a whip curled over his shoulder the same color as his bones.

Billy stuck out a fist, and they bumped knuckles. "Causing chaos?"

"Always. Are you working today?" she asked.

Billy laughed, a throaty sound, considering he didn't have a throat. "Always."

Enee glanced to see if he had any spirits attached to the end of his whip, but it remained free of the dead.

"Did they live?" she asked.

True to his vocation, Billy got called to a scene when someone in the community was on the brink of death. Sometimes, the person had enough life in them for Billy to use his whip to pull their spirit back into their body. Other times, Billy called the time of death and led the spirit to the Charon River. Nymphs took it from there, shuttling the spirit to the closest Charon Well where they could sink into the Midst.

"False alarm. The fifth one this week for the same guy. The Golems haven't quite grasped the notion of waiting to ring the bell for me," Billy said.

"Five times? For whom?"

"A Phoenix," Billy said flatly.

Enee snorted. She doubted Phineas was pleased with the constant calls for Billy's services. Was that what they'd been fighting about when she'd visited the barn last? Curse of being the only Charon in town, she supposed.

Billy looked over Enee's shoulder to where the Lochs sat. "Visiting?"

"For the moment, I'm spying," Enee admitted.

Billy laughed. "Well, good luck. Isaac may be old as dirt, but he has enough stamina to talk your ears off." The faintest and clearest of bells made Billy stiffen. He groaned. "I swear if this is about that Phoenix again—"

But despite the complaint, Billy gave the call his complete attention. The ring of the Charon's Bell resonated against every bone, making the gold shimmer.

"Is it?"

Bill sprang forward, unfurling his whip to capture whatever spirit tried to flee. However, he did not rush back the way he had come.

Instead, Billy leaped towards Isaac.

The Everlass had begun to shake, his head coming

down inches from Arc's feet. Isaac's spirit radiated off him in ribbons, neither entirely formed nor detached.

Enee rushed after Billy to Arc's side. He'd frozen in place, his snake-locks shaking. She grabbed him like a sack of Steed feed and carried him far enough back to stay out of Billy's way. Mountain laurel reached out to the Foblin, steadying him just as Tobias steadied his father.

"We were only talking," Arc croaked.

Enee squeezed her friend tighter. "Billy's going to help him."

But Isaac's spirit was old and stubborn. Lassoing a spirit was easier when they were in one piece, mimicking the shape of the body they came from. The ribbons half-attached to Isaac made Billy's job far more difficult, even when the braid of his whip unwound into branching threads to grab the parts of the escaping spirit.

"Enee, do you mind giving me a hand?" Billy asked calmly.

"I don't know any spells!" she gasped.

Billy waved her over anyway. "That's not important."

She left Arc in the care of the mountain laurel and made her way to Billy.

He pointed her over to Isaac. "Place your hands on Mr. Loch's face and have your Familiar sit on his forehead. We need to anchor him."

Tobias fumbled back to make room for her to follow Billy's lead. Not even Omen argued, jumping onto Isaac's crown.

"What do I do now?" Enee asked.

"Think about Isaac as a whole and talk to him. We need

to focus our intentions on keeping him with us," Billy instructed.

Enee focused on the Everlass' aged face. She thought of Isaac the best she could, but she'd never met him in person. He had moved to the retirement wetlands before she'd moved to Porto Bello, and it wasn't like Tobias spoke of him often. Still, she had a job, and Enee wasn't one to do things halfway.

"Hello, Isaac. We haven't met before, but my name is Enelope Noe. I'm a Chimera. Just as you are an Everlass. You're the biggest person I've ever met, which is saying something because Mama is *tall*. I like your fur. Do you know the MMA fighter Olwen Yule? She has white fur, too. That's what it reminds me of. Are you an MMA fan?" Enee kept talking and described Isaac as she saw him. She had no idea if she was doing what Billy wanted, but he didn't correct her.

"The pieces of his spirit are coming together," Omen said.

Enee spared a glance above, catching the moment when the ribbons of Isaac's spirit merged, creating a mirror image of the Everlass as if it were a reflection in a Churchmere.

He looked down. "Well, this won't do," said his spirit.

Billy's lasso slipped to the ground as the two parts of Isaac Loch stitched together. Enee felt a bolt of pain behind her eyes when the merge finished. She clamped them shut only to find the forest waiting behind her lids. She could smell the damp soil from the belly of a cozy nest.

Another Everlass towered above her, rimmed in the moonlight. Enee cried, but not in pain. She cried because the screams had woken her. The screams of the Pegasus.

"Hush, my little Isaac. It is just a war like all wars before it, born from fear. What a shame the Alchem fear the Chimeras'—" the Everlass mother paused as if her next thought had been lost to the wind, leaving a puzzled look on her face.

The pain behind Enee's eyes vanished so quickly that she staggered and landed on her back. Omen flew from Isaac to her chest.

"Easy there. You took a shot of the old guy's memory. You've got to give yourself a minute," said her Familiar.

Everyone else seemed to have calmed down. Even her landlord looked more at ease, brushing back a few of his father's bangs as the elder Everlass took to snoring. Had he fallen asleep?

"Thank you, Enelope. I'm sorry you had to see that. He'd been having a good week," Mr. Loch said softly. He looked at Arc and uttered a similar apology.

"This has happened before?" she asked.

"A few times. I think the reason he still sticks around is for me. One of these days, though, not even a Charon's Whip will keep him together," Mr. Loch admitted.

The memory of the screaming Pegasus made Enee shiver. She looked at the Everlass as he snored peacefully, centuries removed from the memory that rattled between Enee's hearts like a ping pong ball. Enee remembered to move about the same time Arc remembered to breathe. Billy coaxed them away to give Mr. Loch and his father some time alone.

Billy took a knee when they were within range of the patrolling Golems. "You both did great. Honestly, better than eighty percent of the first-time Charons I've met."

Enee debated whether to ask her question for a quarter-second before doing it anyway. "Do Charons ever see into the past when they touch someone who's dying?"

"Now and then. Life flashes are usually contained inside a body. But when a spirit leaves, it's like opening a box. Anyone can take what's inside," Billy admitted.

Enee nodded. She'd ask more questions if she had any idea how to put the screams in her chest into words. Plus, Arc looked ready to pass out.

Billy put up two fists for them to bump. "See you two at the barn sometime?"

Enee cracked a wild smile. "As if you could keep me away."

"I'm usually not far behind whatever trouble she gets into," Arc croaked.

Billy laughed again. "Fair enough. And, Enee, if you or Mama need anything, ask. I know it may not feel like it right now, but you've got folks in your corner."

Enee offered her best smile. "We have things handled, so don't worry about us. Thank you, though."

Billy looked like he wanted to say more, but let the subject drop. Arc and Enee left silently, leaving their tokens with the nurse at the entrance. They said nothing when passing the Grail Tree or the footpath to the barn. Instead, they just walked, arms looped together as tightly as possible without breaking an arm.

A scrap of paper poked out of Arc's balled fist. He was hiding something, but given what happened, Enee wouldn't push for him to show her. *Later.*

Just before they reached the pastures, Arc pulled up short.

"I think I want to be with my Snails for a while," he admitted.

Enee struggled to let go, still feeling the slight shake in Arc's hand. But his family didn't know when to leave him alone. Enee knew she had to do better. Or, at least, try to.

"See you during the field trip?" she asked.

Arc managed a quick smile before digging out her treasure box from his backpack and handing it over. "Yeah. I'll see you there."

The two of them split. Arc rushed home in a blur as Enee hopped over the Stone Troll Wall with Omen practically glued to her. She ran across the pasture the moment her feet hit the ground, desperately praying for the memory of the screams of the Pegasus to fade away.

CHAPTER FIFTEEN

A DEAL AS HEAVY AS AN ALCHEMIST SALAMANDER

Omen clung to Enee's ear for dear life as they cantered. Knoble may have been stocky, but every step transitioned as smoothly as creamy peanut butter. At least, that's what Enee believed. Omen seemed to think they rode only to provide an excuse in a plot to murder him.

"I told you to sit by his withers," Enee pointed out.

"What are withers?"

She waited another minute before she brought Knoble to a walk. The moment Omen could, he skittered down Enee's arm and knotted himself into a lock of mane at the base of Knoble's neck.

"Do you do this often?" he asked grimly.

"As often as I can."

The Familiar didn't comment, but she could feel him simmering. Enee bet he regretted having her as his mage now. The title still didn't feel right, like having a pair of socks with a thick seam that rubbed over the tops of her toes. And yet, she'd blown up a tree. How could she ignore that?

They reached a part of the woods where the tall birch trees made the Hollow seem yellow and still. She stopped Knoble beneath the thicket and looked up at the canopy, where the branches cracked the blue sky.

"What were they like?" Enee asked.

"Who?"

"The Chimeras who could wield. You said they did, so I'm assuming you've at least heard some stories," she said.

"Not stories."

Omen didn't say it, but something hummed between them. Enee couldn't read his mind, but their connection made her feel more than what he said. A link like that couldn't be completely blind to whatever churned in Omen's brain.

"I had a mage once before," he admitted.

Once?

"When was that?" she asked.

"For you? Uh, I don't know. When did King Gibrias rule the southern cities of Phlox along the Siren Strait?"

Enee blanched. King Gibrias? Seriously? Soundbites of Camphor's history lesson marched forward. King Gibrias ruled so long ago that he existed more as a myth of a myth of a myth than a real person. Enee knew Familiars could be old. But *ten thousand* years old?

"Please don't tell me I'm wrong about immortality, too," Enee moaned. Having Chimeras wield magic was enough for her to swallow in one week.

"I was sort of punished," Omen admitted.

"What kind of punishment keeps a Familiar alive for

thousands of years and prevents them from picking a new mage?"

Softness gave way to guilt, and that guilt bubbled into anger. "The kind that involves being imprisoned and forced into a dead sleep."

Enee didn't even have to ask what he'd done. One look and Omen knew the next question on her mind.

The Familiar lowered his antennae. His anger melted back to guilt. "Ever heard of a legend about an ark and a great flood that swept across the Mundus?"

"No. Why? What happened?"

"I messed up. I let my temper get the best of both me and my mage. Long story short, they died, and I got sent back to my realm. The moment I returned, the other Familiars grabbed me. They said I was too disruptive to be partnered with another and imprisoned me," he said.

Enee tried to take Omen seriously. This pink and yellow and fuzzy Moth was a destroyer of mages, harbinger of a legendary flood, and a menace to Familiar society?

Figures.

Whether she liked it or not, she couldn't return Omen. Plus, wouldn't she want the chance to get a better outcome out of life if she'd been given the opportunity?

"So, did your prison sentence end or something?"

Omen shook his head. "That's just it. I woke up because of a flaw in the imprisonment. A couple of cracks and good post-awakening hyperventilation later, and I wiggled free. I'd been completely forgotten. None of the Familiars I knew before were still alive. They had all been killed during your Crusades, specifically targeted to weaken the mages on either side of the war. So, I sort of just slipped back into the running. Your stone came through, and I seized the chance to do things differently," Omen admitted.

So, she got a potentially unstable Familiar because an entire realm forgot he existed?

Just like everyone forgot about Chimera magic.

The thought flashed into Enee's mind so quickly that she felt the words might leave a scar.

"So, before you were punished, could Chimeras wield?"

"Last time I visited the Mundus, the Chimeras I met had the potential for magic like everyone else. Now you're telling me that it's the standard that Chimeras have no connection to magic at all. If it weren't for everyone saying the same, I'd have laughed *you* off as a liar," he said.

"No offense, but shouldn't you have records about this?" she asked.

"A Familiar's history lives in memory. It's word-of-mouth and survives from one Familiar to the next. The recognition of the families we've touched is instinctual. What about the Chimeras? Don't you keep records?"

Enee bit her cheek. Fair point. The Chimeras were not known for writing down their history. What they didn't remember or forge in steel was forgotten. The only place the Chimera bloodlines could be found written down was in the archived editions of the yearly census. The mandatory document was born out of the Alchem community's obsession with writing everything down, at the order of kings who were even more obsessed with it. Of course, Enee would remember Mama and the one hundred surviving Chimera families until she died, but did Enee know the names of every Chimera who ever lived? No.

Enee's ears sagged. Wasn't it her duty to remember even when their armor rusted to dust and the kingdoms fell to new ones? Wasn't that why Mama read her the census each year, listing the Chimeras who remained so they wouldn't forget? And yet, she'd never learned of the earliest members of the line of Noe. Like Omen, they had been lost to time, emerging only in the deepest recesses of her stupid dreams.

A *crack* brought Knoble to a standstill. His ears flew forward and his velvety nose flared, finding a new scent among the underbrush. Enee found the source just after her Steed.

Pemprin kicked the stick that she accidentally stepped on out of the way. The mage had snuck up behind them with Ramil at her feet.

Knoble spun on his haunches and backed away from the Familiar.

"Did anyone teach you not to come up behind a Steed?" Enee snapped. "It'd be your own fault if Knoble kicked you in the face."

"Maybe he just needs better training," Pemprin complained.

Enee refused to be baited into another fight.

"What are you doing out here?"

"I don't need a reason. The forest is open to everyone," Pemprin said.

"You don't *need* a reason, but most of the time, people have one. What's yours?" she asked.

Pemprin folded her arms, giving Enee another once-over before looking at Omen. "I'm here to talk to you. I want you to be my magic practice partner."

Enee laughed. Then, realizing Pemprin was serious, she laughed some more. "No."

"What do you mean *no*?"

"Are you seriously forgetting what just happened?" Her temper refused to drop below a simmer. If she did use magic, her practice would begin and end with turning Pemprin into a pile of ash. "Why would you even want to practice with me anyway?"

"Perception bends to knowledge, and knowing the extent of a *Chimera's* ability to wield seems like just the kind of knowledge people should have," Pemprin said.

Enee paused. *Chimera.* Pemprin's words felt like a trap. This could be just another excuse to get her to lose control, proving Keeper right.

"The answer is still no."

She wasn't going to fall for it. Trusting a Pendra was like coating her hand in egg fat, sticking it in the mouth of a Crocswallow, and expecting them not to bite. Her very name lived at the heart of the Alchem. Half title. Half lineage. A dynasty that stretched across the Mundus and gave the very soil beneath their feet its conquered name. *Pendra*-North.

"I'd reconsider, if I were you," she said, trying to recenter her perfect posture, as if the angle of her shoulders was the reason why Enee refused.

"And why would I do that?"

"Because if you don't, I'll undo the erase-trace spell I cast earlier today," Pemprin added sharply.

"The what?"

Why would Enee care about her spells?

Pemprin sighed. "An erase-trace spell cloaks the source of wayward magic."

"And?" Enee pressed.

"And, I just so happened to cast that spell around a smoldering beech tree not far from where you love to climb. Nobody, not even the trees, can identify the culprit unless I let them," Pemprin said.

Enee blanched. The fact that Pemprin covered up the incident felt weird enough. The idea of someone tracking her through that magic only made it worse. She gave Omen a stern glare for his *I can't track magic* lecture.

"Just because I said I couldn't find the source doesn't mean others can't, given the right tools," Omen admitted.

Great. Enee clicked to Knoble to leave behind their unwanted guests. As much as she needed to learn of new ways to reach the Grail Stone, she refused to be blackmailed.

"Why should I care if they found out it was me? I've been through the EMD. People know newbie... *mages* sometimes lose control," Enee said stubbornly.

"But do you really think they'd really blame you first?" Pemprin said calmly, even as Enee rode past her.

She brought Knoble to a stop. *Mama.* Parents were the ones who were liable. And by what Keeper said, it wouldn't take much for the town to do more than hand Mama a fine.

I need more time. But for what? To gain enough control to prove she wasn't a danger? To claim the Grail Stone? Both? Whether Enee liked it or not, Pemprin's spell had bought her that time.

The girl wanted knowledge? Fine. Let it be a two-way street. Enee would get what she needed in the process.

"What do you say, partner?" Pemprin asked.

CHAPTER SIXTEEN

THE BREATH OF WHAT PROTECTS US

Pemprin gave Enee just enough time to brush Knoble down and release him to the paddock before collecting on their deal. The mage led the way into the forest with Ramil glued to her heels. Enee stomped along. The times Pemprin echoed her followers, calling out Arc's snake-curse or her temper, jabbed each of Enee's hearts in succession. When Pemprin spoke, she couldn't help but feel as if thorns lay beneath each word. Enee constantly needed a comeback, a defense.

Be a good Chimera and suck it up until you have the Grail Stone, Enee told herself.

She looked for the mage's followers as they walked. She expected to find at least one of them waiting in the wings.

"Where's your gang?" Enee asked.

"At home, I assume."

Pemprin refused to look anywhere but forward. They reached a part of the Hollow sandwiched between Rowbuirin and the school grounds. The area felt private and isolated, with a clearing large enough for the two to spin around without touching each other.

"The perfect place to murder someone," Omen said.

The Dryad Grove didn't stretch this far, and Enee doubted the Drakes would care much if she got picked apart by wayward magic. What did she contribute to their existence besides feeding MuMu bits of cheese and occasionally giving her a nose rub?

Pemprin pulled a branch from a fallen tree and used it to carve a large circle around them.

"What's that for?" Enee asked.

"Protection."

"From?"

"Anything that might want to interfere with the spells we cast when we cast them," Pemprin said. When Enee didn't say anything, Pemprin tossed the branch and put both hands on her hip. "Do you know anything about practicing magic?"

"I know the important stuff."

Granted, when it came to magic, the stuff she'd cared enough to hold onto was, *one*, mages and magic were an explosive mix, and *two*, don't leave an invisibility spell on an apple too long, or it sours the taste. It wasn't like she ever thought she'd be wielding. That information didn't matter in the face of all the other stupid things the Treechers gave her to memorize.

Pemprin sighed. "Fine, the basics."

She directed Enee to one end of the circle while she walked to the opposite side. The Familiars stood by their mages, eyeing each other with as much mirth as a good old-fashioned ghost town standoff.

"Are we really doing this?" Enee whispered to Omen.

"You'll be fine. Just go with what your instincts tell you."

"And if my instincts light her on fire?"

"I bet I can find a shovel," he said.

Enee sighed and widened her stance.

"Before we can cast any spells, we must create a barrier. Otherwise, anyone could come in from the sidelines and mess with our session," Pemprin began. "The circle I've drawn is a reference line. It's just to help us while we build up our guards."

"Like armor?"

Pemprin nodded. "What we need to do is create that armor. I want you to take a deep breath, as deep as you can, and imagine it reaching every part of your body."

"Breathing? That's it?" Enee grumbled.

"Just do it."

Enee reluctantly closed her eyes. She took a deep breath but let it out too quickly to hold on to it for more than a second.

"Again. This time, slowly," Pemprin coached.

She was not a slow kind of person, but she tried. Enee let the air fill her lungs, imagining it pour into her shoulders, arms, legs, and hands. Getting to the fingers and toes posed the most challenging part. Her fingernails felt so far away, farther than her lungs could stretch.

"Imagine all of your bad thoughts and feelings wrapped in that breath. So, when you exhale, those bad things come out as black smoke," Pemprin said.

What if she exhaled, and out came real smoke? Well, Pemprin wanted magic.

Enee let out her breath and imagined the smoke. The dark fumes filled the space like a dangerous cloud until the line Pemprin drew stopped it from expanding.

"Good. Now, keep doing that. Each time you exhale, the smoke gets lighter. Keep doing it until the color is white or gold," Pemprin said.

Enee repeated the exercise until whatever yuck inside her started to clear. The smoke around her slowly turned gray, then cream. The image of Pemprin's smoke entered her thoughts. The mage's breath came out so bright and shiny that Enee could see where her smoke ended and Pemprin's began. No matter how hard she tried, she couldn't get her barrier to match. If anything, the more she tried, the more the forest dissolved.

Pain spread through her hands as the barrier engulfed her.

ENEE WAS ENEE, BUT NOT. SHE FOUND HERSELF BACK IN THE branches of the Grail Tree with the Blood Wyrm.

"Time to hear the proposal for peace," said the Familiar.

Enee's host snorted but held her tongue. She let go of the branches and down and down she went. At the last second, Enee's hands seized a branch to swing herself from the Grail Tree. The Chimera in this dream was far stronger than her, with muscles accustomed to war. It took no effort for her host to swing to the next tree and slink down bark that looked like it had met her nails on more than one occasion. In less than a minute, Enee stood next to the white Chimera.

The gaze from all three of their heads was as solid and unforgiving as polished pyrite until Enee stepped closer. The Chimera wrapped an arm around her shoulders and gave her a noogie.

"*Ah*, Umber!" she moaned.

"Come on, show off, or we'll be late. The Alchem kings have sent us a proposal."

"One we'll accept?" she asked.

Her host's words bulldozed over Enee's thoughts. She couldn't change anything! Each word lived as a legend that Enee had no power to change. The Blood Wyrm chuckled from her shoulder but kept their thoughts to themselves.

"I guess we'll see," said Umber.

The Chimera led Enee to a camp that looked like it had been there for a while. The tents had lost their color, washed to faded gem tones and patched with whatever had been at hand. Uneven stones ringed the fire pits, mounted with cast-iron grills and cooking pots. Around them sat logs worn enough to make the wood look soft and buttery. And—

Everywhere Enee looked, she saw Chimeras. So many! Others joined them on their walk, some twice their height and with fur ranging from charcoal to a near-blue white, copper to russet, and gold. Some had all three heads, others fewer. Enee even spotted a couple with wings. Next to many of the Chimera wandered creatures of the Mundus in all shapes and sizes.

No, not just any creatures. *Familiars.*

Enee shivered. These Chimeras could wield.

"Do you think the truce is real, Umber?" asked another Chimera.

Her guide shrugged. "If the terms pacify the kings enough, maybe."

Enee kept quiet. Whatever script lived inside her had nothing to say. They arrived at an enormous tent at the center of the camp, packed with more Chimeras than Enee had, or ever would again, see in one place. She prepared to be the shortest and most bald member of the group. A sore thumb among legends. But she wasn't.

By the Mundus, did the legends get it wrong, Enee realized.

Some in the dim tent were stocky and smooth-skinned. Others looked more reptilian. Just seeing the spectrum of differences made Enee feel like she... *belonged.*

"Keep going, cub. As far as you can," Umber said, pushing her forward.

The crowd shifted just enough for Enee to squeeze into the front row. Within the ring sat four speakers from the various Chimera bands. At their center stood an emissary with dozens of thick, red snake-locks.

The Gorgon from before.

They were clean of stone dust, but their snake-locks still wore little leather helmets to cover their eyes. It probably wouldn't be much of a peace talk if they turned everyone to stone.

The emissary noticed her and dipped his head in acknowledgment.

She did the same. Enee would have believed in peace if he had made the truce, but the Gorgons were puppets to a final curtain call, where the Alchem kings waited at the end of their strings.

"Say your peace, Gorgon. We are ready," called one of the four Chimeras in the center.

The Gorgon straightened. Even though Enee knew he wasn't Arc, they wore the same intense look that Arc did when he needed to explain a plan. "The courts of Skyrs, Lask, Sears, and Ledean have motioned for a truce. They've agreed to cease all attempts to claim the remaining Grail Stones."

"And what of the ones already claimed?" asked the council member with a coat the color of the basalt-rich sand found on many of the Cemre Islands. Even from where Enee stood, she could smell the jungle on them. They were a long way from home.

The Gorgon's snake-lock coiled ever so slightly. "Those will remain with the kingdoms that claimed them, as will eighty percent of the lands claimed by the respective parties."

The crowd stirred. So, the kings would stop fighting and chopping down the Grail Trees, but they wouldn't return all the land they'd taken—or the Grail Stones.

"And the twenty percent of the land they leave unclaimed?" the council pressed.

"This will be neutral territory, of which the Chimeras will be free to do with as they wish should they not desire to live within the reign of the kings," the Gorgon added.

"And if none here wishes to remain within that twenty percent or be subject to a king, what then?" a Chimera shouted from the crowd.

The Gorgon flinched. "The traveler will be considered a trespasser and dealt with according to Alchem law," he admitted.

The crowd growled, and something inside Enee roared

with them. Death. That was what the Alchem law called for.

"And what if we don't want to be subject to your cage?" roared a Chimera from across the circle who still wore a sword at their hip.

"Those are the terms," the Gorgon said firmly. "Unless—"

"Spit it out. We gave our oath that no harm would come to you while in our company today. This remains true, no matter what the kings have ordered you to say," said the council member with gold beads threaded through their mane.

"The kings have agreed that all Chimeras will be allowed free rein should they attend the signing of the Accords. Upon which, all the Alchem allies vow to never so much as touch a Grail Tree lest they lose their life. And—" the Gorgon took a breath, "every Chimera, of their own free will, vows to relinquish their claim to magic for all time."

The crowd erupted.

∼

"HOUSECAT? ANYONE UP THERE? YOUR MIND DRIFTED AGAIN, didn't it?" Omen asked.

When Enee opened her eyes, only Pemprin and the Familiars remained in her company. The smoke she imagined had vanished as quickly as her dream, but the feeling of its presence remained. She wanted to sink her hands into it, knead the air, and pull it around her.

"I—" What was happening to her? The dreams had invaded her day twice.

Pemprin watched her carefully, her stance wide as if expecting an attack.

"I'm ready," Enee stammered.

Pemprin kept staring. "Since the EMD, have you learned anything as to why you can wield?"

"I've barely accepted that I have access to magic *at all*," she admitted.

"You are the first Chimera to wield, and you've done no research? Seriously?"

"Maybe not the first," Enee risked saying.

Pemprin stilled. "Who told you that?"

"Omen, my Familiar. He said Chimeras used to wield, but the connection is somehow gone today. I have no idea if that's true or why I suddenly have a connection to something no other Chimera does."

Saying *my* Familiar felt strange. But, despite her reservations, it didn't feel horrible. Just different.

Pemprin twisted her fingers around her necklace until the chain cut into her neck. She was either thinking or trying to strangle herself. Enee wasn't sure which was more dangerous.

"Have you talked to anyone about it?" she finally asked.

"Like who? Other than having a Kitchen Drake, it's not like I'm surrounded by people letting me in on spells," Enee snapped. "And Mama is... Their focus needs to be on other things right now."

She did collect MMA cards, but Enee always asked Mama to gloss over the magic bits. And she had the Whittles, but the most they shared revolved around apples and how to grow them.

"Have you thought of asking a professional, like, I don't know, *my uncle,* or visiting a library? You're not going to find answers to anything by lounging around in the company of Snails and snake-cur—"

Enee didn't let her finish the sentence. She rushed forward and shoved Pemprin right off her feet. Pemprin landed hard on her back outside the circle. Ramil hissed, taking a stance between the girls to stop her from approaching.

"What is wrong with you?" Pemprin gasped.

"Don't *ever* call him that again."

Enee found all the smoke she'd tried to purge and pulled it around her. The dark cloak morphed into a battle cape. She wanted the weight of her words to stick. It would never be okay for Pemprin to refer to Arc as a snake-curse. He wasn't a curse, and the curse itself was an inheritance beyond his control. If Pemprin didn't learn that, they could never work together, no matter what she threatened.

When her hearts started to slow, Enee realized what her action might have cost her. But the mage looked *small.*

"Isn't that what he is?" she asked, her words as fragile as the skin beneath an eggshell.

Enee stepped back. "He is Arcamo Balsam Landem the Fifth. He is a wonderful *person,* and an even better friend."

Pemprin nibbled her lip. "Okay."

Enee had no idea how to respond. What did Pemprin think being snake-cursed meant? Everyone said it, but how many of them actually knew the history behind it? What did they see when they looked at Arc? For decades after the last Crusade, Foblins were marked as traitors within the Elemental community. They had chosen the Alchem over everything else. To have a snake-curse was just that. A curse. To *be* a snake-curse was to be a snitch who lived under the thumb of another with no thoughts of their own.

But what thirteen-year-old would care to know the difference unless they had Snakes growing out of their head?

The cloud around Enee vanished as she reached out a hand. Ramil stopped hissing once Pemprin accepted the help and was lifted back to her feet.

"So," Enee broke the silence between them. "Should we practice now, or what?"

CHAPTER SEVENTEEN
THE APPLES ARE INVISIBLE
FOR A REASON

Pemprin had a point. Enee needed to at least *try* to think about what having access to magic meant, especially if it meant learning a spell that'd help her reach the Grail Stone. She just needed a better suggestion on learning how to start than "go to the library."

"Let me sleep on it," Pemprin said after their practice session.

Now, Pemprin rode in the branches of the Treecher behind Enee, her nose in a book. The lack of attention seemed contagious. Arc had barely said a word the entire walk to the school grounds, where the Treechers loaded their branches with students too tired to care that they were taking a field trip. Enee walked beside Treecher Oak, her head caught on a swivel between staring down Pemprin and silently poking Arc.

Was Arc mad? Did what happened with Mr. Loch's father still bother him? The Foblin's brief "I'm fine" clearly meant the opposite, but Enee couldn't crack him like a peanut shell to see what was happening inside. Arc's silence also made it impossible for her to focus on something other than her classmates' complaints.

"Just because Arc can't be in a different forest all day, why do we get stuck going to this lame orchard? Half the trees are always bare," muttered a boy named Hollsee.

"Enee suggested it," Estel whispered from the next branch.

"The trees are not bare. There's an invisibility spell on the apples that are still ripening so the Wyrms don't get to them first."

To Enee's surprise, Pemprin was the one to defend the Whittles.

"I still think going to Redwick would have been better," Keeper argued.

Pemprin looked up from her book. "There's more than one Foblin in our school. Are you saying we should have left them behind?"

"He's the only one who has such a bad reaction to leaving the Hollow. Everyone else can spend a day or two away. Why should we be punished because *nobody left behind* includes a snake-curse?" Keeper pushed back.

"We shouldn't say that. Arcamo Landem is not a snake-curse. He simply has a condition," said Pemprin.

All that knowledge and all that power, and she couldn't come up with something better? Even so, Pemprin's change of tune perked Arc up. That had to count for something. Enee's shove must have really knocked something loose.

"Whatever," Keeper said sharply.

Enee spun on her heels to walk backward and face Keeper. But when she turned, she found Treecher Camphor. He gave her a stern, *remember our talk* look. Anger burned deep in her belly, clawing its way up her throat like fire. The flames raged against the idea that everyone else had the power to completely change her life on the whim of saying or doing the wrong thing at the wrong time. She dug her nails into her palms. If only she could—

Enee's attention snapped to the back of the group, turning her fire stone cold.

Proctor Pendra trailed behind. *Far* behind. The kind of behind that tried to hide the fact that he was there at all, dressed in what Enee could only guess were pajamas. His enormous satchel banged against his hip, throwing him off-balance while he scribbled into a notebook. When he finally looked up, it was right at Enee.

The proctor dropped his pencil. Clearly, he didn't expect her to see him, let alone stare at him. Without bothering to pick it up, he turned on his heels and shuffled back the way he came.

"I think we can safely say we're being watched," Omen shuddered.

Her anger layered over her in heavy, impenetrable scales. She raised her head high and kept moving.

Don't stop. Not now.

"We're here!" Treecher Oak announced quickly.

The Treechers knelt to let the kids walk along the driveway to where the owners of the orchard, Mr. and Mrs. Whittle, waited. Enee tried to keep track of Arc. The Foblin lingered in the back, his fingers looped into his backpack straps, and his hood kept low over his brow.

"It's okay. You can get closer," Arc said.

"Come with me?" She had to tell him about the proctor.

Arc shook his head. "I'm going to stay back here."

Splitting up screamed *bad idea*. But his snake-locks had twisted themselves around his face, making it impossible for him to fully cover them with his hood. He looked exhausted.

"Leave him be. Something's got him all twisted up, and I don't think you'll be able to fix it right now," Omen said.

Reluctantly, she gave Arc his space and joined the other students. Maybe they both needed to take a breath. Could she? Well, if there was ever a place that could make her problems feel far away, it was here.

The Whittles were powerful mages in a backyard way. They didn't wear cloaks or consult with powerful leaders. They didn't carry orbs mounted onto elderberry staffs like a proctor. They wielded shovels, with standard uniforms of denim and cotton sweatshirts patched with their orchard's logo. Work gloves filled their pockets, and their salt-and-pepper hair sported the occasional leaf.

Mr. Whittle shifted on his bare ape-like feet, the hair on them just as gray as on his head. He didn't do crowds as well as Mrs. Whittle, who watched the group with a bright, fanged smile.

The Whittles caught sight of Enee and gave her a big wave. She waved back. Enee was proud to be the one who suggested their place for the field trip. Arc needed a destination inside the Hollow, and the Whittles needed the business. Besides, the place was beautiful. The swath of land the orchard sat on stretched far enough to exhaust even a Chimera.

"Welcome to Hidden Pit Orchard. Is everyone ready to do some picking?" Mrs. Whittle asked.

The response followed a standard monotone *yes*.

"Wonderful. We'll divide you into three groups. Group one," Mr. Whittle sliced the air with his hand, drawing an imaginary line between Enee and everyone to her left. "You get first pickings. Two munching apples, if you please. Trust me. You'll need room for the other activities today. Just make sure not to climb the trees. We've got to protect them the best we can."

"Group two," Mrs. Whittle added, creating a line that scooped out the middle of the class, "you'll come with me to the produce barn. You'll see where we press the apples for cider, make many of our baked goods, and even help turn milk into butter."

The third and last group joined Mr. Whittle to check the farm equipment and test-drive the tractor. When the time came to disperse, everyone in group one ran off to claim their apples with friends who'd been lumped into the same pile or were close enough to the border to choose where they wanted to go.

Enee hoped Arc would be in her group, if for no other reason than to have a good line of sight. She caught a glimpse of his hoodie in the far back. That, she expected. What Enee didn't expect was seeing him next to Pemprin, a salmon-colored book in his hand.

"Are they arguing?" she asked Omen.

If she found out Pemprin was teasing Arc, or that she had anything to do with her uncle hanging around, there'd be serious pain during their next magic practice. Enee tried to push through the crowd, only to lose sight of them.

"Where'd they go?"

She checked the aisle laden with Arc's favorite, golden

apples. Halfway through the row, she saw a flash of red and sprinted after it.

"Arc, wait up," she called into the trees.

Arc didn't slow down.

"Hey!" Enee grabbed his arm. "What's wrong?"

"I need you to stop," Arc said.

He spoke softly, but the words were so sharp they could have peeled the skin off a moldy tomato.

"If you want to be left alone, fine," Enee said, trying to keep the hurt from her voice.

He pulled Enee to a roped-off section of trees. "I don't want to be alone. That's the whole problem. I don't want you to get hurt climbing You-Know-What, forced out of the Hollow, or worse."

"You know why I'm doing this," she said.

"Yes, for Mama. But, Enee, there are other ways to help them. We can come up with a new plan. You don't understand—"

Enee tore her arm away. "Understand what?"

Arc gestured to his book. "Before Isaac Loch had his... *episode*, he told me about a poem."

He found the page he wanted and gave it to Enee. The book itself looked like any other that the Treechers walked around with during history class. Only this one had two sheets of unbound paper sticking from the block. Gold leaf bordered two sides of the first page as if someone had torn the sheet from a larger document. The second came from a regular lined notebook covered in Arc's familiar scribblings.

"He found this scrap in the woods as a kid, near the You-Know-What," Arc said, pointing to the gilded page.

Had this been what Arc had in his hand when they left the retirement wetlands? And yet, the paper looked perfect and uncrumpled. At first, she thought her inability to read the text was just her brain being, well, her brain. Then Omen chimed in.

"I haven't seen that language in a while," he mused. The Familiar crawled onto her arm and gently stroked the page.

"Can you read it?" she asked.

The Familiar nodded. He found his voice just as the sea found the crimson stone cliffs of Antioch County.

"Surrendered magic of a Chimera's roar
is locked away in enchanted ore
until what was given to the pine
is bestowed to a child of the donor's line.

With this debt, honor is paid
to a world destined to be remade.
And what was locked away in enchanted ore
shall finally seek justice from a heartless war."

Enee slammed the book closed and passed it back to Arc. The words sank beneath her skin faster than a cold rain. She'd heard parts of this before. The EMD.

"A poem? So what?"

Words. The poem was only words. Right?

"It means something. You can wield now, and as far as we know, you're the only one who's tried climbing the Tree since the Crusades, a time you said you've been dreaming about. What if it's responsible? Combined with the poem, there has to be a connection. A dangerous connection," Arc said.

Enee doubted she had done anything first. Someone must have tried climbing the Grail Tree at one point. A curious mage layered in protection spells. A determined traveling salesman. A different Chimera.

"When I asked Pemprin to help me with the translation, she—"

"That's what you were talking to Pemprin about? Did you go to her when you told me you wanted to be with your Snails?" Enee asked.

Arc sank into his jacket and nodded. "She's not all how you see her. She helped me out when I wanted answers. And, you heard her today, she's... I don't know, different," Arc said.

Only because I made her, she thought bitterly.

"And I know you don't read well."

Enee flushed. "I manage just fine."

The thought of Arc telling Pemprin about the poem before her hurt, even if she wouldn't have been much help. Did Pemprin only want to practice wielding with her out of curiosity? A prodigy hungry for a legend of her own?

"I'm scared, Enee. What if something bad is destined to happen? What if the You-Know-What wakes up and poisons everyone? Have you looked at it lately? The sap isn't white, and its needles cover the ground around the trunk. If people link the cause back to you, especially with all the rumors, they won't think twice before sending you and Mama away. What if your magic is a sign of what this poem is saying? What if your dreams are a sign? What if the Tree has given you something that could explain why you can wield?"

Enee winced. *But Omen said—*

"I asked for Pemprin's help because the Pendras have the oldest collection of books in the county. She'd never seen this poem before and told me the paper had been enchanted to keep it from being destroyed. Truly enchanted, not just saturated in a temporary charm. I've crushed, thrown it, and dipped it in Glamour Snail slime. Nothing damages it," Arc said.

Chimeras with no magic. Chimeras with magic. Chimeras *given* magic. Enee felt sick. She had almost wrapped her brain around wielding, but the idea that she stood as the puppet of a column of wood and Wyrm poop was too much.

"Stop it. It's just a poem, not a doomsday prophecy," Enee said through her teeth.

The look on Arc's face froze her from the inside out. "Why do I have to fight to be heard by you, too?" he whispered.

"It's not like that—" Enee tried to reach out, but he brushed her off with a hiss.

"Why don't you see the danger? Everything points to the idea of your climbs being *crazy*," Arc snapped, his snake-locks shaking.

Crazy?

Enee couldn't speak. Couldn't move. All that ran through her head was *crazy*. How could he say that? All Enee wanted was to find a way for Mama not to need anyone—to live without asking for permission to stay or leave, to get hired or fired. Did he not see how worn Mama had become? Did he not see the cracks?

She wanted to scream and scream until the Grail Tree shook, dropping its Stone. Maybe then Enee would be—

Useful.

"This has always been about you and your guilty conscience. Never have I heard Mama complain to you about work. I get that it's hard, harder than I will ever truly understand, but did you ever think that maybe there were other ways to make their life easier? Ways that won't give people a reason to look at a Chimera like a Sselesu Retsnom," Arc said.

Useless monster.

Omen tried to stop Enee before she did it, but the Familiar wasn't fast enough. She went in for a shove just as one of Arc's snake-locks coiled and struck, biting her hard on the wrist. She didn't know who looked more shocked, her for being bitten or Arc for doing it. They froze with his snake-lock's toothless mouth around her wrist.

"That's enough."

Mr. Whittle touched Enee's shoulder and gently tapped the nose of Arc's snake-lock. Whatever magic pooled in Mr. Whittle's old, worn hands was like water to the fire that flickered in her chest. The two of them separated, unable to meet each other's eyes.

"You alright, Arcamo?" Mr. Whittle asked.

Arc nodded. "I'm fine, sir."

"How about you go for a nice walk?" Mr. Whittle suggested.

The Foblin barely nodded before shuffling into a different aisle, leaving Enee and Mr. Whittle alone.

"And you?" he asked.

Enee's breath came out in ragged, hot bursts as if she had stuck her face too close to a sandstove. She would not cry. She would not.

"I could use some help. Want to show my group how to drive a tractor?" Mr. Whittle asked, a gentle smile folding up all the time that gathered around his eyes.

She stood straighter and gave Mr. Whittle a brief nod. Enelope Noe could at least try to do that right.

CHAPTER EIGHTEEN
THE BUSINESS OF KNOWLEDGE

While Mr. Whittle gave directions, Enee pointed out the different parts of the tractor that had faded to a color between a bruise and a baby's gums. He called the family heirloom the Chow Hound, which she figured was because his forefathers had haphazardly enchanted the metal beast over the decades. When a person, mage or not, claimed the driver's seat, the tractor ate up their energy to keep it running. Did it work? Sure. It just left the driver on the brink of passing out afterward.

It was exactly what Enee needed.

When it was time to move the Chow Hound, she went first. The students who wanted to try followed, with Omen keeping watch from above to observe the demonstration. Enee stayed close by to ensure nobody exhausted their energy and accidentally dozed off at the wheel. More often than not, her classmates' eyes began to droop, and she would take over. She had plenty of energy to burn. So, if something heavy needed moving, Enee moved it. If Mr. Whittle asked her to run and get something, she ran. It was similar to when she volunteered during the summer. Sure, she mostly did it as an excuse to be around Mama, but she never slept more soundly than after a long day of farm work.

Enee started to feel better by the time the first group left to pick apples. She decided to stay with the tractor one more round. Better safe than sorry.

"How does it feel to wield?" Mr. Whittle asked while they waited in the shed for the next group to arrive.

Enee shrugged. The only magic she could conjure involved fire, a spell simple enough for a Drake. To her, magic only burned. Did all mages feel like this when they started to wield? Enee tried to imagine Olwan Yule with gnarled magic bubbling in her chest, but the Yeti always looked composed and solid. Why couldn't Enee be that?

"Like I'm turned around, if that makes any sense," she admitted, digging the tip of her shoe into the dirt. *Like I'm losing control.*

Mr. Whittle chuckled, which made her smile because his laughter was wickedly contagious.

"It does. Wielding is like being lost in the wild, especially when you don't know any spells. You can have the potential, an anchor to keep you grounded, and the magic waiting to be shaped, but *understanding* how those pieces fit together is a completely different story. And that takes time."

Enee rubbed where Arc had bitten her. The snake-lock had left only a slight bruise. The memory would last longer.

"Maybe I'm just *bad*," she said.

Life would be easier for Mama if she kept her head

down. If she did the dance and had her own version of Arc's *school quiet*, maybe there would be fewer looks. Maybe there would be less of a reputation Mama had to do everything in their power not to uphold.

Enee sniffed. Life would be easier, but it wouldn't be her own. Every inch of her screamed against the Mundus. The Grail Tree was the answer because it was the only one she had. Enee knew she wasn't strong enough to be the person Mama needed without it. She wasn't strong at all. She was a mess that breathed fire.

"Is that what you and Arcamo were fighting about? You're thirteen—a thirteen-year-old Chimera who can wield. Tell me the name of a single teenager who doesn't cause a few problems," Mr. Whittle said.

Enee frowned. "I'll take that as a yes."

Mr. Whittle sat on his workbench and patted the seat. Enee plunked herself down beside him.

"What everyone notices isn't all a person is," he said.

"What if I'm just a wrecking ball?" Enee paused. "What if I'm doing something that others are telling me is stupid, but I keep doing it anyway?"

Mr. Whittle didn't look concerned. Then again, it's not as if Enee had told him she was actively trying to steal a Grail Stone. Nor did she mention the dreams about the Crusades and the loss of Chimera magic or the potential doomsday prophecy found by an Everlass at the foot of the Grail Tree.

"Well, I guess if you know that's what everyone else is telling you, and you know that it might be bad, I suppose the real question is why you feel you need to do it. Why does Enelope Noe, the hardest working kid I know, and cub of the biggest help this farm has seen in twenty years, need to do this when everyone else says *stop*?" Mr. Whittle asked.

Enee looked away. She didn't deserve to be lumped in with Mama's praises. They were the one who ran errands for the Whittles and did most of the farm work when the time came to scoop up the old apples that the tourists left behind. Enee barely qualified as an extra pair of hands.

"Chin up, Enee. There are great things ahead," said Mr. Whittle.

"Like?"

Mr. Whittle only winked before welcoming the next group of kids. Throughout the demonstration, Enee let all she'd said and done swing in her mind like a punching bag.

This had all started last summer. Mama's job kept them away from Porto Bello most of the time, and Arc couldn't hang out while he dealt with family drama. So, she took to enjoying the woods alone. Then, she passed the Grail Tree. She'd seen it hundreds of times, but she'd never touched the Grail Tree.

She remembered how the bark felt in that first moment. Electric. A drum beat in her veins. The shimmer of scales of a sleeping Drake. Time. If time had a feeling, it'd feel like a Grail Tree.

Enee had looked up and up to where the Grail Stone waited and knew she had to touch it. Only later did she ask Mama about the legends. The Chimeras had given up so much to help the Grail Trees. Couldn't she be a little selfish now? Couldn't she use that Grail Stone to help Mama? From that point on, Enee had one purpose.

The hardest part of remembering this was if she took away the part about Mama, all that remained was the desire to climb. Did she do it out of guilt? Did she climb out of a reckless need to do something? The feeling seemed too strong for that. But maybe Enee created that feeling so she could lie to herself.

"Cheer up. You didn't hurt the Foblin," Omen offered, finally flying down to join her.

"Not setting him on fire and not hurting him are two different things."

She had no idea how to make things right with Arc. When she thought of no longer climbing the Grail Tree, Enee felt as if she wore a suit of armor made of Night-crawlers. If she really couldn't stop, what could she offer Arc? Nothing.

If I can't change, will Arc leave?

To make matters worse, Pemprin raised her hand to be the next on the tractor.

Enee tried to be professional and shove her feelings as far down as possible. She guided Pemprin to the track like all the other students.

"I think we should try some defense spells next practice. What do you think?" Pemprin asked, adjusting her grip on the wheel to accommodate Ramil, who'd curled around her shoulders like a pudgy shawl.

Enee bit her tongue and focused on the track.

"You're a ray of sunshine today," Pemprin remarked.

"I guess it's the company. Backstabbers with creepy uncles make me itchy," she grumbled.

"What are you talking about?"

"I know about that poem. Funny that you forgot to

mention it yesterday while using me as a practice dummy. And I saw Proctor Pendra following us on the way here. He's been watching me ever since the EMD."

Pemprin stiffened. Her eyes swept back and forth as if reading her own thoughts to try and keep them straight. "I see."

When she pointed her attention back to the task at hand, Enee could swear it was like watching someone put on a costume, layer by layer, until only a perfect Pendra remained.

"The only reason you want me as a practice partner is because you think that poem means something. You're like the proctor, researching. Only, you have the guts to do it to my face," Enee growled.

If Pemprin had really wanted to practice magic, the kind that challenged her, she had an entire family to pester.

"That's it. You've got me all figured out," Pemprin said, gripping the wheel.

Enee needed to take a slow breath to keep her roaring fire at a steady, non-murderous burn. She ran the names of the Chimera families in her head, timing them to the turn of the tractor's tires.

Giles, Gomer, Halon, Hild, Imre...

"Am I wrong?" she asked after a good dozen names.

"No, you're completely right. I blackmailed you because I want to know what's going on."

Pemprin squirmed in the seat. Everything she said *sounded* true, but only because the words were vague enough to leave a gaping hole that could be filled with anything the mage wanted. Lies included. Yes, Pemprin wanted to know what was going on. But—

"Why?"

"I already told you. I'm in the business of knowledge. A Chimera gains magic. A Grail Tree loses its Stone. Arc's poem proves that something bigger is happening. That sounds to me like the makings of a legend. What could be more momentous than that?" Pemprin said.

Another totally believable speech. And it stank like a big fat lie.

Pemprin didn't look like someone on the verge of a quest. Where was the spark? The mischievous wonder of possibility? Instead, Pemprin tried to sit straighter. Any straighter and Enee guaranteed her head would pop off.

"That's it? You want to be a part of the excitement?"

"Don't you? You're always the center of the noise at school. You bite our classmates when you want and run around the room when you get too antsy."

"Shows how much you know," Enee said.

Pemprin stayed silent. The tractor rolled to a stop for the next kid to get on. As she got off, she met Enee's eye.

"I've lived my whole life by one rule: perception is everything. Legends have always been a part of that. If one is really unfolding, here and now, that means the perception we live by could be changing." Pemprin looked to her group, only to find Keeper, arm-in-arm with Estel and Myra, making their way to the next activity. "And maybe that's a good thing."

Enee looked at the girl before her and the Familiar who clung to her shoulders. Was that a compliment?

"What does that mean?" Enee asked.

"It means, if you want those spells, check your pocket," Pemprin said.

CHAPTER NINETEEN
CROCSWALLOW THOUGHTS

If Pemprin ever decided not to be a High Mage, she'd make an excellent thief. Without Enee realizing it, she had slipped a book no bigger than a deck of cards into her pocket, along with a pink note smelling of lavender and two quartz crystals the size of a thumb.

"Find pages 43 and 67. Try the spells on the ground first. Or don't and go splat. Your choice.

P.S. We will have a practice session after school tomorrow. Be there, or else."

Omen laughed after reading the note. "Or else? This kid's a riot."

Enee had never wanted to open a book so much in her life. Yet, the one occasion she was willing to spend the time to figure out what it contained, she had to wait. The Treechers refused to let her walk directly home despite how close Porto Bello was to the orchard. Enee had to march back to the school grounds and complete the mandatory check-in with all the other students. She didn't see Arc, nor did she go looking for him once they were dismissed. Pemprin had also pulled a disappearing act.

"Where are we going?" Omen asked.

"Porto Bello, first. Then we need to find a place to practice," Enee said.

As she walked, Omen glanced at the book and read over the gold foil embossing the title, *"Bartell Lerner's Fledgling Fundamentals for The Novice Mage: Hexes, Hoaxes, and Hazes Vol. II"*

When she opened it, the spine crackled in her hands. Enee had to count out the pages to find the ones Pemprin mentioned in her note. Not that it mattered. The words were gibberish. A slamming free-for-all that she'd have to rip apart, letter by letter, until she could identify each one by sound, squish them back together, and maybe hear an intelligent word come out the other side.

I don't have time for this.

"Do you mind?" she asked.

She hated asking. She hated even more that she couldn't bring herself to ask properly. Omen caught the tail end of her point and settled near the book. To the Familiar's credit, he didn't tease her. He saw the problem and started to read, no questions asked.

Out of the spells Pemprin bookmarked, the second of the two seemed the best. The first spell detailed how to levitate inanimate objects. Pemprin probably thought it'd be helpful if Enee wanted to try and pry the Grail Stone from the Tree. But the farther away and the heavier the object, the more complex the spell became. Plus, she had to be on a flat surface while conducting the spell. Enee bet there were ways around that. Those ways just existed somewhere other than a first-year student's spellbook.

Pemprin's second suggestion appeared far more flexible. Enee needed a few special objects, concentration, and something solid to levitate off of. Flatness not required. If Enee climbed to the thickest branches of the Grail Tree, she could activate the spell and float upward in increments. If she had to move other than in a straight line, she could climb onto a branch and start over.

The principle seemed straightforward. Too bad the incantation sounded ridiculous.

"*By the sun, I am light. By the moon, I take flight,*" Omen rehearsed.

"Is that what it means to be a mage? To speak in bad poetry?" Enee asked.

Omen shrugged. "It could be worse. At least the supply list looks manageable."

At the bottom of the instructions was a list of objects Enee would need to complete the spell. Two charged quartz crystals, one left to bathe in the sunlight and one in the moonlight for two days. Check, courtesy of Pemprin. One Crocswallow feather, at least ten days of age. And one talisman sacred to the person conducting the spell.

Enee had the crystals, and her MMA card remained nested in her pocket. The tricky part came with the Crocswallow. Did Mr. Loch still have that hatchling? Maybe. He did say he was waiting for a relocation crew to do a sweep.

She made it to Porto Bello and snuck to the side window of Mr. Loch's office. She didn't see him inside, but she did spy a back table covered in an old crate—a crate with a baby Crocswallow.

They snapped at the bars, stripping away the white plastic covering the metal. They didn't look happy.

"I'm not sticking my hand in there," Omen said.

"Scared?" she teased.

"I think the words you're looking for are *not stupid*."

Enee entered the building silently and rounded directly into the office. Porto Bello didn't do high security, so even the door to the office was left open. What made things difficult was that she needed one of the Crocswallow's feathers, and they didn't seem at all impressed by how Enee looked at them.

"Hey, nugget. Remember me?"

The Crocswallow opened its sharp-toothed jaw and let out a little hiss. They hadn't grown much since she last saw them, but that didn't mean they couldn't remove one of her fingers.

"Oh, stop. I need *one* feather. You can live without it," Enee snapped back.

She looked at the Crocswallow's golden wings, still fluffy with bright yellow down. One feather stuck up at an odd angle, probably on the cusp of falling out in favor of a flight feather. Just as she readied to reach into the cage, Enee stopped. How was this fair? The Crocswallow had been captured, trapped, and now stood as an ingredient for a spell.

"What are you doing, housecat?" Omen asked nervously.

Enee knelt to meet the creature's mossy-green eye. "I'm going to open up this cage, and you'll be able to escape, but I'm going to need a feather in return," she said.

"What? That thing might not look like much now, but it will get huge! You want to let it go?" Omen said.

"Yes," Enee said.

Enee looked for something to wrap her hands in should the Crocswallow decide to make a snack of her.

"At least use a glove," Omen said, fluttering to Mr. Loch's desk.

The pair of gloves on top was the last thing Enee would want to wear if she planned to use her hands for anything more than punching someone in the face or prying open a Crocswallow cage.

As she fitted on the gloves, Omen snooped.

"Don't mess up his paperwork," Enee scolded.

"It's not my fault. Who can resist a big, red DENIED stamp?" Omen said. He started reading out a housing application. *Mama's* housing application. They'd been rejected for a new placement. Again.

This time, Mr. Lock had attached the application to a cluster of notes.

"*D85, shRoom C may be open next year. Nothing else available for the time being. Also, don't forget to sign the paperwork for Mrs. Whittle,*" Omen read.

Enee frowned. Of course not.

Omen couldn't help himself and kept going. To be fair, Enee didn't exactly stop him from reading the miscellaneous letters addressed to Mr. Loch.

"*Mr. Loch, we appreciate the Noes' situation, but, seeing as we are also tenants of your facility, it would be remiss if we didn't point out the unfairness of your request for a housing swap. Their presence, to date, has posed as a serious disruption in the day-to-day lives of the community.*"

Omen stopped reading. When he dug into the pile of letters below, each one became less about the idea of swapping apartments and more about them being in Porto Bello altogether.

Danger.

Liability.

Disrespectful of public walkways.

Enee owned up to the fact that their hair had caused some plumbing issues when they first arrived and the fact that she and Mama nearly flattened a few of their neighbors during their morning races. But was this really how her neighbors saw them?

"You okay, housecat?" Omen asked.

Enee squared her shoulders.

Bear it. Let the neighbors talk and move on, Enee commanded herself.

Mr. Loch wasn't listening to their drivel, and, for the moment, that was the only person whom Enee needed to ignore the gossip. She took in a deep breath and directed her attention to the Crocswallow. The nugget stepped back far enough for Enee to feel comfortable wrapping her hands around the bars. Even with her fingers in the cage, the Crocswallow didn't move. She pulled until the bars warped enough for the Crocswallow to fit through. If she opened the door, Mr. Loch would know someone had done it intentionally. This way, the escape looked like a determined flying reptile concocted it.

"Be free," Enee said, slipping off the gloves to put them back onto the stack of letters.

For a creature set on escaping, the Crocswallow took its sweet time walking to the hole Enee made. The hatchling climbed up onto the bars and over the edge. Without anything else to stand on, they fell snout-first to the floor and landed with a *splat*.

"Oh. Right." No flight feathers.

The fall barely fazed the Crocswallow. While they marched, Enee came over and plucked off a feather. The Crocswallow snapped its jaws and thrashed its head as if to bite her, but it never reached her hands.

Enee had the feather, and the Crocswallow had their freedom.

"Hop to, nugget. Unless you want Mr. Loch to catch you," Enee said, jumping over the Crocswallow.

She slipped from Mr. Loch's office before she and Omen got caught, leaving the creature to escape. If they were smart, they'd sneak outside and never look back.

CHAPTER TWENTY
WHAT DO YOU DO IF YOU'RE A BREAKER?

A s soon as she opened the front door to the apartment, Enee could smell eggs and hot sand. Mama was home. And making lunch? She reached the trapdoor to the shRoom and stuffed everything into her pockets.

Mama stood at the sandstove. A bandage covered most of their right paw. "Want food?"

"Yes," she said, eyeing the bandage. "Please."

Mama took two eggs off the pan and plopped them onto a halved sandwich.

"I can make my own if you leave the bread out," Enee said quickly, trying not to stare.

Mama finished the sandwich and placed it on the table. They even set out a dish for Omen, with the ingredients laid out so he could pick what he wanted. "Eat."

Enee didn't know what would spill out if she spoke, so she sat and waited. When Mama's sandwich finished cooking, they ate together in silence. The more Enee chewed, the greater the pressure built in her hearts, making her heels bounce against the floor.

"Did something happen at work?" she finally asked.

She stuffed another bite of the sandwich into her mouth to keep the rest of her thoughts from spilling out.

"Nothing for you to worry about," they said.

Their words rang as true as the day stretched long. And yet, Enee *knew*. Mama was breaking. And, if Mama broke, Enee didn't know if she could put the pieces back together.

"But—"

"Nothing," Mama repeated.

She couldn't help but think of one Mundus-breaking, roar-burning, tree-shaking thing. What if Mama was wrong?

She needed to claim the Grail Stone, no matter what some prophecy said.

Needed. The thought clung to her like sap. No other answer mattered in the face of that need. Enee shivered. Why did that scare her?

A knock came from the bottom of the stairs, breaking the moment like an egg.

"Expecting someone?" Mama asked.

Enee shook her head. Arc? She doubted it. He wouldn't use the front door even if she hadn't destroyed their friendship.

Mama went to the door and looked down at whoever stood below. "Mrs. and Mr. Landem, come in."

Enee choked on her sandwich.

"This isn't good," Omen said, stuffing a piece of egg into his mouth.

She rubbed the spot where Arc's snake-lock had bitten

her. Would he go as far as to tell his parents about the Grail Tree to get her to stop climbing?

No. *Never*. Right?

The Landems made it up the stairs far more gracefully than most, but scowled when they realized they had to touch the floor to finish the climb into the shRoom.

"Would you like some coffee?" Mama asked. Even though Mama and the Landems weren't friends, it was against a Chimera's principles to be inhospitable.

They both lingered on their bandaged hand.

"No, thank you," said Mrs. Landem, brushing the dirt from her palms.

Enee wouldn't have guessed they were related to Arc if she hadn't met them. Delsie Landem was willowy, with spidery arms, dark-gray eyes, and hair as black as pine pitch. Her husband, Arcamo the Fourth, stood nearly as tawny and muscled as Mama—minus the height.

"Enelope," Mrs. Landem said curtly. "Would you mind giving the adults a minute to speak?"

Enee glanced at Mama, who nodded to their bedroom. What could she say? No? She scooped up Omen and ducked into the next room.

"I wasn't done!" he complained as she drew the curtain, leaving only the tiniest of cracks to look through.

"That's as private as you will get," Mama said, positioning themselves between the Landems and the curtain.

Mrs. Landem clasped all six hands together. "Arcamo came home upset after the field trip. When we tried to speak to him about it, he stormed off."

"He's not here," Mama said flatly.

"Clearly," she said, taking in the entirety of the shRoom

in one glance. "Where he is isn't the issue. We'll find him soon enough. The issue is your daughter."

"Excuse me?"

The room dropped ten degrees. Even the Landems took a moment to check the exits.

"You see, Arc has never done anything like this before. Although he didn't tell us what happened, our sources say he got into a fight with Enee during the field trip," said Mr. Landem.

Enee ground her teeth. Nosey apple trees. They better not have told them why they were arguing.

"Kids fight," Mama said.

"Not our son. He has never run off without telling us, keeping in the blin—"

Mrs. Landem stopped herself before saying *blind spots*. Despite what most Foblins wanted people to believe, their knowledge of the forest wasn't omniscient.

When Mama didn't say anything, Mrs. Landem continued. "We believe that this attitude has been building for some time. He stays late after school without telling us and, among other things, has been stalling on important decisions about his future. This is a delicate, finite time. There is no room in Arc's life for things that could cause him greater harm."

Enee clawed her arms to keep from tearing the curtain. How dare she? Arc kept everything to himself because the Landems didn't have room for him to be anything other than perfect. Arc didn't have the space to make a fuss in the chorus of a house with six other kids.

Enee owned being a bad influence. She admitted being reckless, stubborn, *illogical*, and even a bad friend. But she was the only person in this shRoom who could honestly say she cared about what Arcamo Balsam Landem the Fifth really wanted, and not what he was *supposed* to want.

"This kind of recklessness comes from one place. Enelope," said Mrs. Landem.

"Excuse me?" Mama said again, slowly.

Mr. Landem stepped forward, trying to defuse the wrath on both sides.

"Chalice, you see—"

"I go by Mama," they said sharply. They briefly touched where Nama's head had been. "Chalice is not my name anymore."

Enee's chest burned again. Mama had been Chalice Noe before they lost Nama and Oma. Mama couldn't bear the name that had been theirs together without them. They were Mama. The only one Enee had ever known.

"Right," Mr. Landem said, clearing his throat. "We know Enelope is a good kid, but she's reckless."

"*Wild*," Mrs. Landem corrected. "Biting kids. Breaking arms. Riding off into the woods, unsupervised."

Mama kept very still as Mrs. Landem went down the list of Enee's sins. In her defense, she always wore a helmet when she rode Knoble, and the kids she bit deserved it.

"I don't recall Arc being supervised when I've seen him," Mama said.

Mrs. Landem straightened, but the woman was at least two feet shorter than them.

"The forest is always with him."

"Like now?"

Mr. Landem intervened. "We just think that Enelope's behavior isn't the kind of influence Arc needs right now.

Now that she can wield, the consequences of her presence are *unstable*, more so than before. Please, we're simply thinking of our son's safety. If she were on stabilizers, maybe—"

"*No*," Mama's voice rumbled like a death threat, making the Landems shake.

"I've appealed to your daughter before, but she cannot handle such a mature decision. As such, we are coming forward to clarify that we do not condone their friendship," Mrs. Landem said, trying to keep her voice steady.

Finally, they'd reached the point.

"Noted," Mama said.

"Does that mean you will respect our wishes and keep Enelope from our son?" Mr. Landem asked.

"It means I heard you. I believe the matter of who your son is friends with is not our decision."

Before Mrs. Landem could protest, a Wax Wyrm fell onto her shoulder. She flicked the creature to the floor and drew a long breath.

"I understand things have been difficult. Perhaps a fresh start is what all of us need." Mrs. Landem said. She stepped forward, her gaze held steady. "I have friends across the country who have done the same, choosing lands away from home to give them a life they wanted. Friends with *thriving* businesses who wouldn't think twice to offer help to another looking for the same chance."

Enee's stomach dropped.

Mama's status as a probationary citizen depended on being a model of lawful behavior. That, and the annual fee that prevented them from taking *advantage* of Pendra-North's hospitality and required them to be employed only by businesses with stable earnings. Or ones with enough vouchers to prove that the job wouldn't implode and prevent Mama from paying their dues. What Mrs. Landem was offering wasn't just a bribe. She was offering a solution.

"Noted," Mama said again.

By their tone, that meant *this conversation is over, please remove yourselves from my shRoom*. The Landems got the message and left as quickly as they came.

When they'd gone, Mama stood silently. Enee couldn't calm the fire in her chest, but she couldn't hide, either. They had essentially asked her to choose: Mama or Arc.

Omen stroked her ear.

"Friends come and go," he tried to console her.

Not this kind of friend. But Mama was *Mama*. The impossible choice wasn't impossible. Just impossibly hard.

She pushed aside the curtain and went to Mama's side.

"You fought with Arc?" they asked.

Enee nodded. "I don't blame them for hating me. I break things, Mama. I think I broke my friendship, too. Maybe that's how it has to be."

"Is Arcamo your best friend?" Mama asked.

Even after their fight, Enee only had one answer for them. "Yes. But they said if I stopped being his friend, they would help you. *Really* help you."

"What they're offering doesn't guarantee anything. I am fine. *We* will be fine," Mama pressed. They dropped to a knee and took Enee's hands into their own. "Is. Arc. Your. Best. Friend?"

Enee nodded.

"Things break in life. They just do," Mama said, lifting

Enee's chin. "Sometimes we are born to be breakers, lion-heart. When you are, life can get messy and difficult. In the end, there is only one question you must remember to ask yourself. What do you do when you break something?"

Enee sniffed and shrugged.

"You do what you can to fix it."

CHAPTER TWENTY-ONE
PHOENIX FIRE

Enee had so much going on in her hearts that she couldn't imagine what would happen if she only had one.

"Hang it all," she hissed.

She should have stopped, turned around, and waited for Arc to come out of the woodwork. But going after him felt the same to Enee as climbing the Grail Tree. She *needed* to do it. Every cell in her body refused any other answer.

She pressed onward, keeping as close to the mountain laurel as possible in case it recognized her enough to offer some of the same stealth it provided to Arc. If the Landems hadn't found him yet, it was because he had gone somewhere the trees of the Hollow couldn't spy on him. A blind spot. And what was the best blind spot around?

"Why would he visit the Grail Tree when he was against you being near it?" Omen asked.

"Arc's a planner. He likes to gather as many details as possible if there's a problem. You can't get specifics about a

You-Know-What without going to one in person," Enee guessed.

Even if Arc stopped counting her as a friend, he had a maddeningly big heart. The kind of heart that could befriend a cub who basically introduced themselves by mauling a classmate. Arc would hunt for answers to keep her safe, no matter what.

When Enee arrived at the spot, even she had to admit the Tree looked worse for wear. Dry needles blanketed the ground, giving each step an extra crisp spring. The lowest branches were practically bare, and the bark looked ready to peel off in some places.

Nevertheless, the urge to climb sang to her like a Siren's song.

She stepped up to the Grail Tree and placed a hand on the trunk like she had the day she decided to climb for the Stone. Only now, when Enee lifted her hand away, it came back sticky and black. The war from her dream whispered to her, filling her ears with the sound of a battle from centuries ago. She could feel the clang of swords, the stomp of hooves, and the breath of wings taking flight.

Arc had been right. Something was wrong.

She shivered. Were her dreams even her own? Was her ability to wield? Escaping the desire to climb felt impossible. Whether it was for herself, Mama, or something else entirely, Enee needed to reach the Grail Stone.

"What is happening?" she whispered to the Grail Tree.

Enee looped around the trunk slowly, letting her fingers trail over the rough bark. She made it halfway around before stopping. Near the Grail Tree's roots slumped a body covered in sap.

A body with red snake-locks.

"Arc!"

Arc laid inches from the Grail Tree. His skin smoked and bubbled, and a glob of black sap covered his chest. A large burl had split open on Arc's side of the Tree like an infected sore.

"We need to get the sap off," Omen said quickly.

But how? Water wouldn't cut it. She rushed to Arc's backpack and dug through the contents for his stash of Slime-Be-Gone. She lathered what remained of the jar on the worst spots, but it wasn't nearly enough to cover the Foblin.

"What do I do?" she begged.

Arc started to shake. A misty double of the Foblin peeled from his body like a hand-hewn wood shaving.

"No!"

Enee threw her hands into the mist to keep it from moving, but the spirit slipped right through. Omen flew over Arc's spirit and began to flap as if his life depended on it. Fine scales from his wings sprinkled over the mist and weighed it down.

"This won't last long. We need a Charon," Omen said.

There wasn't a Charon's Bell close enough to help them. Nor could Enee leave Arc side to find Billy. If she left, Omen would have to go with her. If he left, Arc's spirit would untether.

Whatever had to be done, Enee would have to be the one to do it.

"Listen up, Arcamo, you will not make me responsible for orphaning your Snails," Enee snarled.

She yanked the golden cord from her hair until her curls

burst in every direction. Enee unraveled the binding to its full length and created a loop on one end. The material was close-*ish* to a Charon's Whip. Granted, Billy's had his forged from the purest harvest of Golden Fleece, while Enee's came from the unusable bits sold at the hardware store too crappy to make it into charmed appliances. Same difference.

Enee stood back far enough to throw the loop over Arc's spirit. For a split second, she feared the cord would fall straight through him.

"Snail caretaker. Swift runner. Plan maker. Best friend."

Then, the loop snagged, and the slip knot fitted to the shape of the escaping spirit. Enee wrapped her end around both fists and brought the spirit down with all her might.

"Remember when the wards to your kingdom of slime broke, and we spent the day hunting down all the Glamour Snails? What about when we went into the swamps and collected buckets of algae to throw at each other?" she gasped.

Enee coaxed the spirit with all the memories they had created together, layering them one after another until its form began to flicker.

"Please, Arc," Enee prayed, unsure of what more to say. "There are still so many questions left to ask and plans to break. *Together*. So, please. Stay."

Slowly, the spirit came down and settled back beneath Arc's skin.

The Foblin shuddered, and his snake-locks coiled tightly around each other for warmth. Enee finally allowed herself to breathe. One problem down. Another to go. She needed to get the sap off him.

"You have to use your fire," Omen said.

"What!"

All she could imagine was incinerating Arc. How in the Mundus would setting him on fire help?

"I know I'm not winning any Familiar of the Millennium awards, but I'm still a Familiar. Please, trust me," Omen said.

So said the Familiar who admitted to getting his last mage killed. The same one who only got another chance because everyone else had forgotten what he'd done.

And yet, who was Enee to judge? "What do I need to do?"

With Arc's spirit secured, Omen flew to Enee's head.

"A fire made of magic doesn't have to burn. A roar of anger, frustration, or fear is a faster spell to cast. Let's be honest, how often did people meet the Dragons when they were in a good mood?" Omen said.

"How does that help me?" Enee pressed.

"What other being do you know uses flames?"

She didn't have time to be annoyed about Omen's teachable moment before realizing what he meant. "A Phoenix."

The Phoenix was a being of near-immortality that, upon its death, was engulfed in flames only to rise again from its cocoon of ashes.

Omen bowed his head. "The intention behind your roar is everything. Spells, charms, and even enchanted objects only help you find or obtain that intention. Find the right intention and use it to shape the magic that's here, right at your fingertips. Roar, Enee, but not with anger. Roar for what Arc needs right now."

How?

"What do you fight for, lionheart?" Mama said after her first scuffle.

To fight was to decide. Enee's job was to determine whether it was worth it. Arc was worth every fight, including the one to go beyond her anger and frustration. She conjured her breath, layering herself in the protections Pemprin had instructed her to do. Within that mist, she imagined the one thing she wanted. The one thing worth fighting for.

Save him.

This roar began as a hum, no stronger than a Bee's prayer to a flower. As the hum grew, the roar became a hive. A blue fire spread over Enee's body. The longer the roar droned, the farther the flames traveled until she and Arc were covered.

"That's it, keep going," Omen said.

As the fire burned, even the thickest sap pools turned to dust. The flakes wicked into the air and drifted away as poisonous snow. The wounds beneath the sap sealed, leaving behind patches of raw skin, and the pain in Arc's face softened to a deep sleep.

"Excellent job, housecat," Omen praised.

There came a point when Enee lost her voice, and the flames petered out. She was exhausted, but Arc still needed help. He couldn't stay here. She drew herself up and pulled him away from the Grail Tree.

"You can't drag him all the way home," Omen said.

"I don't have to. I only need to get Arc away from the Tree."

No other roots dared to encroach on the Grail Tree's

space. That's why the forest couldn't spy on him. Or, in this case, save him. To gain the forest's help, Arc needed to go beyond the bounds of the Grail Tree's roots.

Enee brought him to a looming hemlock and pressed her nails into the trunk. "One of your own is hurt. Please bring Arcamo to the Landem Estate."

The ground rumbled. Enee had barely enough warning to jump out of the way before roots shot up from the ground. The tree formed a cage around Arc until she could no longer see him. Once enclosed, the hemlock pulled him down into the soil.

"It's eating him!" Omen cried.

"No, it's carrying him home," she said. Hopefully.

With Arc on his way to the estate, Enee finally let herself collapse. She looked up into the canopy and began to laugh.

"What's so funny?"

Everything. She laughed because her muscles felt like noodles. She laughed because it seemed better than worrying about how much the Landems would hate her after this. She laughed because that was the only thing she wanted to do.

Eventually, Omen caught on and let her laugh until her throat refused to give her anything more than silence.

"Uh, should we take his stuff?" Omen asked.

He had a point. They couldn't leave Arc's journal where anyone could find it. She crawled over to the book and inspected the damage. It, too, had been touched by her healing fire. The pages were stained, but the sap itself had been stripped away. She forced her focus to the words, only to have the letters flounder and die before her. She sighed.

"Omen?"

The Familiar didn't miss a beat.

"Surrendered magic of a Chimera's roar —
    Enee's roar? Magic was surrendered by whom? Why?

is locked away in enchanted ore —
    Just ore? Or something made from this ore?

until what was given to the pine —
    Did the Chimeras give their connection to magic to the Grail Tree?

is bestowed to a child of the donor's line.
    Was the donor a Noe?

With this debt, honor is paid —
    Is Enee's ability to wield a reward for the Chimeras' role in fighting for the Grail Trees?

to a world destined to be remade.
    That doesn't sound good.

And what was locked away in enchanted ore —
    The Chimera's ability to wield, right? Or, was it more than that?

Shall finally seek justice from a heartless war.
    Is that what Enee is really searching for?"

Enee looked at the burl that'd caused the whole mess.

The bark looked as if it had burst open. The black sap still oozed from the wound, creating a dark trail to the ground. Despite everything, she still wanted to climb. It was the last thing she should have wanted, and yet, the call grew until her hands hurt and her hearts galloped.

She turned her back on the Grail Tree and refused the call. Enelope Noe was nobody's puppet.

She looked for Arc's backpack. He had hung it on a nearby branch. Prying the bag from the mountain laurel's clutches was harder than Enee wanted to admit. The branches fought her the whole time. When she finally pulled the bag free, it nearly knocked her over. What did he pack? Rocks? The backpack weighed a ton.

She slipped his journal behind his lunchbox and hoisted the beast onto her back.

"Are we returning to Porto Bello?" Omen asked.

Enee shook her head. There was more to do, and she needed every ounce of daylight left to do it.

Omen groaned. "Great."

CHAPTER TWENTY-TWO
LABYRINTH FOR A LIONHEART

E nee marched from the Grail Tree like a soldier going into battle. She would not turn back. She would not climb. At least, not right now.

"Where are we going?" Omen asked.

"To make sure Arc made it home. Plus, I owe him an *I'm sorry I ignored you and almost got you killed*," she said.

"Didn't the Landems just ban you two from being friends? What makes you think they'll let you see him?" Omen pointed out.

Enee shrugged. Even if Arc's parents wouldn't let her see him, she wanted to make sure he made it back okay.

Getting to the estate, however, posed a different problem. The energy spent healing Arc had left Enee exhausted. She had to stop every few minutes to rest. When she did, Enee tried to tie her hair back, but using the cord as a Charon's Whip had pushed the material to its limits. Half the line was riddled with kinks, while the other half had become stiff and brittle. Eventually, she gave up and stuffed the whole thing in her pocket.

"I vote we stop at Porto Bello for a nap," Omen suggested.

A nap? She hadn't taken naps since she was a baby. Mama had banned them after realizing that if Enee didn't wake up naturally, she'd be meaner than when she'd gone to sleep.

"You take a nap," Enee retorted, pushing on.

"At the rate you're going, I might as well."

She would threaten to make him walk, but he had a point. Enee's legs were not giving her the speed she needed. She needed reinforcements.

"Time for a detour," Enee declared.

REACHING THE BARN TOOK LONGER THAN ENEE THOUGHT. When the Stone Troll Wall came into sight, she dreaded the idea of walking up the hill to the barn. That is, until she heard a whinny.

Knoble waited for her by the wall, close to where her spare helmet was stashed. By some miracle, his coat looked spotless. Enee laughed despite herself.

"Such a good boy."

In an instant, all the speed Enee had lost came back. She knew every shortcut that'd take her to the estate as if they were the lines in her palm. At least, she thought she did.

No matter the path they took, the estate refused to appear. The same trails she'd known for years shifted. No. The *trees* shifted. Every direction Enee took changed the forest beyond what she recognized. They should have been near the outer edge of the estate by then, if not right on top of Arc's Snail empire. Instead, Enee saw only more trees, bowing and shifting with the land. Omen crawled from Knoble's withers to the top of the Steed's head and waved his antennae like a pair of fans.

"The forest is keeping us away," he said.

"How are they—" *Foblin magic.*

"Those sap-sniffers set the forest against us!" Omen snapped.

"Maybe I can use magic, like I did with Arc?" Enee suggested.

"Do you think you've got enough *oomph* to try?"

Not a chance. They needed to regroup, rest, and devise a better plan. Enee steered Knoble in the direction she guessed would lead them back to the barn. Then came problem number two.

The trees didn't just keep Enee away from the estate. The forest made it impossible for her to know the way out. Porto Bello, the school grounds, Hidden Pit Orchard—every landmark Enee relied on became useless.

"Because that's what I need today," she grumbled, guiding Knoble into another shifting grove that expanded and contracted like an enormous pair of lungs.

"I'm going to fly above the canopy and see if I can find a way out," Omen said.

She could feel the tug of their bond the moment he launched from Knoble's mane.

"Do you see a way out?" Enee asked.

"I can see the main trail from here, but any time you move, the land shifts to keep you inside," Omen relayed. "It's like your own personal prison. I don't know if you'll be able to escape until the spell burns out."

Would she have to wait until Mama realized she'd been

gone too long? Or her Treechers? Or even the Landems? What if the spell didn't burn out? What if they didn't check the labyrinth? Enee suddenly felt like a Wax Wyrm stuck in a forgotten mercy trap, left to mummify.

"Oh," Omen exclaimed.

"What?"

The Familiar didn't explain. She felt Omen land, stretching their connection enough to make her wince. A hum hit the back of her skull as if he spoke from the bottom of a lake. She couldn't make out what was being said or to whom. When the humming stopped, Knoble stilled. He flicked his ears in the direction Omen had flown and flared his nostrils. A bulge in the leaf litter covering the ground sped towards them, making the Steed prance. Enee had to circle him twice and massage his neck to get him to stand his ground. What had Omen done?

Two feet away, the bulge stopped. From the leafy covering popped a snout covered in bright yellow spots.

"Ramil?" she exclaimed. "You plum guppy, didn't I tell you not to sneak up on a Steed?"

Ramil chirped, betraying the seriousness of his stoic face. From the forest came the Familiar's mage, a pair of sticks in her hands with a glistening web between them.

"What happened to your head? Did you kill and skin a Yeti?" Pemprin asked.

"What are you doing here? Now you're stuck, too!" Enee snapped.

"Please. I can find my way out." She looked over her shoulder and watched as the trees shifted. "Come on. We need to find a tree to help us."

"What do you mean?" Enee asked, pushing Knoble forward.

"*Come on,*" Pemprin repeated, looking at the web between the twin branches she carried.

As they traveled along the shifting path, Omen returned to Enee's shoulder. She was about to complain about him getting Pemprin of all people, but decided to let it go. It wasn't as if they had many options. Enough luck had decided to join the party to have someone, even her, nearby at all. That didn't mean she'd admit to being grateful for Pemprin's so-called rescue. But at least, she could keep Knoble from stepping on Ramil.

"What exactly did you do to get stuck in this mess?" Pemprin asked.

Enee shrugged. "Be a magical thorn in the side of the Landems."

"I can't say I blame them. You are the definition of *wayward.*"

"If keeping Arc from dying with only a roar and some magic fire is what it means to be wayward, I'll take it," Enee snapped.

Pemprin stopped.

"You used healing magic?"

Enee pulled at Knoble's mane. She never really thought about magic in terms of *healing.* Why? Mama. Before Mama could finish the Guard's cadet program, they had a serious accident. They spoke vaguely about what happened, but afterward, they started suffering from migraines. To stop the pain, they were given medication to help, but the new medication conflicted with the stabilizers they were on. The medications didn't mix and sent them into a crippling fit of seizures. To put a stop to the seizures, a mage surgeon decided to take two heads out of the equation in the hope of giving the strongest of the three a chance to survive. A chance for *Mama* to survive. When all was said and done, the surgeon thought they'd done a stellar job and sent Mama home with scars and a refill for more stabilizers.

Healing magic had taken two parts of Mama and pushed them to leave a whole life behind. And yet, without magic, Arc would have died at the foot of the Grail Tree.

"Are we getting out of here or not? What's with the web anyway?" Enee asked, hoping Pemprin would stop staring at her.

"It's a Mage Map. You can confuse a mage in a labyrinth, but not a map crafted by an Obolos Spider. By looking through it, Pemprin can find the patterns in the labyrinth," Omen answered in Pemprin's stead.

"If the web can show her the way out, why not just lead us to the road?"

"Just because you can see the way out doesn't mean the forest will clear a path for us. We need a tree that hasn't agreed to be a part of the Landem's trap," Omen explained.

Enee wanted to laugh. Even the hardwoods seemed eager to keep them trapped. If the Landems could convince them to intervene, what chance did they have of finding a tree that had resisted?

"Bingo," Pemprin said, pressing her lips into a puckering smile.

"Of course," Enee realized, suddenly feeling incredibly stupid.

A Rood Tree.

The Rood Tree stood half the size of Pemprin and grew

in the middle of a small clearing. The top half of a suit of armor encased the trunk, while turquoise stones the size of melons guarded its base. A helmet rested on the Rood's crown, making it appear like a person had been cut across the middle and left to decompose in the woods. A pair of clunky gauntlets rested by the turquoise stones, both within reach of a sword whose blade plunged deep into the rocky soil.

"Pardon the interruption. But we are lost and need a clear path to free ourselves," Pemprin said.

The Rood remained unmoved, but the orange Ave perched on the sword's diamond-shaped pommel began to stir. When the Ave adjusted their grip, Enee realized it wasn't an Ave at all. The Drake's head, front legs, and tail had camouflage to match the sword's metal, while its bright orange and black rump made it seem like a pudgy Ave sat in its place. The Drake flicked a forked tongue at Pemprin. Neither it nor the Rood Tree seemed particularly motivated to give them directions.

"Please, we are travelers in need of assistance," Pemprin stressed, raising her head higher.

Neither answered. If anything, the Drake looked bored.

"Was that supposed to do something?" Enee asked.

"My uncle told me a Rood Tree grows wherever a truly noble knight fell during the Crusades. They're born out of the oaths the knights made, since oaths can't be broken, even by death. They became guardians of the wood, who provide aid to anyone who gets lost."

Enee grimaced. "And we all know how reliable a stalker is."

"He's not like that!" Pemprin snapped, sending the

forest silent. "He's just like the rest of us, picking up the pieces and trying to figure out what to do with them."

Enee squirmed. What was she supposed to do with that? She half-slipped, half-jumped off Knoble. "Let me take a whack at it."

"You can't beat a sacred guardian!"

Enee fixed her footing and marched past the mage. "It's a figure of speech. Relax."

"What are you going to do then?"

She removed Arc's bag and fished around until she found his lunchbox. The remnants of a banana and some unwanted tofu jerky remained. She took the banana peel and left it at the base of the Rood's armor. Their roots reached from the soil, grabbing hungrily at the banana peel and pulling it into the ground. As for the jerky, Enee stuffed two slices into her mouth before handing the rest over to the Drake. One whiff, and the Drake wrapped its long tongue around the dried tofu and pulled it into its mouth.

As the pair ate, Enee took a moment to sit.

"I'd get fed up with people if they only ever asked me for help," Enee said, swallowing the salty jerky.

"So, bribery is your plan?" Pemprin asked.

"I didn't give them the food as a bribe. I gave it because I could. They don't owe us anything."

Pemprin rolled her eyes.

The Rood Tree twisted to face Enee. "*Asssk.*"

The word hissed from their helmet like the wind at the mouth of a cave.

"Will you help us out of the labyrinth?" she asked.

The helmet turned again, this time to face the Drake.

The creature turned up its snout and let out a warble that echoed through the forest.

For a moment, all fell still. Not even the breeze stirred as the trees thought over the Drake's cry.

Then the path began to shift. An opening, as clear and flat as any bike path, opened to their left. Enee couldn't see where it led, but it was where the Rood Tree thought they ought to go.

"Thank you," Enee praised, bowing her head.

"That was so totally a bribe," Pemprin grumbled.

Once Enee got to Knoble's back, she removed her helmet and held it out to the mage. Mama wouldn't be pleased, but Enee wasn't about to risk being responsible for nearly killing someone else.

"Hop on," she said.

"B—both of us?" Pemprin stuttered.

"Knoble's all muscle. He can take us both, even with Arc's backpack."

Pemprin took the helmet. Ramil curled around her neck just before she struggled onto Knoble's back, looping her arms around Enee's waist. Enee clicked, sending Knoble down the road that the Rood Tree had opened. It took time, but the pieces of the trail they passed began to become recognizable.

"I think I should have been more specific," Enee admitted.

"Why, where are we?" Pemprin asked.

The trees parted to a stone embankment.

"The Churchmere."

The pond beyond the stones stretched longer than it was wide. Nothing disturbed the surface, making it as smooth as polished glass. With the sun slowly hiding behind the trees, the shade allowed them to look beneath the surface. The pond transformed into a cathedral crafted entirely from glass shards of every color imaginable.

Pemprin's grip tightened. "We can't cross that. We're not supposed to be here."

So said every Treecher who was ever asked about them. Churchmeres were only mentioned in terms of the EMD or to warn the students not to go poking around their waters.

"The Rood Tree might be giving us a way out, but the labyrinth somehow sent us around to the *far* side of the Churchmere. To reach the main road, we have to cross. Unless you've thought of another way to get out of the labyrinth," Enee said.

Pemprin held her tongue.

"No matter what, don't jump in. I don't care if you need to slap yourself or squeeze my guts out," Enee said.

"Why would I jump in?"

"Because it's tempting to meet the echoes of the dead," Enee admitted.

A row of broad, flat stones created a shoddy land bridge to the other side. She gave Knoble a loose rein, allowing him to bring his nose to the stones to help him cross. When she looked to her left, Enee saw in the colors of the cathedral the face of every member of the Noe family line who'd died. Well, almost everyone. GrandMama had their back turned. Mama and GrandMama had a falling out just before Enee's birth. Even though the Churchmere only reflected the echoes of the once-living, the echo GrandMama's spirit left behind still held a grudge. Enee shouldn't have cared. Why care about someone who didn't want her to exist? And yet, Enee's hearts pounded. Would they think of her differently if they met her in life?

Maybe I deserve it.

The Chimera from her dream came to the front of the line, looking clearer than in the reflection of the Swan. Their lips moved as if trying to tell her something. Enee felt the temptation to lean closer. What was she saying? It felt important, as vital as air. Her ancestor cupped their hands as if to hold an invisible ball. An orb?

Enee shook her head. She refused to be lured and forced her attention on Pemprin.

Thousands of years of the most powerful mages in the Mundus watched them pass. At the front of the line stood a woman with a single horn on the left side of their crown as white as marshmallows. She held a baby who reached out to Pemprin with a newborn hand. Before the woman could put their hand down, Pemprin leaned forward.

"Don't!" Enee snapped.

Too late. Pemprin lost her balance and grabbed Enee's shirt. The weight of both of them sent them sliding off Knoble's back, tumbling headfirst into the cathedral of the dead.

CHAPTER TWENTY-THREE
LAURELS OF THE LEFT BEHIND

The echoes of the dead could neither pull them into the depths of the Churchmere nor save them. More than anything else, the Churchmere was a mirror. Without a spell or enchanted object to create a portal, they had a better chance of interacting with the afterlife by simply drowning. The silence of water filled her ears like the opening chord of an organ while the fire in Enee's chest roared, burning through what air she had left. Which way was up?

Enee blindly reached for Pemprin, grabbing hold of what she hoped was the mage. Swimming in the Churchmere, especially for two people, took more strength than climbing any Tree.

"Enelope!"

Omen's voice tore into her mind like a set of claws, cutting through the deafening absence of noise. The Familiar used his words like a lure, guiding Enee to the surface. *Up.* Enee needed to go up. But to go up, something needed to give. Enee shook off Arc's backpack while keeping hold of Pemprin. The backpack was replaceable. Pemprin wasn't.

The arm she'd broken burned against the strain of dragging them through the water, following the pull of Omen's words.

"Keep hold of my voice. Ramil and I can't go to you, the Churchmere won't allow it, but you can come to us. Swim! Follow our bond!" Omen said, his words becoming clearer. *Stronger.*

Among the Churchmere's colors, Enee finally made out the sallow blue of the sky. She pushed harder, holding fast to Pemprin's limp body.

Malin. Maud. Mete.

She counted her strides with the Chimera family names, forcing her mind to follow the rhythm away from panic.

Nassor. Noe.

"Come on, housecat, you're almost to the surface," said Omen.

The silence of the Churchmere ripped open to a string of Omen's curses. Enee knew she couldn't stop there, no matter how much she coughed. She dragged Pemprin until they were far enough from the water to keep them from being lured back.

"Pemprin?" Enee wheezed.

The mage didn't move. She remained stunned, barely coughing up water while her eyes stayed locked on the Churchmere. The ripples they left behind obscured the dead from their line of sight. And yet, Pemprin stared. Ramil crawled into her lap and pawed for her attention. When that didn't work, he curled against her to try to keep her warm.

"Pemprin, look at me," Enee ordered. She grabbed the mage's shoulders and shook.

Her eyes were unfocused. Something *inside* remained trapped.

"PEMPRIN!" Enee repeated, grabbing the girl's face and squishing her pale cheeks together.

Nothing.

"She's wandering," Omen said.

"How do I make it stop?" Enee asked.

Neither Familiar seemed to have an answer. Would Enee's roar help, like it had Arc? How could it? Enee had no idea what Pemprin needed. Arc's wounds had been easy to spot. Whatever the Churchmere had done affected a part of Pemprin that Enee couldn't see. If only Pemprin had been bleeding or lost a limb.

Enee paused. *Well—*

She leaned in close, lips inches from Pemprin's porcelain skin.

"Sorry, not sorry," Enee whispered and bit the mage's wrist.

Pemprin's pupils shrank instantly. She ripped her hand away and beat at Enee's head until she let go. On instinct, Enee slapped her back hard enough to leave a mark to match the one on Pemprin's wrist.

"Are you back to the land of the living?" Enee asked.

Pemprin rubbed her wrist, massaging the perfect print of Enee's teeth. It wasn't like Enee bit hard enough to draw blood. Give a Chimera more credit than that.

"I guess that's a point for you," Pemprin said.

"What do you mean, a point?" Since when did they

keep score? And since when did saving a life count as only one point?

Then again, Enee had gotten her into this mess.

Pemprin didn't answer. Instead, she cuddled into Ramil's warmth until she could stand up. For a second, her eyes strayed towards the Churchmere.

"That's enough swimming for today," Enee said, pushing her and Ramil towards Knoble to help the pair mount.

Adrenaline buzzed through her body like magic. She led Knoble onto the path that extended past the bank.

"There were so many ghosts," Pemprin whispered as they walked.

The mage clutched the ring she carried over her heart like a talisman.

"Not ghosts. Churchmeres only hold the echoes left behind by someone who's died, which are pulled into focus when a living relative is close by. They're keepers of—" Enee needed a moment to remember what Mama said, "—*kinetic* memory. All actions cast an echo. So, when actions themselves are forgotten by *living memory*, their impact on the Mundus can't be erased."

"How do you know that?" Pemprin asked.

"Mama told me."

They also told her to "leave it alone" after she found the Churchmere for the first time a few years ago. No wonder. Enee thought of the people who'd appeared for Pemprin. She hadn't expected the echoes to reach for them. If they loved you in life, wouldn't their memory want you to live? If they hated you, why would they want you bothering them in the afterlife? But the boy who'd reached for

Pemprin had been a baby. *Reaching* was probably the only memory he ever made.

"Did you know them?" Enee asked.

"They're my mom and brother. At least I think he was my brother. I never got to meet him, but my uncle was there when they died. He talked to me about it, even when no one else did," Pemprin admitted.

Enee hadn't known she'd lost someone. She never cared to ask. All she knew for sure was that Pemprin's family was powerful, making her the youngest of her dynasty. Youngest alive.

"Does your uncle tell you everything?" Enee asked.

"I thought he did. Since the EMD, he spent hours in the family archives, locked up with that orb. When I asked about it, he refused to talk about what he was doing. And that's not—" Pemprin's twisted her fingers into Knoble's mane. "That's not what we do. We talk, even if the rest of my family won't."

They rode in silence as the last of the labyrinth gave way, and the familiar sounds of the wild creatures filled the Hollow.

"Why did you help me?" Enee asked.

"I knew I could get out. Besides, if I'm to be the next High Mage of Pendra-North, I can't have my allies stuck in magical labyrinths. It reflects badly on me," Pemprin said curtly, finally loosening her grip.

"We're allies now?"

"It's better than having friends. Friendships fall apart."

"Real friendships can be put back together again," Enee said, remembering what Mama told her.

"Keeper's friendship was real! So was Estel's and

Myra's and—" Pemprin tried and failed to keep her voice steady.

The dregs of Enee's adrenaline made their way through her system. The hole it left behind took the fight out of her, leaving a dull ache in her arm. Maybe Enee would make a better ally than a friend, considering what happened to Arc.

She brought Knoble to a stop at the edge of the main road. She knew exactly where the Rood Tree had led them. Turn left, and they'd arrive at the school grounds. Turn right, and Enee would eventually hit Porto Bello.

"Well, that's enough excitement for today. I'm going home," Pemprin said.

She slid off Knoble's back like a wet blanket and handed over the helmet. As much as Enee hated to admit it, she couldn't agree more. She wished she could just ride Knoble to Porto Bello and collapse onto her bed, but he needed to return to the barn. He'd earned his dinner ten times over.

As she mounted, a new path emerged at the edge of the forest.

"Well, that's not creepy," Omen said.

Enee stared at the path. Mountain laurel. The entire trail was lined with mountain laurel.

Arc?

"Don't tell me you're going to go back in after what we just went through," Pemprin cried.

"I think it'll take me to Arc," she said. The path was just wide enough to fit a Steed and tall enough to hide them from the spying trees. Arc had to be responsible.

"You don't know that."

Enee pointed to what grew along the edges. "Arc hasn't officially bonded to the Hollow. He doesn't wield the same influence over the trees as his parents. But there's one plant he's always been on good terms with. Mountain laurel."

Pemprin groaned. "Fine. But I'm calling the Guard if you're not at school tomorrow." She turned on her heels and began the trek home.

"Forgetting something?" Omen prompted.

Enee rolled her eyes. "Hey, Pem?"

"What?" Pemprin snapped, not turning around.

"Thanks."

The mage stopped. "You're welcome."

Enee, Knoble, and Omen were the only ones left to follow the mountain laurel. The path circumnavigated the estate, bringing Enee close to Arc's Snail empire at the last possible second. She took it as a good sign. If Arc led them to his Snails, it meant he was healthy enough to go outside.

Enee tied Knoble to one of the laurel branches and traveled the last stretch on foot. She found Arc by the moat with both hands clutching the roots of a mountain laurel tree.

"Arc?" she whispered. Seeing him gutted her. Burn salve made his face shiny in some places and lumpy in others, where the skin had begun to peel.

The Foblin released the roots, but couldn't bring himself to look at her. They both had regrets. Enee, however, hadn't come all this way to hold onto the shame. She sprinted to him and wrapped him in an angry-sorry-relieved hug.

"Ow," he moaned, hugging her back twice as hard.

They let the hug cover all the bases of an apology.

"I'm so glad the tree got you here in one piece. I didn't

have the strength to carry you home after getting the sap off," Enee admitted.

Arc beamed. "I knew that was you!"

"Don't get too excited. I didn't save your backpack."

"That's all right. I'll try to salvage whatever I can once my parents set me free," Arc said.

Enee let out a nervous laugh. "I wouldn't recommend it. Not unless you have a special way to reach the bottom of a Churchmere."

Arc's jaw dropped. "How did my bag end up in the Churchmere?"

"I had to let it go when Pemprin and I fell in while crossing," she admitted.

Arc noticed her wet clothes and rubbed his temples, smearing the salve. "Why were you at the Churchmere?"

"It was the only way out of your parents' labyrinth."

"They snared you?" he gasped.

Enee nodded. "If you haven't gotten the message yet, we've been banned from seeing each other. Your parents hate me."

As sore as Arc's snake-locks must have been, each one coiled and hissed. He'd never say a bad word about his family, but that didn't mean he'd never think about it.

"I guess it's a good thing I didn't mention the idea that you were the one who saved me or that I'd been visiting the You-Know-What," Arc said.

"You didn't tell them?"

"Are you kidding? They'd never let me leave the estate again. As far as they know, I was checking on Mr. Loch's dad when I startled a nest of Sun-Stinger Drakes. It's not like I had any sap on me when I popped out of the ground like a mushroom. And you know trees. They paint pictures in broad strokes," he said.

Maybe Arc's parents had a point about her being a bad influence. Arc's silver tongue was getting sharper.

Enee's mood sobered. "Maybe they're right to separate us."

"Don't say that. I choose to be there. I choose to be your friend, as you are now, with all the recklessness that comes with it. I choose," he said. "If anything, it's you who I thought wanted to leave, to get you and Mama away from the town."

"Leaving is the last thing I want!" Enee cried. Yes, she wanted Mama to be free. Yes, she wanted them to be together. But, to leave the Hollow? To leave Arc? "My thing with the Tree—I can't stop. I know you're right, and that something is wrong, but something inside me says I have to climb. I think you're right, and it's not all about getting the Stone for Mama. But realizing that hasn't changed the feeling that climbing *is* the answer. I don't know what this means. All I know is that I don't want to hurt you again."

Arc's face flushed. He went to say something, then paused.

"The only thing that'll hurt me is being left behind."

Enee stuck out her pinky, "I wouldn't dream of it."

A commotion broke out from the main house, growing louder with the swing of one of the kitchen doors. Enee could smell flour and garlic and hear the shuffle of tiny feet across the grass.

"Arc! Food!" one of his siblings called.

"We'll find a way to talk at school," Arc whispered.

"I doubt your parents will be pleased about that," she said.

"Don't worry, I have a plan. A bargaining chip, so to speak."

She didn't have time to ask what that meant. She dashed back into the mountain laurel, the path collapsing behind her as she returned to Knoble's side.

"Are you alright, housecat?" Omen asked as they rode toward the barn.

Enee nodded. "You were right earlier. I need a nap."

CHAPTER TWENTY-FOUR
THE LEGACY OF A PENDRA

T he vague memory of her ancestors extending their hands softened the time between when Enee fell asleep and when she woke up.

MuMu's whine cut through the haze. The Drake begged Mama to hurry with breakfast, and Enee could hear the usual "put your fast pants on" from the neighborhood parents. Even Omen was up, taking the time to groom his fur in the reflection of the window.

"Do I have to go to school?" Enee moaned.

Mama chuckled. *Yes.*

She intended to launch from bed and begin her morning workout, but the blankets were warm, and the sky was dark, and her eyes were so heavy—

Tap tap tap. Tap tap tap.

The noise broke her trance. Arc? Enee rolled to the window and looked down at the balcony.

A Messenger Drake with green scales and reflective red spots flapped against the doors. They wore a Green Squirrel Mail Company vest and a saddlebag stretched to bursting to make room for their morning deliveries. Mama opened the balcony door and reached out their unbandaged hand for the messenger to land on.

The Drake accepted the perch long enough to remove a single letter from its pack. They handed the delivery to Mama and swiftly flew back into the waking forest.

"Who's it from?" Enee asked on her way downstairs.

"Work."

Mama tore the letter in two and crumpled the pieces before tossing them into the trash.

"Will you be home late?" Enee asked.

"Maybe."

Enee grabbed the jar of peanut butter from the table and kept her hands busy scooping absurd amounts of the spread onto a plate of apple slices.

"Maybe we can talk to the Landems, find some way to—"

Mama walked to the counter and wrapped their arms around Enee. The smell of coffee, rosemary, and warm dust encased her like armor.

"All is well," they said.

If Enee had one wish, she'd use it to make herself believe them.

When Mama let go to finish getting ready for work, Omen jumped at the chance to fly into the trash can. He didn't need a psychic message to tell him what she wanted. Enee knew reading the note violated Mama's privacy. Still, she needed to know.

MuMu chirped from their breadbox, a piece of cheese in the corner of her mouth.

"*Shh*," Enee warned.

MuMu chirped again, so Enee handed over another chunk of cheese to buy her silence.

"I'm having trouble uncrumpling it," Omen said.

Before Enee could move a muscle, the floor creaked, and the curtain to Mama's room began to shift. Omen leaped from the trash can with barely a wingbeat to spare before Mama made their way to the table.

Their mind was elsewhere as they chewed their scrambled eggs. Usually, mornings were marked by a comfortable silence. This was far from comfortable.

"I could only read a few words. *Topher, Owner & Operator, The Mitey Bean.* The paper felt thick and fancy with an embossed logo," Omen admitted.

She knew that paper. Dove Topher custom-ordered the stuff. Whatever the letter said, she knew the message wasn't the casual, "Hey, can you come in early, please, and thank you."

Enee forced herself to finish the last of her peanut-drenched apple. Otherwise, Mama would know something was wrong. She got ready for school as if her thoughts weren't screaming, convinced the letter meant Mama would receive their two-week notice before the day was over.

It's too soon, Enee thought.

The desire to act swallowed her whole. She filled one pocket with Pemprin's spell book, the Crocswallow feather, and her favorite MMA card. In the other pocket, she hid the crystals.

As she packed, Omen gave her a look.

"What?"

"I've seen enough destruction to know when trouble is brewing," he said.

"Is that a pep talk?" Enee asked.

The Familiar flew to her shoulder. "As if. I'm not your conscience. But I'll be here when the chaos starts."

Enee offered him a smile. Knowing Omen would be there, no matter the outcome, made her feel better. Maybe having a Familiar wasn't so bad after all.

If Mama was worried, they hid it well. They pedaled straight toward town when it came time to leave, despite what likely awaited them. Enee, on the other hand, had to force herself to go in the opposite direction of the Grail Tree. Missing a day of school would draw too much attention. Somehow, she needed to find the will to wait until after school.

"Where are you going?" Omen asked.

He stopped her just before she took the usual shortcut through the woods to the estate.

"This banishment thing is already a pain," Enee grumbled.

She was so used to looping through the woods that taking the bike path felt wrong. Not only that, but Enee arrived at school *early*. She arrived at her English class to find only one other student in attendance. Pemprin.

"I guess this means I don't have to call the Guard," Pemprin said, glancing up from her book.

"I aim to please," she said.

Seeing Pemprin in class felt stranger than the notion of her being at school early. Enee felt *glad*. She claimed the stump next to the mage and sank to the ground.

"What are you doing?" Pemprin asked.

"My workout. My routine fell apart this morning," she said as she began doing sit-ups.

"Is that why you're here so early?"

Enee paused. "I just ran faster than usual."

"As opposed to any other time?" Pemprin pointed out.

She didn't answer. She needed to focus on one thing at a time.

Pemprin looked ready to prod her for a better response when Ramil placed a gummy foot on the mage's ankle. Pemprin looked around and finally put the pieces together. Enee had walked to school without Arc. Pemprin looked back at her book, which could have been older than Isaac Loch by the state of the cover, and had a silver orb pressed into the leather.

She thought of the proctor's staff during the EMD. Enee shivered. Seeing the orb had made her feel raw. She switched to push-ups to try to choke out the memory. At least her arm felt better. A small win compared to the fact that her life was unfolding and collapsing simultaneously. She could feel an acrid heat in her mouth, the taste of metal leaking between her teeth. Omen tried to help, but because they were connected, he reflected those feelings like an echo. Even as he stroked her ear and tried to calm his own quick-to-anger heart, Enee's fire refused to quell.

Run. RUN. RUN!

A handful of wood chips fell on Enee's back and snapped her out of the spiral.

"Let's get out of here," Pemprin said, dusting off her hands.

She picked up her backpack and let Ramil crawl onto her shoulders.

"Where are we going?" Enee asked.

"We're taking a mental health day."

Enee blanched. "We can't leave."

No matter how much she wanted to, leaving would only cause more trouble.

"Come on, before the bell rings," Pemprin pushed.

Once the bell rang, the wards would go up around the school grounds and alert the Treechers to anyone who left class without permission.

"The Treechers will stop us," Enee pointed out.

Even if they did slip beyond the wards in time, the Treechers would notice if students went missing.

"No, they won't."

Pemprin stepped to the side and pulled out the enchanted Prayer Nut Enee saw her carrying the day she fell from the Grail Tree. She opened its shell. When the time came to close the Prayer Nut, the click of the latch echoed in Enee's thoughts as if it were the only sound in the world.

Two perfect copies of the girls occupied their seats. The Pemprin-copy flipped through the pages of her book while the Enee-copy scowled at the dirt. Enee stepped up to her copy and poked it in the shoulder. Her double slapped the hand away.

"Don't touch me," they said before digging their toes into the soil.

Enee gulped. "This is insane. They can't possibly replace us."

"Yes, they can. Our copies will go about the day as we would and vanish the moment I let go of the Prayer Nut. Now come on—or do you have a deep desire to sit through a lecture on the structure of a sonnet?" Pemprin asked.

Enee wondered how often the mage made a double of herself to cut school. Before Enee could ask, Pemprin started walking toward the one place she most desperately wanted to go—the Grail Tree.

"Well, go on," Omen prompted.

She cracked a smile and followed Pemprin into the forest.

The mage pulled another object from her bag as they walked. This time, she retrieved a string of beads that glimmered like a Unicorn's horn. They swayed back and forth from her fingers in rhythm with a chant Enee couldn't understand. They pulled into a patch of thick brambles past the main entrance of the school ground for Pemprin to finish the chant.

"We can't have the forest tracking us, right?" she said with a faint smile.

An erase-trace spell?

"Wait, we need Arc, too," Enee said.

"For what? To scrapbook our journey? Bringing him along is going to strain the erase-trace spell because of his connection to the forest," Pemprin said.

"He's my spotter," she argued.

"I can be—"

"You want to know how friendships last? This is what it looks like. He comes."

Pemprin quieted. She didn't tell Enee yes or no. She simply turned her attention to where their classmates filed along the road toward the main entrance. They waited in the bushes, hoping to snag Arc before he passed the threshold.

"Why are you doing this, anyway? There is no way

you're going through all this trouble to help me just because you consider me an ally," Enee asked while they waited.

Helping her out of the Landem's snare was one thing, but this? If anyone found out what they were doing, it would definitely reflect badly on a future High Mage. Why would she risk that?

Pemprin kept her eyes forward. "I figured out what happened."

"How what happened?"

Arc came into sight with both thumbs looped into the straps of a new backpack. Pemprin readied herself to catch him before he reached the entrance.

"I know why Chimeras can't wield—"

Enee's hearts stopped.

"—and the Pendras are responsible."

CHAPTER TWENTY-FIVE
THE LEGEND NOBODY REMEMBERS

I f Enee counted her natural talents on every finger and toe on the people of the Hollow, patience would not make the list. Stubbornness, however, ranked among her top five qualities. Enee used it to muster enough patience to keep from running after Pemprin as she pulled Arc to their hiding spot and conjured a doppelganger to take his place.

"Stick to the mountain laurel," Arc whispered as they left the school grounds behind.

When the trio made it to the safety of the Grail Tree, Enee ran out of willpower. She grabbed Pemprin's shoulders and forced the mage to look at her.

"Enee—"

Omen waved Arc off. Nobody, not even him, was going to stop her from getting answers.

"Explain. Now," she demanded.

Pemprin didn't try to escape.

"The Pendras have been key players in Alchem society since before the Crusades, tasked with knowing how to solve problems, often with magical means. I have all these enchanted objects because my family created them. Some kids get brooches and ugly couches as heirlooms. The Pendras acquire enchantments. The orbs used for the EMD are one of their creations," she started.

"And?"

"They made the orbs to hold the Chimeras' connection to magic," Pemprin admitted.

Enee held her gaze, carving every second into memory.

"I thought the orbs were just decorations," Arc said.

"The first orbs were created during the last Crusade and were incorporated into the EMD by accident. Most of the orbs we see today were made afterward and are only meant to be ceremonial objects," she clarified.

Whatever orb the proctor used didn't feel ceremonial, Enee thought. It felt alive.

"What do you mean by accident?" she asked through clenched teeth.

"Do you remember the phrase from Arc's poem that mentioned enchanted ore? The book you saw me reading is one of my family's archived journals that my uncle dug up after the EMD. According to the book, the Pendras of the time crafted the orbs from a special ore. I may not know everything, but I do understand what they intended to make."

"Tell me," Enee said.

"The orbs were paired with an intricate spell. By themselves, they were designed to displace a target's connection to magic and contain it. In place of that connection, an invisible tether forms that links the orb to its target, which, in this case, are the Chimeras. This link keeps each Chimera bonded to a specific orb and automatically ensures that the moment their children are born, they're also robbed of their connection. The partnering spell made everyone forget what the orbs had taken. That part seems like a one-off. Otherwise, I'd forget the moment I learned about it."

Enee finally let her go. Chimeras weren't jars of peanut butter. You couldn't just scoop out what you wanted and leave the rest behind. At least, not without a whole lot of consequences.

"Wouldn't that process kill a person?" Arc asked.

She knew he must have been thinking about a Foblin's temporary blood pacts with the Mundus. Those pacts never let a Foblin live out their full life.

"If I'm being honest, yes. If you weren't connected to magic, you wouldn't exist. It's everywhere and lives in everything," Pemprin said.

"Except in Chimeras," Enee pointed out.

"No, that's my whole point." Pemprin's gaze fell. "All the history I thought to be true was wrong. *I* was wrong. We've always been told that Chimeras don't have magic and that there's evidence to prove that it cannot be detected."

She was aware of the resonance tests doctors could perform to detect magic. Mama told her they'd both been tested at birth. Not that Enee remembered. All she remembered was what came after.

"Being able to wield only happens when a connection to magic is anchored strongly enough to allow a person to manipulate it. Those with dormant magic have a connection to live, just not to wield. Elementals and those who receive clear, tangible anchors, like a Familiar, have a greater *gravity*, giving them sway over the magic that's already there. If a connection is too weak, the person will die. So, if this happened to someone in the Alchem or even an Elemental, their body probably couldn't withstand it. I think that the only reason the orbs work is because of who the Chimeras are. Something about them makes it possible for them to survive," Pemprin admitted.

Chimeras were built to take whatever the world threw at them. Somehow, that fact didn't make Enee feel better about the situation. It only left her with more questions.

Arc's snake-locks bared their toothless gums and hissed, "Why would anyone do such a thing?"

Pemprin shrugged. "The Chimeras kept the old kings from getting what they wanted. With a threat like them, what do you think the solution would be? When a Drake becomes dangerous in a household, what happens?"

"They take their fangs and claws," Arc croaked.

Enee felt her chest tighten. By the look on Pemprin's face, there was more.

"What else?" she dared to ask.

"If all of this is true, what if the reason so few Chimeras are left is because their lives have been shortened due to being separated from magic? My uncle told me there are grave consequences for kids who have the potential to wield but don't participate in the EMD. They *need* a Familiar. That's why it's the law for everyone to test. So, what if, like them, the consequences of not acknowledging whether you can wield are more than just legal?"

Enee started shaking. The kings of the Crusades hadn't simply shifted the life of Chimeras into the shadowed hands of the Alchem. They planned their extinction. One that happened so slowly that nobody blinked twice over the disappearance of an entire family line.

Genocide in slow motion.

Until then, Pemprin had one hand on her enchantment and the other on her necklace. She pulled so hard on the chain that the clasp snapped.

"There was a catch," she whispered, staring at the ring in her palm.

"What catch?" Arc asked.

He put a hand on Enee's shoulder. It was the only thing that kept her fury anchored, burning deep in her belly as if trying to eat itself.

"The Chimeras had to agree to give up their connections for the enchantment to work, both for themselves and in the name of every member of their family born afterward," Pemprin said.

She tucked the ring away and looked at Enee. *Really* looked, without all the posturing and her high chin, blue-eyed conviction.

Enee had never seen someone so sad. Well, almost never.

The Gorgon who visited the Chimera camp had those eyes when he'd told them the terms of the truce. He didn't just offer a deal. He sold a lie. A big, ugly lie that bled into Enee's life, boiling down her history into an old sword and a list of a hundred names.

"How did the Pendras remember if the second part of the spell made everyone forget?" Arc asked.

"They didn't. Making exceptions to a spell weakens it. They forgot, like everyone else, but, like I said, that part of the spell only erased the world's memory *once*. Journals, the objects themselves, *evidence,* survived. I managed to piece things together because my uncle has been hunting for clues. I doubt he's the first, since we're not the only branch of the family to have access to the archives. But after the Crusades, the Mundus entered an age that tried to distance itself from the war. Since nobody remembered, nobody was at fault. And since there are so few Chimeras left—"

Her voice trailed off. Enee suddenly realized why Pemprin had gotten involved. *Guilt.* If she were a good person, she'd tell the mage that she shouldn't feel guilty for something her ancestors did. But.

Ophis, Ottolie, Patton, Pearl…

One hundred names out of thousands, hundreds of thousands, wiped out not just during the Crusades, but in the aftermath. Her whole life, Enee had thought this was normal. But with so few families remaining, nobody thought the truth mattered. They thought she and Mama didn't matter.

And that made her want to burn the Mundus to the ground.

Enee looked to the Grail Tree. Was that why it continued to call to her? Every time she climbed, she learned about a past nobody wanted her to know.

"Climb?" Omen guessed.

"I'm going up. Spot me?" Enee asked.

"Like we have a choice," Pemprin said, slinging her backpack to the side and using it as a seat.

Arc nodded. "We'll be here."

Enee climbed until she'd gone farther than she ever had before. Farther than the perch that showed her the whole of

Rowbuirin and the hills beyond. This time, though, Enee couldn't see the town, the worn bricks, or the fields dotted with the Night Mares of Rowbuirin Castle. A fog had swallowed the land below, cold and thick, making her feel as if she, the Grail Tree, and the sky above were all that remained of the Mundus.

Omen kept quiet. She could feel his concentration mixed with hers. The Grail Stone looked so close that she could hardly believe it. If only she were taller.

But the branches had grown thin and brittle. They may have been able to hold Omen, but they definitely wouldn't carry her.

Now's the time, she thought.

Enee braced herself against the last of the branches she knew could take her weight. She took out her MMA card, the Crocswallow feather, and the two crystals. She pressed them between her hands like a prayer.

"Don't forget your protection circle!" Pemprin shouted from far below.

"I'm not!" Enee shouted back. She'd totally almost forgotten.

She did the breathing exercise until the smoke she exhaled was as creamy and warm as fresh milk.

"By the sun, I am light. By the moon, I take flight," she said, first quietly. Then, again, with even more force. "By the sun, I am light. By the moon, I take flight."

Nothing happened.

She tried again, each chant louder than the next. Not a single spark.

"Forget the words. Words suck. Find the intention behind what you want to happen," Omen coached.

What could make her light as a feather? What could make a Chimera soar when everything else felt heavy? Enee saw Mama in a thought as bright and sharp as the summer sun. Their mane was wild, gilded with light. The where and when didn't matter. Those bits and bobs were as useful as the spell. What mattered was how Enee felt engulfed in Mama's enormous, effortless smile.

It felt like—*home*.

Enee felt her feet lift. It took all her concentration not to flail with excitement. Enee kept her body locked, straight as a pin, so she hovered over the same branch. The closer Enee got to the Grail Stone, the more she could make out the beautiful lattices within the crystal. The Stone wasn't just purple, but blue and green, seafoam and silver. After all, who could describe the moon, the sea, and the sky at night through every season in every part of the Mundus? Who could describe rain and Obolos Spider webs and the dreams caught in them like a secret trail on a Mage Map?

Carefully, Enee tested to see if she could put the items for her spell back into her pocket. It took time, but she managed it with minimal rocking. When the Grail Stone came within reach, her hands were free.

The Stone sat right in front of her. *Right there.*

Enee reached out her fingers. Inches. Centimeters. After all this time, every answer came within her reach.

"You all right, housecat?" Omen asked.

A raw sob sprang from her. The Stone was within her reach. Obtainable, ownable, sellable. They could stay in Rowbuirin to build a life rather than run through it. They could stay and discover the history they'd forgotten.

And yet, Enee had a sharp pain in her hearts, a feeling that told her a terrifying truth.

Taking the Stone would change nothing. And it would change everything.

Her fingers waved over a crack so fine it almost looked like a strand of silk.

Cry, her hearts told her.

Touch, the Grail Tree whispered.

Enee cried as she touched the Stone.

She cried as the Stone cracked in two.

CHAPTER TWENTY-SIX
IN THE NAME OF POSSIBILITY

Dozens of Chimeras laughed around her.

"You want us to give up wielding?" the council teased.

The Gorgon suddenly looked a lot less sure about their proposal. Did they expect outrage? A fight? Enee certainly hadn't expected anything so *merry*.

The Gorgon reached for the case he'd left behind his heels and opened it for the camp to see. Inside waited an orb.

"A spell is written on the lid of the box. If you agree, utter the words in unity, and your magic will be taken. This is the same deal being proposed to all the known Chimera gatherings, who must make the decision unanimously and present the orb together at the signing of the peace treaty held in their region," the Gorgon said.

"Why not? It's not like we wield much anyway," jeered a smooth-scaled Chimera from the crowd.

Enee looked to Umber. "Why would the kings ask for this?"

Although she had no power over her host's words, the same question burned in their collective hearts.

Umber grunted. "Because they are cowards and fools. Yes, most of us born since the time of the first Crusade can wield, but—"

"What if the spell takes more than our ability to wield? What of our Familiars?" her host demanded.

A growl rumbled in Umber's throat, making Enee flinch. They said nothing, leaving only the future to run through her thoughts, beating to a broken drum of time and knowledge she had only just begun to unravel.

"Please, Umber. Don't we need our Familiars, as the Alchem mages do?" she asked, brushing a finger along the crown of her Blood Wyrm.

Umber paused. "If we were of Alchem blood, perhaps. But we are not. Chimeras will always remain, even when the Mundus loses heart. Our communities were long built by the strength of our bodies, and will not be bent to the rules in their books."

Their words curdled in Enee's stomach like a bad stew.

She wanted to warn them that the Gorgon had explained only one part of the spell. Giving up their connection to magic meant they'd forget about ever having had the potential to wield. Their children and their children's children would never know the extent of what they were capable of.

"How are you so calm? They are giving us the option to be collared or caged. We can't accept that!" Enee hissed.

"The war has been long, cub. No creature, not even a Chimera, is meant to fight forever," Umber said.

It's a trap!

Enee's scream died inside her. She could not change the past. The bulk of the Chimeras continued to tease the Gorgon while a few others had slunk into the shadows and left the war tent. The council raised their paws for silence.

"When will this signing take place?" the Chimeras asked.

"During the next full moon, before the Grail Tree, so that it may bear witness to the Accords."

The council murmured amongst themselves.

"You will have our answer then. If we attend, you'll know we have accepted your proposal. Should we fail to meet under the mother moon, we will pay heed to the truce and accept your twenty percent of granted lands."

This left the matter unresolved for the Gorgon, who looked more uncertain about returning to the Alchem court than staying at the camp. Still, the Gorgon bowed and promised to relay the message.

The crowd parted, allowing him to make his way to the exit, leaving the orb behind for the elders to ponder. The gap behind him filled in with Chimeras, each with their own thing to say about the Alchem. Most of the words were so colorful, even Omen would blush. If only the council could hear Enee. She'd speak of the future, where the Chimeras were far and few between and free to roam only until passports became a thing in the Era of Revolution. The deal was rotten from the start and would only get worse with time.

Enee slipped through the crowd and followed the Gorgon outside.

"Wait," she called, catching up to him.

"I suppose this wasn't the outcome anyone hoped for," the Gorgon said, offering a nervous smile.

She could tell that her ancestor knew him as more of a friend than an enemy, even though part of her suspected they'd stabbed each other once or twice.

"What about the Elementals who fought? Do you have to do something similar?" Enee asked.

The Gorgon fiddled with his armor.

"We all have to make sacrifices for the chance for something better," he admitted.

"How will this make things better?" Enee growled.

"Because it'll bring change. The kind of lasting change that can only happen in an age of possibility."

The Age of Possibility. Enee's time. Enee's life. The Gorgon looked up, and she swore that it was *her* he saw.

"And what do the kings have to sacrifice for this *possibility*?" her host snapped.

"Us."

The Gorgon left the camp. Enee wanted to follow, but couldn't. This Noe's path had been written in legend and would not be thrown off-course. No matter how hard she fought, nothing she did changed the routine.

Enee was trapped.

With the battle at a standstill, being trapped meant pitching in with the chores around the camp. Scrubbing wrecked armor and oiling saddles wasn't exactly thrilling, but Enee couldn't help but feel good about working in the company of others like her. When a task became too sedentary, they'd switch spots, allowing another who'd been clearing brush or beating the dirt out of old garments to take over. The Chimeras accomplished each task, but nobody had to sit for more than thirty minutes at a time. It was *wonderful*.

But how would Enee's mind return home? Her previous glimpses into the past had been brief. This one didn't seem to want to let go. Would she need to visit the Grail Tree and touch the Stone again? That posed a problem since Umber kept a very close eye on her, sending her from one place to the next as if afraid that if given an inch, she'd get into trouble.

"Best to keep busy until the council decides," Umber told her.

The Chimera clapped a paw onto her shoulder, and—

The camp vanished.

The landscape changed as quickly as a snuffed candle. Enee's mind had returned to the Grail Tree. The mother moon shone overhead, illuminating a night still seven and a half centuries ago.

In Enee's hands sat the orb.

The Chimeras had accepted the deal.

CHAPTER TWENTY-SEVEN

HOW TO DRY POISONOUS TEARS

E nee's host stood at the roots of the Grail Tree with the other Chimeras. Nobody spoke. Nobody had a Familiar.

The mother moon rimmed the trees in bright silver while glowstones hung in macrame slings to fill where the moonlight couldn't reach. Across from the Chimeras waited the forces of the four Alchem kingdoms. The Gorgon who'd given them the orb stood at the forefront of the Ledean soldiers, others like him standing to his back.

Enee screamed and thrashed and roared inside her host. She knew this part of the legend and had zero desire to live through it. But Enee's host refused to budge. They stood silently with the orb in their hands as the Dragons kept watch over the Knights of Sears, and the Griffins waited patiently within the ranks of the Kingdom of Skyrs. Even the one Siren drafted to the army of Lask refused to hum as Alchem soldiers wheeled her forward on a wooden cart barely large enough to keep her feathery, multi-finned tail from dragging in the dirt.

The orb was filled with the same swirling smoke she remembered from the EMD. She hadn't witnessed the Chimeras agree to the truce, but she had the evidence. She carried the connections of all the Chimera families who fought in the region. And this was only *one* orb, presented beneath *one* Grail Tree. Enee's heart hung heavily under the thought that, at this moment, such a deal was taking place under every remaining Grail Tree in the Mundus. Peace would be unanimous at the Chimeras' expense.

Enee stepped away from the Tree and brought the orb front and center. As she walked, four squires dressed in full armor stepped into the gaps that separated each kingdom.

"Today, we make a motion for peace that will last from our children to their children's children. A peace that will unite the Alchem and strengthen the kingdoms through friendship. Today we sign the Pendra Accords," said the squire who wore the shiniest plate.

Enee scowled. Of course they'd named the treaty after the Pendras.

The Gorgon she had spoken with stepped forward, holding a long, scrolling document in his hand. He held out the Accord with a quill poised to make history. One by one, the squires signed as representatives of their respective kings.

Enee felt every hair on her body bristle. The magic in her hands rumbled like thunder. She hadn't seen the point of wielding, but that was before the Grail Tree showed her what the kings had taken from them.

A mage stepped forward and claimed the document. They laid it on the ground and poured spiced oil over the parchment. They muttered a spell, sending the parchment into cold flames.

"No Elemental shall touch a Grail lest they poison their spirit. No Alchem shall touch a Grail, stealing for profit, lest they give their life and land. So shall these rules stand until the end of time, so the Grail Trees cease their poisonous tears and slumber," the mage boomed, citing the terms of the Accords.

Once the flames turned into a smolder, leaving behind a document already enchanted to survive the test of time, it was Enee's turn. She stepped forward and presented the orb.

"The Chimeras offer magic as their sacrifice for the sake of peace," she said stiffly.

The mage took the orb and motioned for her to step back. Looking at the Gorgons didn't help Enee's mood. They stepped forward, along with all the Dragons and Griffins, ready to take a knee to show they would honor the accord.

No! Get up! Enee begged.

Nothing. She wanted to close her eyes, but couldn't. It wasn't as if she didn't know what was coming. Everyone knew. But knowing something would happen and seeing it were two very different things. She looked for the Foblins, who waited by the trees until the squires signaled for them. The kings had made a backroom deal with the Foblins in exchange for their freedom. War made the leaders of the four kingdoms too uncomfortable with the idea of each side having powerful allies. So, what were they to do but balance the scales?

In the name of peace, of course.

The mage began to chant and raised the orb above his head. Enee could feel a new part of the orb's spell take effect, making her tired and slow. Too slow to do anything but watch.

And forget.

The Foblins may have been the weakest of the Elementals, but they were the fastest. They came up behind the other Elementals with blades of Dragon scales, the strongest material known in the Mundus. After two hundred years of war, the Foblins slayed the Dragons with very weapons they had gifted. After two hundred years of violence, the Griffins were roped down, their wings cut, and the rest burned.

After two hundred years of service, the Foblins speared the Gorgons. They fell and took the dream of a better future to their grave.

Finally, Enee's roar came through.

Perhaps it was because her ancestor was the youngest of the group. Maybe it was because she was small. But even as this Noe forgot why she was so angry, she pushed through the chains of the spell and grabbed the orb. She yanked it from the mage's grasp, shoving him into the fray. In the corner of her eye, she watched as the Gorgon who wore Arc's face fell to the ground. He pulled himself to the abandoned Accord. A knife had been jabbed deep into his side, but his eyes still glistened as if filled with stars—as if filled with magic, glimpsing the possibilities he believed worth dying for. He seized the dragon-scale knife from his ribs to tear a corner from the document. With the abandoned quill, he wrote a prophecy on parchment that the mages had intended to keep *their* words alive forever.

Surrendered magic of a Chimera's roar —

Enee's host ran with the orb to the Grail Tree and cracked it against the trunk. The connections of a thousand Chimera families erupted from the orb, still inextricably tangled in the orb's spell, and engulfed Enee in light.

Suddenly, she was no longer inside the body of her ancestor but floating around them. Enee could see the damage done on all sides.

She saw the birth of the Pegasus. These winged creatures came out of the blood of the Gorgons, growing faster than any colt. They bit some of the Foblins who'd attacked, infecting them with a curse as penance for their betrayal.

A snake-curse.

She saw the Dragons fall and the gathering of cloaked mages who'd emerged from the forest like shadows. They used their magic to stop the hearts of every Chimera they touched. And they were all touched, save for the smallest of the Chimeras who'd collapsed at the foot of the Grail Tree. A little Chimera from the house of Noe who'd never remember what she'd done or the Familiar she lost.

The force of the shattered orb sent Enee away from the scene, pulling her up into the canopy where everything was quiet and distant. The Tree swallowed the entangled spellwork whole and sent it to where it believed it could keep it safe. They owed the Chimeras at least that.

The trapped magic burned inside the Grail Stone, carving the memories that the spell had intended to steal into the Grail Tree's heart. Was that a blessing or a curse?

All the Grail Tree knew was that the spell coiled around the Stone like a ravenous Drake, hoarding what it stole and feasting on any connection belonging to the Chimeras' descendants who survived the slaughter. One day, the Grail Tree knew it'd have to let the magic go. Otherwise, it would rot them from the inside out.

Until then, all the Tree could do was hold on until it wore the bonds of the orb's spell thin enough for the Chimeras' connections to be freed.

A process that would take centuries.

A process that would only release generations of magic devoured by *one* orb.

A process that the Grail Tree couldn't do alone.

The Tree searched with its deep, ever-reaching roots for the others who lived across the Mundus, hoping to find a happier ending. They found the same scene, this time with the other orbs left intact. The Chimeras had lost magic. The Elementals who'd chosen sides lost their lives.

The Grail Tree needed it all to stop. It dried its tears of poison sap and begged for sleep. Perhaps they could dream of a world still with Dragons, Gorgons, and Griffins. They could dream of a place where the Sirens didn't retreat so far out to sea that the only evidence of their existence came from the jewelry that washed to shore once in a blue moon.

As Enee's mind traveled closer to the Grail Stone, she wished she could do something. But there was only one thing Enee could do. She could remember.

Surrendered magic of a Chimera's roar
is locked away in enchanted ore
until what was given to the pine

is bestowed to a child of the donor's line.

With this debt, honor is paid
to a world destined to be remade.
And what was locked away in enchanted ore
shall finally seek justice from a heartless war.

Her hand rested once again on the Grail Stone. The day Enee first touched the Tree, the spell attached to that orb had finally grown thin and tired enough to present them with the long-awaited opportunity to let a connection go.

The connection Enelope Noe was meant to be born with.

Upon that first touch, the Stone had cracked. The split was as delicate as a line drawn with a sewing needle, nearly invisible but big enough to do the job.

Upon the second, she dissolved the last of the orb's spell, releasing all the connections that belonged to the Chimeras who had died in the Hollow centuries ago, and to the descendants of the one family that had not.

A family by the name of Noe.

What better champion could a Grail Tree ask for?

THE MUNDUS REFOLDED. ENEE FELT THE STRINGS OF TIME shift around her until the landscape returned to how she remembered it. She floated at the top of the Grail Tree, her fingers on the split Stone. The purple hue had changed to magenta, as if the weight of the past had lightened the color once it had been shared. Omen clung to her ear as all the connections found a new home within her. Well, all but one.

Enee felt the last connection flee from the Grail Stone to find the one other surviving member of the family of Noe, a Chimera who'd once called themself Chalice.

CHAPTER TWENTY-EIGHT
MAMA

Mama frowned into the bowl on the downstairs altar.

They couldn't quite sort out how they felt when their parent's face didn't stare up at them. Relieved? Angry? Sad? Time had mangled the emotions surrounding their relationship into a mass as thick as scar tissue. Why did Dove need to add water from the Churchmere to the space? Did the woman really need to have a memorial to their EMD, complete with her ceremonial stone as a reminder of the magic they couldn't wield? Some people really couldn't let go.

Still, upon Dove's request, Mama cleaned the area *again*. And again, they were careful not to spill the water as they wiped the outside of the bowl. What if Mama just dumped it down the toilet? Why not? The tidying job had just been an excuse to get them downstairs anyway.

They sighed. No. A job was a job. They needed to do it right.

When Mama went to light the incense, the old match

flared, burning their fingers. They growled as static pulsed through their hand hard enough to force them against the altar. Dove's stone tumbled into the bowl, taking Mama's threading bracelet with it.

"*No.*" They clawed greedily through the water only to come up empty-handed. The cathedral of the dead stole the little braid Enee had woven years ago on the rare occasion when the cub found the desire to sit and make something. She could have chosen to do anything, and yet had decided to make a bracelet for them.

Why couldn't the bowl eat one of the nasty sticks of patchouli? Mama wondered, not feeling sorry for the loss of Dove's stone.

"Chalice, can we have a minute to talk?" Dove asked. The cafe manager made her way down the stairs with a fat folder in her hands.

Here we go, Mama thought.

Mama didn't correct Dove on the name and took a chair. They'd stopped asking such a thing from their bosses after a while. People got too flustered about calling them Mama, including their own parent, who thought naming a part of themselves *Mama* before they could even walk was ridiculous. Not that it mattered now. Mama had been through this conversation before and knew what came next.

"I want to thank you so much for your work. You've been a dedicated employee—"

But. There was always a but. Usually, this conversation went along the lines that they were downsizing their staff. A perfectly rational explanation on paper. No. A better way to phrase it was "a perfectly *legal* explanation on paper," if not taken literally. A five-foot-two, ninety-pound high schooler named after a plant or a body of water would stand behind the espresso machine in a few weeks.

Mama imagined them. River Daily, barista. Jasmine Mill, foam art aficionado.

This time, Mama had been the one to slip up. They could blame it on the lack of sleep or the long hours surrounded by people, but anyone can come up with excuses. Excuses didn't change the fact that Mama had lost their temper.

"We've decided to let you go," said Dove.

"Okay."

"Okay?" Dove waited for more.

What else could be said?

"Would you like to explain yourself?" she pressed.

"Would that change the outcome?" Mama asked, fighting a burn in their chest.

Dove put up her hands as if she'd grown exhausted by Mama's attitude. "You slammed a fist into a mirror. You're lucky I haven't reported you."

Yes. *That.* In Mama's defense, they'd only destroyed the mirror in the back room. There had been one rumor too many that day. Call Mama a beast. Call them unstable. Mock them. Work them to the bone. Hurt *them.* Just leave Enee out of it. Changing jobs may have become a form of routine in recent years, but these new rumors were an outrage. How dare they joke about taking their cub, as if she'd been stolen in the night from a royal tower?

But what could Mama do? Break a customer's face? Absolutely not. So, Mama broke the mirror. Now, it was time to accept the consequences.

"I replaced the mirror this morning," Mama offered.

Dove sighed and turned to deal with the necessary paperwork. Mama knew Dove wouldn't report them to their case manager. As much as employers toed that line, nobody wanted to get wrapped in the legal storm of having, on record, an *unstable* Chimera on their payroll. Let alone one from another country. Regardless, Mama sat quietly while the manager crossed the cafe's legal *t*s and dotted all the *i*s, her face doing little to hide how she saw Mama as nothing more than a giant with a hair-trigger who, apparently, kidnapped children.

If the Mundus didn't believe Enee to be a full-blooded Chimera, they'd never met her. She was the best thing to come out of the mess of Mama's life, and they would do anything to ensure she received a better lot than they did.

They'd thought a new town that hadn't had Chimera residents for years, nor knew of Mama and their history, would give Enee a blank slate. What a fool Mama could be.

But they were *Mama*.

And they would be Mama until their last breath, foolish or otherwise.

A customer meandered downstairs before Dove could hand over Mama's termination notice. Despite the situation, they smiled. Mrs. Whittle.

"Oh, sorry. I—*Mama*? Fancy seeing you! So sorry, dear, I'm just looking for the ladies' room," said Mrs. Whittle.

Once she slipped behind the bathroom door, Mama found it hard to sit still. The burn inside their chest had sharpened their temper, and looking at the daisy stickers spread across Dove's folder didn't help. Losing a job wasn't the end of the Mundus. After you lose two heads from a *necessary* medical decision, as the doctors so elegantly put it, and nearly a third due to poor coping mechanisms and a prescription for stabilizers, the bar for the end-of-the-Mundus gets pretty high. Mama would find a new job, somehow. They would because they refused to think of the alternative.

The first time the rumor mill made the community unbearable and work had dried up, Enee had been too small to remember the town, much less get attached to the quiet corner of Camoya. Now, Enee had friends. Well, *a* friend, but one was enough in Mama's experience. And she had just discovered her ability to wield, the first Chimera to do so since... *forever*?

The burn inside Mama's chest flared. They tried to shake it off and find their line of thought. Magic wasn't the point. *Choice* was. Mama had chosen to leave Ledean rather than try to dig themselves from the ashes of their old life. Then again, in Camoya. Now, it was Enee's turn, and Rabot County had the kind of schools to help her explore this new ability without being locked in a city. Keeping rural did put them in a bubble. One that, by virtue, was prone to gossip. But gossip only killed when the authorities got involved, and nobody lived in the woodlands without having a family cautionary tale about the Guard. The Hollow was a blind spot. After all, nobody talked about the hometown of the High Mage. Not even him. People only talked about *other* places. *Other* problems and fights across the sea.

That's why they'd chosen Pendra-North to begin with.

So, Mama needed to find a way to stay put. Fixed. They needed a way to stand their ground even when all the forces of Rowbuirin shoved back. Whatever the job, however the hours, Mama would take it. They didn't have to be suited for the work. Not much in life had been built with Chimeras in mind anyway. They just had to convince their employer that they were worth taking a chance on, so Enee could have a place to call home for a while.

Mama's hearts started to hammer. That wasn't normal. They knew anger, and the burn in their chest felt nothing like it. Instead, Mama felt full of emotion. *Every* emotion, all at once.

They looked up from the folder to find Dove still discussing employee rights and final payments.

Had the patchouli been mixed with something?

The more Dove talked, the faster they looked for a way out of the basement. Then something inside Mama clicked. Whatever had happened, they needed to keep it under control.

Don't be the beast they expect you to be.

Mama looked for any form of distraction. A texture. A smell. An—Ave?

A pied Kingfisher sat on the rim of the altar's bowl, placid as a sunbeam with Mama's bracelet in its talons.

"Hello."

After so many years of only one voice in Mama's head, having another sound cut through their thoughts felt like touching a newborn star.

A roar in Mama's hearts erupted. The incense on the altar burst into flames, catching on the vase of dried flowers. Dove launched out of her chair like a spark from a firecracker while Mama rushed for the extinguisher.

"Put it out!" Dove ordered from halfway up the stairs. "I'll evacuate the cafe!"

Mama smothered the flames in a thick layer of suds.

The Kingfisher was the only thing not drowning in foam by the time they'd finished.

"Hi," Mama said back.

They held out a finger for the Kingfisher to perch on. Mama went to stroke their crest but held back. The Ave was small, light, and crushable. Mama's hands were large, blocky, and crushing. The Kingfisher cocked its head to regard them with an eye as black, shiny, and impenetrable as its beak.

"You won't break me," the Kingfisher promised, offering up the bracelet.

Mama took it and stroked their marbled feathers. They felt the creature's heart hum like it were in Mama's chest alongside the others.

"Now I've truly seen it all."

They turned to find Mrs. Whittle by the bathroom door. The woman stifled a cough from the smoke that left the room with a thick and bitter taste. She stepped around the tables to marvel at the Kingfisher. Her Familiar, Lucy, crawled out from the collar of her jacket to sneak a peek.

"Certainly not the day you were expecting to have, eh?" Mrs. Whittle said.

"No," Mama admitted.

Getting fired and getting a Familiar at the same time? The incense absolutely had to have been laced with something.

Still, as Mama stroked the Kingfisher's feathers, they wondered how Enee had felt during the EMD when her Familiar came forward. Mama remembered their ceremony back when they had Oma and Nama for company. It hadn't felt like this.

Mrs. Whittle regarded them for a minute.

"Do you want to grab some lunch?" she offered.

"Here?"

"By virtue, no. At home. I've got better food and some news that I'd like to discuss with you," Mrs. Whittle said with a starlit smile, the kind that had helped Mama land every job they'd applied for since moving to Rumfoot Hollow. "So, what's their name?"

Mama looked at the Kingfisher and stroked their crest. Whatever was happening, they decided to roll with it.

"Tama."

Her name was Tama.

CHAPTER TWENTY-NINE
FOR A WORLD REMADE

Enee ached as if every cell in her body had shifted. A little click here, a flash of cold across the back, and *boom*. The new connections fit into place.

"Are you coming down?" Arc asked.

"In a minute!" Enee called back.

She needed more than a minute. She had barely managed to grab one of the Grail Tree's branches in time before her spell burned out. At least the Tree seemed better. The spots where the black sap oozed had hardened and begun to crumble.

"We need a different plan to get her down," Pemprin said.

The mage's words landed like a whisper, but even the distance between them couldn't hide the pinched worry in her voice.

"We can't go up," Arc pointed out.

"No, but we might be able to give her something better to fall onto if she slips."

Enee rested her head against the trunk just as

Rowbuirin began to emerge from the fog. She could finally see the town square and the white steeple of the meeting-house. Enee traced her eyes along the town hall, the cafe, the fire station, and the WyrmMart. She gazed out at the balding swaths of farmland tended by the salt-white Stone Trolls. They lumbered between the fields, gathering the early autumn harvests.

This is nice, she thought. Being with the Grail Tree felt nice.

Enee flinched as she started to nod off. She tried to think of ways to keep herself awake, but the view was ridiculous. One look and even the grouchiest Sun-Stinger Drake would become a pacifist.

"I could pinch you. Repeatedly," Omen offered.

Given how the rest of her body felt, she doubted a pinch would do the trick.

"Do you still think being my Familiar was a good idea?" Enee mumbled.

"It was the best decision I've made in a millennium. Granted, the bar was pretty low," Omen admitted.

Enee snorted. They all had to start somewhere. She looked back at Rowbuirin, wondering if it'd be the last time she'd get a view like this. Mama needed to know the truth. Everyone needed to, at least to some degree. The moment that happened, Enee doubted she'd get away with climbing the Grail Tree again.

What will Mama and I do now? She wondered.

The Tree may have given Enee back her connection to magic, but it would not give up its Stone—not even to a Chimera. It remained firmly attached to the crown. Only now, its color had changed, and the crystal had split into two pieces.

Enee's head bobbed. She didn't have the energy to worry about that now. First things first. She needed to get down.

A black haze swept the Rabot County hills, flexing like a broad ribbon caught in the breeze. Enee tried to make out the haze. Smoke? Drakes?

No. *Moths.* Thousands upon thousands of Moths.

"Are you doing this?" Enee asked.

"Do I look like a Moth whisperer?" Omen snarked.

The swarm flew directly toward the Grail Tree. A biblical plague? An unleashed curse? Enee glanced down. Below, Pemprin cupped both hands to her lips. A spell? Magic padded the air with static. She was calling a swarm to her aid, but Enee felt as if it wasn't for the first time. This spell had been used before.

Sneaky mage.

"When they reach you, start climbing down," Pemprin called.

Were the Moths supposed to be a safety net? A swarm was better than nothing. Maybe. In seconds, thousands of Moths blanketed the Tree. She took a deep breath and began her descent.

Careful. One step at a time.

Eventually, Enee ran out of branches. The bare trunk stretched for a good twenty feet below. Would her hands be able to hold on for that long? The Moths adjusted so they could fly under Enee. They obscured the ground like the fog that had fallen over Rowbuirin.

"I guess I have to get down somehow," she mumbled.

Enee took another deep breath and continued.

She made it two feet.

Her grip faltered, and she slipped away from the trunk. The Moths came to the rescue, flying up her backside like an upside-down waterfall. Moth guts spewed everywhere. They slicked her neck and brushed her cheeks. Enee landed on a bed of corpses when she hit the ground, a groan locked in her throat.

"Are you alive?" Pemprin asked while Arc rushed to her side.

"Do I have to answer?"

They helped Enee to her feet. There wasn't much either of them could do about the Moth guts. Before either of them let go, she tightened her grip. First, Pemprin.

"It was you who conjured the Snakes when I broke my arm," Enee said.

Pemprin blushed. "I couldn't let you plummet to your death. How cold-hearted do you think I am?"

When Enee looked at Arc, he hung his head.

"I told you I didn't do anything," he whispered.

Enee pulled her best friend into a hug. "You did everything else."

"Enee—"

"Oh, suck it up. They're just Moth guts," she teased, finally letting him go.

"No, it's not that," Arc said. He looked at her face for a long time. "Are you feeling okay?"

"You're such a worrywart," she said in place of a lie.

Being on the ground didn't make Enee feel better. Too hot and cramped on the outside. Too cold and stretched on the inside. The fire in her hearts kept burning, only now it stayed in her chest like the pilot light of an old stove.

"What happened up there?" Pemprin asked.

A lot. More than a lot. Just thinking about all Enee had seen made her sway. She wanted to answer but knew she'd miss something if she tried now, and the whole story would sound insane. Arc retook Enee's hand and began walking away from the Tree.

"Lunch first," he declared.

Lunch sounded like an excellent idea. Enee let herself get pulled along, Pemprin coming up behind. The mountain laurel guided them through the woods towards Porto Bello. They reached the edge of the woods and crouched in the leaves to give them time to check if the coast was clear.

"This is ridiculous. It's midday on a Monday. Nobody is going to be—" Pemprin shut her mouth.

Ahead stood Mama with an Ave on their shoulder and Mrs. Whittle by their side. All three of them stared directly at the hidden trio. Mama looked ready to tear the Mundus into three pieces, one for each of them to stand on. But when Enee met their eyes, Mama flinched. They marched up to her and put both paws on either side of her face.

"There's a lot we have to remember."

She tried to unfold the story in her mind, but it was too much, too fast. Enee buckled.

And Mama caught her.

WHEN SHE OPENED HER EYES, ENEE WAS ON A BED ABOUT AS soft as a rock covered in a quilt of granny squares. Her hair was damp, and she wore a clean pair of flannel pajamas.

"Feeling better?" Omen asked.

The Familiar sat on the headboard next to a black and white Kingfisher.

"I think so," Enee said.

She still felt strange, but not a *wrong* kind of strange. Just *different*. The Kingfisher jumped to the bed and observed Enee closely, not taking her word for it.

"Hi? Who are you?" Enee asked.

The Kingfisher chirped. By all accounts, they sounded and looked like an Ave, small and light, with feathers laid in perfect order. But Enee knew as surely as she knew she had toes that this wasn't an ordinary Ave.

"That's Tama. Mama's Familiar," Omen clarified.

Mama's Familiar. The thought settled among all the other impossible things that had begun to surround Enee as if they had always been true.

Tama chirped again and flew through the door.

"Time to face the music, housecat," Omen said.

Enee would have known they were at the Whittles' farmhouse by smell alone. She followed the scent of buttermilk biscuits and soup across the worn floors that gave with every step and the eggshell walls trimmed with stenciled hills dotted with lollipop-shaped trees. Voices came from the kitchen. Pemprin's, Arc's, the Whittles'. Enee didn't hear Mama's voice but knew they'd be there. Tama disappeared around the last doorway that opened to a yellow-painted kitchen with white lace curtains.

"Marvelous. You're up," said Mrs. Whittle, placing a fresh bowl of soup on the table.

It looked like everyone had finished lunch a while ago. Mr. Whittle stood at the sink with his Familiar, Bob, pumping water into a bucket to wash the dishes. The others had moved on to nursing steaming cups of tea and a platter of maple cookies.

Mama pushed out a chair. "Sit. Eat."

Enee didn't need to be told twice. She nearly cried over how good the food tasted. The only sour part came from everyone's stares.

"What is it?" she asked, tearing into a second biscuit.

"Nothing," Arc said until Pemprin elbowed him. "Not really. It's just... your eyes."

Mrs. Whittle handed Enee a mirror so she could see what everyone meant.

Her eyes were gray. Their color seemed to have been stripped and spun into thin threads, netting each iris in a different color. One in a web of green. One in a web of hazel. The lines were so fine that, at a distance, all they did was make the gray shine like lightning behind a storm cloud.

Enee put down the mirror. Weird eyes. Okay. She added it to the list of impossible things and grabbed a third biscuit.

"Ready to explain?" Mama asked.

There was no point in stalling. She took a deep breath and told them about everything, starting with her resolution to climb the Grail Tree last year.

The climbing. The overwhelming desire not to stop until she reached the top. The black sap. The dreams about the Chimera. The sneaking around. The time she burnt down a tree and Pemprin's extortion. Proctor Pendra's snooping. The Crocswallow. The poem. Arc's near-death experience.

Everything.

By the time Enee got to the part about all she'd seen and felt when she touched the Grail Stone, even Mr. Whittle had taken a seat. Nobody interrupted her. Nobody called her a liar.

"Perhaps fate truly has been at work lately," Mrs. Whittle said. "By virtue. All those connections, in all those orbs, trapped. Should someone choose to shatter them, the living descendants of those Chimeras would regain their potential to wield."

Enee stirred the last of her butternut soup into a vortex. This discovery felt like the beginning of more problems. The only thing that kept those problems at bay was that everyone who knew about it sat in the same room, except for the rest of the Pendras. But seeing how they hadn't said or done anything in centuries, Enee doubted they would change their minds overnight.

"Well, I suppose that'll all be dealt with eventually. Just not today," Mrs. Whittle said, bringing Enee a cup of ginger tea.

"Why didn't you come to me?" Mama finally asked.

"I didn't want to until I was sure I had a way to give you the freedom you deserved. If I claimed the Stone, maybe then I could change things so life would be better without getting you in trouble in the process. Maybe I could save you from—" Enee choked, "—*me*. I'm not good at dealing with what others say about us. I'm certainly not worth what the rest of the Mundus makes you put up with every day. The Stone was my way out, too. A way for me to stop being a burden."

"Who are you?" Mama asked.

They said it so bluntly that Enee thought Mama had meant it as one would when calling out a stranger. But their face didn't carry an ounce of judgment.

"Enelope Noe."

"And?"

Enee tried to think of what else. A walking hazard?

"*My cub,*" Mama stressed. "It's my job to worry about these things."

"But—"

"No. Everything I've done, I give willingly. There is no charge, no tally, and no score. You owe me nothing. Your only job is to be Enelope and discover what that means to you. Everyone else can stuff it."

"How is that fair?" she asked.

Mama stepped around the table and knelt before her like a knight.

"It's not about being fair. It's about what I chose. I chose to fight these battles so you can be *you.* By doing this, living this way, I can give the person I love most what I never had. Don't you see? Being able to be completely and utterly yourself with every breath you take, despite the rumors and expectations, is the furthest thing from a burden. *You,* my lionheart, make me free."

Enee sank into Mama's paws.

"Dare to live free, my love. Live free for all of us," they whispered.

Every oath came with a sacrifice. Time. Loyalty. *Something.* Enelope Noe, the two-thousand-three-hundred-and-first Chimera of her family line, chose fear. She sacrificed fear and said, "I give you my oath."

But what would they do next? Would Mama keep on as

they always had? *Could* they? Would Enee go to school and try her hand at being a mage? Could she even study spell-casting the way Treechers expected, given *her way* of learning? Was she supposed to wait and become strong enough to speak the truth about what everyone had forgotten? Climbing a Grail Tree had been so much easier. Only one thing felt certain. Until her final breath, Enee would remain faithful to her oath.

For she was a Chimera, and a Chimera never broke their oaths.

Their brows touched. Enee's fire flickered in her chest, warming her fingers and toes. She didn't understand how she knew, but one day, her fire would burn down the Mundus and bring it back as something new.

That was what breakers did, after all.

"Well, that makes our news all the sweeter," Mrs. Whittle said.

Enee looked to the Whittles. "What news?"

Mama cracked a smile.

"I have a new job."

CHAPTER THIRTY

A CHIMERA OF NOE

The Grail Tree could be blamed for a lot of things, most of which should have earned them a medal. What the Tree could not be blamed for was the mountain of secrets Enee chose to keep. Now that the truth was out, Mama had to put their foot down. And there was only one reward for that.

Enee was grounded.

In her world, being grounded meant following a regimen that'd make the Guard cry. Until Mama said otherwise, if Enee wasn't at school, she needed to report to the Whittles or Phineas for chores. If they didn't have work for her, she'd go to Mr. Loch, where Enee's sole purpose in life involved hunting down Wax Wyrm nests and patching the damages caused by an *escaped* Crocswallow hatchling.

No riding.

No climbing.

No wandering the woods.

Enee couldn't even practice magic with Pemprin after school. Pemprin gave her a pass until the end of the month.

Then, their sessions, according to the mage, would be raised from thirty minutes to an hour.

"With your potential, I'm providing a public service," she said.

The mage loaded a bundle of Enee's blankets into the carriage parked outside the entrance to Porto Bello.

"You make me sound like a menace to society," Enee said, sliding her treasure box safely between the rest of the stuff they removed from the shRoom.

Ramil had already made a nest out of the pillows, watching leisurely as Omen and Tama fluttered around the carriage. Although the sun was up, the mornings had gained a frosty bite. Ramil seemed to appreciate the change as much as Pemprin. She raised the zipper on her jacket until the hem swallowed everything up to her ears before hopping onto the back of the carriage.

"You now have a bazillion new ways to wield magic. Even if each of the connections you got from the Grail Tree only allowed you to wield a *pinch* of magic, what do you think would happen if all of them responded to a spell at once?" Pemprin asked.

Enee blanched. "And you want to be in the middle of that?"

Pemprin straightened. "If you haven't noticed, I'm pretty good at spellcasting. I can protect myself. It'll be a learning experience."

"Learn at your own peril. And don't think I'm doing it your way just because we'll train together. If I'm learning to wield, it will be how I want to learn," Enee said.

"Which is how?"

She smiled. Whether Pemprin liked it or not, her way involved a whole lot of running.

Mr. Loch passed the entrance of Porto Bello with the last box of Enee's things.

"What? I've got to do all the work?" he complained as he placed the box in the carriage.

Laughter came from the driver's bench. Phineas and Billy sat up front, having volunteered to help with the move.

"That's your second load," Billy said.

"You try going up and down those stairs," said Mr. Loch.

She and Mama didn't have a lot of stuff. The beds and furniture belonged to Porto Bello. They had MuMu, some kitchen supplies, clothes, the family armor, bedsheets, blankets, and Enee's treasure box. Pile on the boxes of documents Mama tucked in the back of their closet, and their whole life packed together in a cart pullable by two of Knoble's brothers. They probably could have moved everything themselves, but Mr. Loch refused to hear of such a thing. Phineas, Billy, and Pemprin had all volunteered afterward. Arc couldn't be there, but not entirely for the reasons one would think.

By some act holier than a Rood Tree's oath, the Landems had compromised. Sort of. Their opinions of Enee remained unchanged, but Arc did have a plan. She just couldn't tell if it was a good one. He argued that, one, Enee had saved his life, leaving out the bit about the Grail Tree, and, two, if his parents stopped actively trying to undermine their friendship, he would bond to the Hollow earlier than his sixteenth birthday.

Enee didn't like it. The entire bargain left holes for the Landems to exploit. Even so, the terms worked. His family agreed to place her on probation. Only supervised visitation on *their* property or in a pre-selected location was allowed. The win was negligible, but it was the only "Thank you for saving our son's life" Enee would ever get. Seeing Arc, even supervised, was better than not at all. Plus, Pemprin seemed confident that they could find a workaround. Unfortunately, no pre-approved supervising adult had been available on the day Enee finally moved out of her shRoom. Instead, Arc had been *asked* to stay home and left in charge of his younger siblings to ensure he wouldn't sneak off.

"Ready?" Mama called, mounting their bike to take the lead.

"Ready," said Phineas.

He clicked to the Steeds, moving their crew towards Enee's new home. *Home.* Part of her still didn't know if living at Hidden Pit Orchard would be permanent. Would the Whittles rescind their offer in a year, forcing them to leave Rowbuirin? Enee didn't believe they would. To her surprise, Mrs. Whittle had spent the last few years trying to convince the local governing powers that the orchard could be a steady employment sponsor.

Combined with the testimonies from Billy, Phineas, and Mr. Loch, the Whittles finally dulled Mama's latest case manager's worries about whether they could submit their probationary citizen dues on time. Enee was sure that having Charon vouch for them went a long way in mitigating the fact that the business of an orchard was at the mercy of the weather, Wyrm infestations, and whether people wanted apples.

They took a chance on us, Enee mused as she looked at all the people in her corner.

Billy, Phineas, Mr. Loch. Even Pemprin. She felt more a part of Rumfoot Hollow than ever before. Still, she needed to be sure. Until then, what could she call the cottage on the far side of the orchard that the Whittles had cleared out for them? What would she call the place Mama now worked, tending to the trees and ushering the orchard through the seasons until one day, when the Whittles retired, the land became their own?

The orchard seemed like a good option. Equal parts hopeful and ominous. Like the future.

Mr. Loch waved to them as they left.

"Don't think moving away means you're off the hook from helping me with the Crocswallows this spring," he called.

"I gave my word, didn't I?" she said with a guilty smile.

Seeing how the Crocswallow she'd released still evaded their efforts to capture them, helping him protect Porto Bello from a spring infestation was the least she could do. Besides, with everything changing, Enee wanted some of her routines to stay the same.

A new place to live. A new curriculum at school. A new morning routine, now that going to the Landem Estate was no longer an option. A new ally, as Pemprin put it. And a new responsibility to carry a history that the Mundus had forgotten. What was she supposed to do with that?

"You're making that face again," Pemprin said.

"What face?"

Pemprin scrunched up her face into some half-scowl, half-pucker. "Your *I'm thinking of biting off more than I can chew* face." When Enee didn't answer, Pemprin's expression softened. "Relax. You're sitting with the future High Mage of Pendra-North."

"Are you sure you want to get involved?" Enee asked.

"I'm already involved. I'm a Pendra, after all. Right?"

Enee snorted. "What does that make Arc and me?"

Pemprin shrugged. "Allies. Material witnesses. Take your pick."

"I'm not going to be your ally," Enee said. "Or your witness."

Pemprin's face lost its color as she thumbed over the ring hanging over her heart by a new chain. "What are you, then?"

"I'm your friend."

Pemprin froze. "Friendships don't last."

"A Chimera's friendship does."

Enee jogged within Pemprin's reach and stuck out a pinkie. She kept pace and waited. Eventually, Pemprin touched it with her own.

For now, Enee didn't need to be more. She just needed to remember. Remember and be Enelope Noe.

"Race you, slowpokes!" she called as she broke into a sprint.

Enee ran past the carriage as fast as her legs could carry her.

And then some.

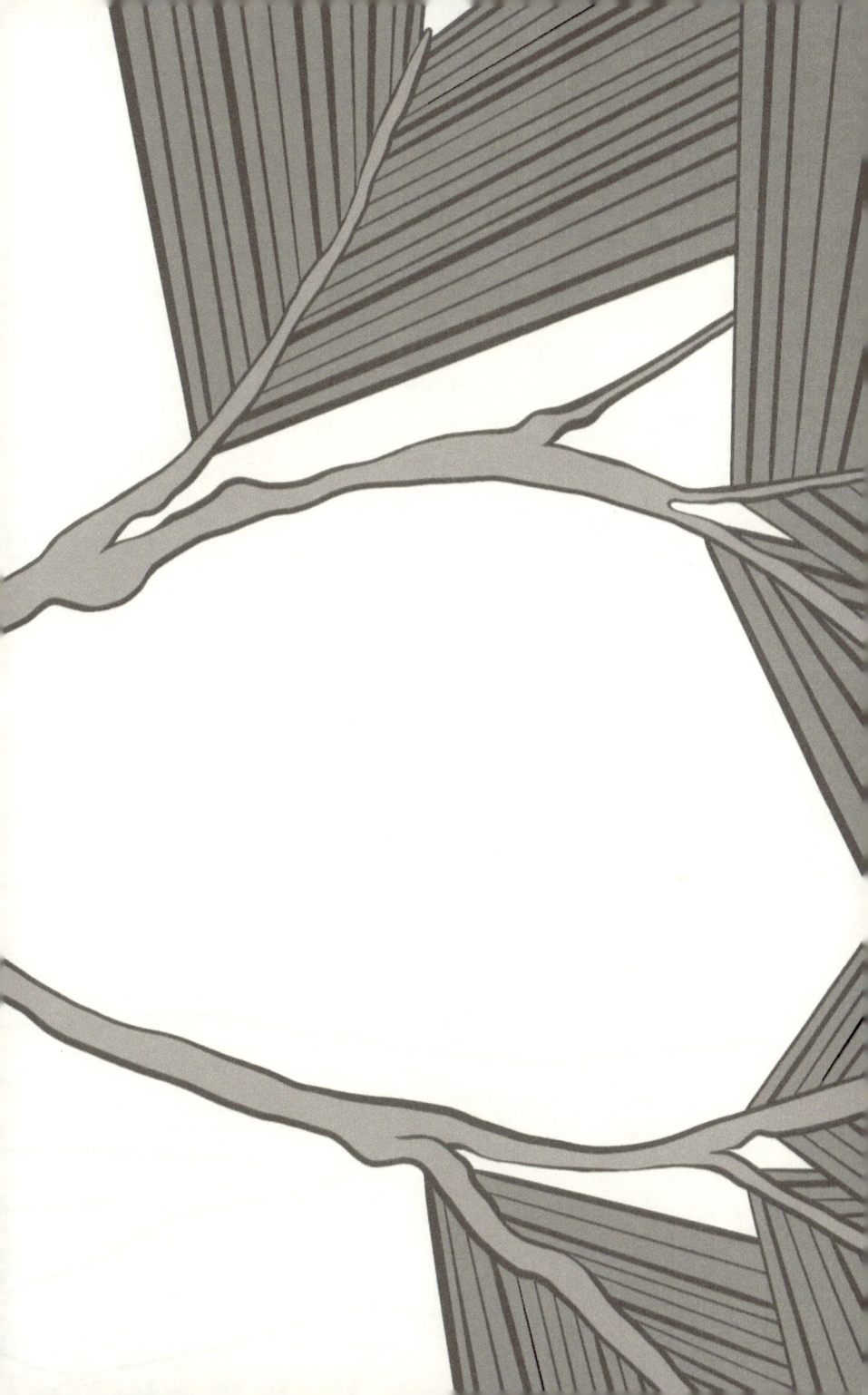

ACKNOWLEDGMENTS

Writing requires heart—a lot of it. So much so that more than one is usually required.

I am beyond grateful to have the unwavering support of a select few who dedicated some of their passion to help bring to life a project I feared would never reach the published page and made it possible for me to follow the beat of my own drum.

Here's to the heart of my father, whose quiet support is the undercurrent of everything.

To the heart of my mother, who looked at the musing of her *where angels fear to tread* child, and said, "I wonder if this is what the beginning of greatness looks like."

To the hearts of my siblings, the original beta readers, and my partners in creative crime.

And to the hearts of all my literary allies like Trisha Wooldridge, whose guidance has been invaluable, Laura Ownbey and Richard Storrs, whose editorial gifts saved me much embarrassment from my inability to spell, and Pegi Deitz Shea, the teacher who went above and beyond to let her student know that she had the potential to be so much more.

Thank you.

ABOUT THE AUTHOR

Corlis C Fraga lives amid the old magic of Connecticut's wetlands. Even as her eclectic resume has evolved—whether earning a master's degree in the Rare Book and Digital Humanities, preserving Tibetan sacred texts as a bindery operator, or nurturing plants in a heritage greenhouse—her mission remains the same as the child raised to run where the wild things are: to be a storyteller who inspires others to believe in the power of limitless wonder.

The Chronicles of Noe: The Chimera & The Grail Tree is her first novel.